Praise for *Aspen*

"This is a tight, impeccably paced story with well-defined characters and intriguing relationships that will resonate with older teens."
—*School Library Journal*

"Aspen is funny, raw, and uniquely romantic. With an eclectic cast of characters, it's an uncompromising look at tragedy and trauma, perception and reality, and how the worst accident of your life might just be the next best thing to happen to you."
—Jessica Park, Best Selling Author of *Left Drowning and Flat-Out Love*

"Aspen is a literary gem. This is a great representation of what YA should be. Poignant, earnest, and inspiring."
—*The Quirky Reader*

"A funny, thrilling story that made me smile, laugh and thank my lucky stars I wasn't that popular in high school!"
—*I Love YA Fiction*

Praise for *Playing Nice*

"Hilarious, heartfelt, edgy."
—Rory O'Malley, Tony-Nominated Actor from *The Book of Mormon*

"I love this book as an adult but as a teenager I would have been obsessed. Rebekah Crane captures perfectly and poignantly the thousands of feelings, thoughts, dreams and desires of that wonderful creature called a teenager."
—Lili Taylor, Actress

"This book is a must read for anyone who is or has experienced any form of bullying or has ever been a teenager girl… Smashing."
—Meagen Howard Fox, *Page Turners Blog*

ASPEN

Rebekah Crane

IN THIS TOGETHER MEDIA

New York, New York

For my mom

THE BEGINNING

Katelyn Ryan sat in front of me in chemistry. I'd stare at the back of her head and wonder what it would be like to have straight brown hair instead of the curly, dirty blonde mess that protrudes from my head, like a perm on a troll doll. I bet she used one of those big paddle brushes instead of a pick and ran it through her hair at least ten times before school.

We even spoke once.

"Do you have a pencil I can borrow?" she asked, turning around and tossing her hair over her shoulder.

"No, sorry."

"That's okay," she said, and smiled.

I dug into the front pocket of my backpack and felt the pile of No. 2 pencils at the bottom. I'm not good at sharing.

One other time, I almost asked her what conditioner she used, but the class ended and I didn't.

Last month, Katelyn Ryan's baby blue Honda Accord crashed into my white Volkswagen Rabbit. We hit head-on and she flew through her windshield. When I was getting stitched up at the hospital afterward, all I kept thinking was that I should have given her a damn pencil.

Newton's first law of motion: Every object in a state of uniform motion remains in that state of motion unless an external force is applied to it.

Katelyn Ryan is dead. I know that. I just can't figure out how to get her to leave me alone.

CHAPTER 1

"Aspen Yellow-Sunrise Taylor, get your gimpy butt down here," Ninny yells from the bottom of the staircase. "I can't believe I have to drive my 17-year-old daughter to her first day of senior year like you're still in kindergarten."

I roll my eyes. "Real sensitive, Mom," I yell back as I pull my tie-dye T-shirt over my head. Its spiral rainbow matches the royal blue cast still suctioned to the bottom half of my right leg.

When the doctor asked me what color cast I wanted, I stared at him and said, "She's really dead?"

"Yes," he replied in that flat, no-nonsense tone only doctors have.

"I guess I'll take blue."

"Good choice."

It itches underneath. I stuck a marker down it last night to scratch my calf and went too far. Now one of my Sharpies has gone into the abyss of flaked-off skin and mildew.

Good choice.

On the plus side, I got to ditch the crutches a few days ago. Now I hobble around on both my legs, like a proper troll, thanks to the rubber bumper on the bottom of my cast.

"You know that's not what I mean," Ninny yells, her voice turning sweeter. "I'm still sad that girl died. I just have stuff to do this morning before work."

I hear her walk into the kitchen and pull out the coffee maker. Our house is so ramshackle, I can hear everything. Including her and Toaster doing it.

"Like what?" I bellow back.

"I need to refill my prescription."

I groan, pulling my cutoff jean shorts from my bottom dresser drawer. She got a medicinal pot prescription five years ago for anxiety, even though pot is legal in Colorado. It's sold on practically every street corner in our town. But Ninny said buying it on the street just didn't seem like a good example to set for her teenage daughter. I'm convinced the only thing she's anxious about is the prescription running out or Colorado changing its marijuana laws. She'd have to go back to scoring her stash the old fashioned way, and then what kind of example would she be?

"I'm almost ready." I look at myself in the mirror, at my curly, tangled bird's nest of blonde hair, and something moves behind me. Turning around, I check my room, searching the corners for the girl who has taken up residency here. Katelyn had this habit of running her fingers through her hair every day when the bell rang at the end of chemistry. It was like clockwork and drove me crazy. Inevitably, long strands of brown hair would fall on my desk.

My eyes shift around the small space, looking on either side of my double bed and behind the desk nestled against the wall next to my closet. An old computer, the kind from the '90s with a huge monitor and keyboard, sits on top, turned off. Ninny's ex-boyfriend gave it to me two years ago for my birthday. Uncle Hayes only lasted about four months, which was good. He refused to use deodorant, claiming it caused cancer. I'm not sure about the cancer bit, but not using deodorant definitely causes a person to stink.

I bend down and check under the bed. Nothing. Standing back up, I stop in front of the Grove. A few of my sketches rattle in the breeze coming through the window.

I started taping my sketches to the wall a few years ago. They've grown to the point where almost no space is left, each picture feeding into the next. My best friend, Kim, coined it the Grove because each tree in an aspen grove connects to the rest through a collective root system to make one the largest living organisms in the world. And each picture on my wall connects to a piece of me. It helps that my name is Aspen, too. Kim's pretty damn smart.

As I take a breath, my chest pinches, pulling tight. It's the side effect of my steering wheel banging into me like a horny teenage boy. I loosen the neck of my shirt, pulling the cotton until I hear a few threads pop.

"She's not real," I say out loud to all the sketches as they flutter in the breeze.

Aspen

In the kitchen, Ninny leans back on the counter, sipping a cup of black coffee and staring at the vase of dead daisies. Each stem has only a few dried white petals left. She brought them and a container of mint chocolate chip ice cream, which she accidentally left in the car to melt everywhere, to the hospital that night. I forgot to water the flowers when we got home.

"Ready," I say, grabbing a sponge to wipe down the counter where Ninny spilled coffee.

She snaps out of her trance. "Salvador's coming over for dinner tonight, so would you please be on your best behavior?"

Ninny licks her hands and runs them over the top of my head.

"Your spit isn't going to make it straight." I pull back from her and take the empty coffee cup out of her hand. Rinsing it, I place it in the drying rack next to the sink.

"You're so pretty, baby. Your dad would be proud." Then she looks me up and down, and puts her finger on the bottom of her chin. "Maybe it was Andy Romaine?"

I groan and pull the full garbage bag out from under the sink. "How many people *did* you sleep with?" I say, tying it closed.

Ninny waves her hand through the air, jingling the silver bangles stacked up to her elbow. "It doesn't matter. What does is that I got you." She squeezes me to her boney body, her patchouli oil tickling my nose hairs. "My sweet Aspen-tree."

My mom had no idea she was pregnant with me, like one of those terrible shows on TLC, *I Didn't Know I was Pregnant* or *Crazy, Young and Stupid* or something like that. The summer before her junior year of high school, Ninny went to a four-day-long Widespread Panic show in Winter Park and did drug after drug until one morning her stomach felt weird.

"I thought it was gas. Altitude does that," she told me when I was little. She lay down under an aspen tree and tried to push the gas out. Instead, she pushed out a baby. She was seven months along. A man saw her and called for help. When he asked what the baby's name was, she said, "Aspen Yellow-Sunrise Taylor." Clearly a rookie mistake made by a high school student who had no idea what a name like that would do to her daughter in the future. I may have to change it in a few years when I want a real job.

I've asked her numerous times who my dad is, but Ninny claims she was in a "free love" phase and doesn't want to be judged on her openness. I'm not trying to judge her. I just want to know if I'm genetically inclined to cancer or heart disease when I'm older. I keep waiting for the day I start seeing dancing bears or have kaleidoscope vision, but Ninny swears she only did drugs that weekend. If you don't count pot as a drug.

The first time I saw Katelyn, I cursed Ninny a thousand times over, sure she was some residual hallucination from Ninny's bad decisions during pregnancy. A few weeks ago, Katelyn appeared in the corner of my room, like one of the ghosts in *A Christmas Carol*, except she didn't move or talk or anything. She just stood there in her soccer uniform, looking alive. I screamed at the top of my lungs and squeezed the entire tube of blue paint I was holding onto the floor. Ninny wasn't home to hear it or see the mess. Thank God. I scrubbed most of the paint out of my beige carpet. No one would notice the blue mark that's left unless they were looking for it. I haven't attempted another oil painting since that day. I prefer sketching with charcoal pencils anyway.

As much as I'd like to blame Ninny for my current hallucinogenic state, I can't. It's not her fault.

"Does Toaster really have to come over for dinner tonight? It's the first day of school," I say.

"Please don't call him Toaster." Ninny lets me go and grabs the car keys off the cracked-tile counter.

"Mom, he brought you a toaster from someone's trash."

"We needed one," she yells.

"He plays the drums on Pearl Street for a living. And they're not even proper drums. They're upside-down white buckets." I put my hands on my hips as we fall into our usual role reversal. Me, the mom, and Ninny, the petulant child.

She shakes her head and plugs her ears. "La, la, la, I can't hear you and your negative vibes."

"Whatever." I sling the garbage bag over my shoulder and take one last look at the dead daisies. Maybe today Ninny will finally throw them out. "Let's get this over with."

"Dinner to celebrate my baby's senior year. You, me and Salvador. It'll be great." My mom kisses my forehead before grabbing her patchwork bag and walking out the door into the warm sun.

Opening the garage, I fling the garbage bag into a half-full can and drag it to the end of our driveway for pickup.

The engine in Ninny's minivan putters on and a cloud of exhaust blows out the tail pipe. Her minivan looks like a meth lab, all dark blue and rusted around the bottom. These types of vans are usually on the side of the highway, abandoned. Ninny needs a new car, like, yesterday.

My car is still in the shop. The entire front crumpled like an accordion. Those were the exact words the guy at Boulder Bump Shop said when he called to say it would take at least a month to fix.

"Your car is old as shit," he said. I'm still not sure how old "shit" is, but I'm guessing it's at least as old as the '80s, when my car was built.

I yank on the van door, forgetting the lock is broken, and the pinch returns to my chest. I rub the spot right between my boobs.

"Indigestion, baby?" Ninny asks as she pops open my door, leaning across the passenger side. She took out the middle row of seats so she and Toaster could lie down in the back and do God knows what.

Before I climb in the van, I check the side mirror to see if Katelyn has followed me outside. Nothing is there but my shadow. I haven't told anyone that I see her. What would I say—"I see dead people," like I'm living in some terrible horror movie with Bruce Willis and that kid who no one hears about anymore, probably because he got un-cute during puberty? I'm already the illegitimate daughter of a teen mom who smokes more pot than Willie Nelson. I'm weird enough without the ghost.

"Something like that," I say, sliding into the seat and catching a glimpse of the green stain from the melted mint chocolate chip ice cream.

Ninny and I are quiet as she drives to school, both of us allowing the stereo to take over. Ninny taps her hand on the steering wheel, beating out the rhythm to "Peace Train" by Cat Stevens. Both of us clap at the same time in the song, right after he says, "Ride on the peace train." *Clap, clap, clap, clap.* She looks over and smiles at me.

We pull up in front of the old brick buildings of Boulder High, as throngs of kids walk in the front door. A spirit rock sits in front of the school, spray-painted all gold and purple with the words *Miss you, K* on the front. I pull a frayed thread from my shorts, yanking some denim loose, and my stomach rolls with nausea. It's like a tapeworm slowly eating away at me. Can you miss someone who's supposed to be dead but keeps popping up everywhere and scaring the shit out of you? Someone you didn't know beyond the intimate way she played with her hair? Right now, I just really miss the ability to itch my calf.

"Are you listening to me, Aspen?" Ninny barks.

"Yes," I say. "Dinner with Toaster." I jump out of the car, the marker in my cast moving further down my leg, and slam the door shut.

Ninny rolls down the window and leans over the passenger seat. "Don't leave mad. It's a new year. Who knows what could happen." She smiles, her dark brown hair falling straight over her shoulders and clear down to her waist.

REBEKAH CRANE

"Couldn't you have slept with a dude with straight hair?" I pull on my curls, and they bounce back like a slinky.

Ninny waves her hand to clear the air of my negative vibes. "At least you got my fashion sense," she yells as she pulls away.

Ninny's van disappears around the corner, but my legs don't move. My toes start to shift in the direction of the Unseen Bean Café, just down the street from school. Kim, Cass and I went there practically every day for the past three years. Then Cass found out that massive amounts of caffeine might shrink his balls and he made us stop. "Penis-to-ball ratio is important to college girls. No one will do me if my balls are the size of peanuts," he said. I still go there sometimes and order the largest espresso size on the off chance it will shrink my ovaries.

I scuff my cast along the ground, running the rubber bumper into the cement, and stare down at my feet. I count all my unpainted toes. A pedicure might help the situation down there. People stare at my leg all the time. Their eyes start at my feet and travel up my legs to my waist and then my face. They usually end up focusing for a few extra-long seconds on the scar that runs across my forehead before the creep-factor of staring kicks in and they look away. I don't blame them. After all, I'm the girl who lived, like a fuck-up Harry Potter with no magical abilities. I'm sure even Harry would say that sucks. I'd stare at me, too.

"Don't even think about it, gimp," a stern voice says from behind me. "I'll tackle you to the ground if you try to leave. I'm not going to school without you. I hate this place."

I clench my jaw and huff, turning around to see Kim. "An Asian saying she hates school is like Ninny saying she hates dope: impossible."

Aspen

Her eyes are blocked by a pair of small, round John-Lennon-esque sunglasses, which she pulls down on the bridge of her nose. "That's a racist stereotype, you fatherless hippie."

Kim Choi and I glare at each other, locked in a stare war until I can't handle the sun anymore and blink.

"Sucker," she laughs, wrapping an arm around my waist. "Sorry I'm late. Uma gave me the first day of school speech and it took longer than usual."

"Speech?"

"You know: 'I didn't come to this country for you to fail. I send you back to Korea in a heartbeat if you fuck up,'" Kim says in her best Korean accent. She loves the word "fuck." "Uma's a Nazi."

"I'll trade you. You can have dinner with Ninny and Uncle Toaster tonight."

"No way. I hate drummers."

"Can I ask you something?" I stop, putting my hand over my forehead to shield my eyes from the sunlight. "Would you ever call me A?"

Kim shrugs. "I might call you an A-hole. Why?"

"Nothing." I link my arm with hers as we walk past the spirit rock. "So did you decide what name to use?"

Kim claps her hands together, a wide grin across her face, "I did and it's fucking perfect. I really think I nailed it this time. My new name is Jasmine."

"Jasmine?"

"I think it suits me." She brushes her black hair over her shoulder. "Anything is better than *Kim*. Kim Choi is just so Asian. I'm more unique than that."

Kim convinced me to pierce her nose this summer. I told her I didn't think a nose ring was very "peace, love and happiness," which is kind of our thing. She told me to shut the hell up and do it. I held ice on her nose until it went numb, and then pressed the needle through. She has a hot pink hoop now. Uma saw it and almost had a heart attack. "Korean girls not supposed to have nose rings," Uma yelled. "You grounded forever!"

Kim threatened to tank her grades so badly that she'd never get into Stanford, where her older sister, Grace, is studying, and Uma backed off. Kim's been trying to change her name since junior high, when Uma sent her away to a Korean summer camp in California. Seven other girls were named Kim Choi, and each hoped to go to Stanford. "And that's only the Korean girls!" she shouted. "What about the Chinese? I'll never stand out in college." She's been using different names ever since in hopes that one will stick. They never do.

"You are unique," I say. Jasmine smiles.

We walk to the locker that's been mine since freshman year. Students pass on either side of us, people slowing for a second as their eyes move from my cast to my face. I stare at the ground and grit my teeth. Pulling the rubber band from around my wrist, I tie my hair back to control the frizz. If the staring continues, I might splurge on one of those treatments that'll straighten my hair. The curls make me too noticeable.

At my locker, I plug in the familiar combination without having to think about it. Then, digging in my backpack, I find the same picture I hung up last year of Kim, Cass and me

13

riding the Boomerang at Six Flags. Kim insisted we ride it and then screamed the entire time. Cass stuffed his face into Kim's chest and I sat on the end, a huge smile on my face, as my hair blew up behind me. I tape up the picture where it hung last year, smiling at the moment captured so perfectly.

"I heard they're holding a memorial for Katelyn at Friday night's football game against Prairie View," Kim says, leaning back against the wall.

"It's a good thing we don't go to football games, because that might be awkward."

"You know it wasn't your fault."

I was on my way to Kim's house that night. When I didn't show up and didn't answer my phone, she called Ninny, who was at the grocery store buying ice cream and flowers, apparently to make me feel better. I've never told Ninny this, but punctuality is better than ice cream in my book. Kim actually made it to the hospital before Ninny. She burst into the ER wearing rainbow pajama pants, her hair pulled into two high ponytails.

"I'm going to fucking kill you!" she screamed, launching herself onto the bed and grabbing me in a tight bear hug. "I can't believe I just said that. I'm a terrible friend. The lowest." Her breath on my ear felt so warm. At that moment, I couldn't have imagined anything better, even though her embrace practically cracked my already bruised chest.

And then I laughed. What else are you supposed to do when someone brings up your death right after you almost met your maker? She washed my hair in the sink until no blood was left in it.

"I know," I say. The nausea from earlier comes back just uttering the words.

Kim squints as she looks at me, like she can tell my words are bullshit and she's about to call me out. I keep steady. Her narrow eyes get even narrower, until they almost look closed. And then she says, "Wanna go to Cass's after school and play *Just Dance* to piss him off? I promise I won't make fun of you for looking like a drunk hobbit." Kim flicks the bun on top of my head and taps my cast.

"Tempting," I exhale my held breath. "But I can't. I have to work, and then it's dinner with Uncle Toaster, remember."

"Right. That'll be a banging good time." Kim plays the air drums. "You know you can talk to me if you need to. Today can't be easy."

"Thanks, but I'm fine," I say, unloading notebooks from my backpack and putting them into my locker.

"Hey, Aspen." Tom Ingersol sidles up next to me, opening his locker, his shiny blond hair shaped into a faux-hawk. It takes a second for a response to actually cross my lips. Tom's locker has been next to mine for three years and he's never spoken a word to me. Literally. Last year, my entire backpack spilled over the floor, tampons and all, and he just stared at me before stepping on my English book and walking away.

"Hi." My voice has an upswing.

"You look tan. Did you go on vacation?" Tom smiles, his white teeth so straight they almost look fake.

"No. Must be from mowing the lawn."

He nods, his grin never wavering.

"You look tall," I finally say to fill the uncomfortable silence.

Tom puffs out his chest. "Runs in the family." He glances at Kim, who's staring at him like he has a third eye. Then, like everyone else, Tom looks down at my cast and then up at my scar. "Well, if you need anything, just let me know. We're locker buddies after all," he says, before walking down the hallway.

"Oh, my God," Kim says in her best valley girl voice when Tom's out of earshot. "Did Tom Ingersol just talk to you? You are *so* fucking cool."

"Did he say 'locker buddies'?"

"Seriously, how much gel do you think it takes to get his hair to stand up like that?"

"Half a bottle, at least," I say as the first bell rings, starting our senior year.

Before I slam my locker closed, I take one last look at the Six Flags picture. How is it possible to want to go back in time and at the same moment to want to forget everything?

As Kim and I turn down the hall, a poster catches my eye. Someone has plastered Katelyn's smiley-faced junior year picture, her soccer number written beneath it in purple and gold, to the wall like a paper gravestone. The caption reads: *Boulder's best and brightest, lost but not forgotten.*

"Let's go to Moe's for lunch. There's a new guy there and he's fucking hot. Uma would hate him. He's perfect," Kim says, but her voice sounds muffled in my head. I can't peel my eyes off Katelyn's picture. "Aspen, are you okay?" Kim follows my gaze to the poster.

"I'm fine," I stutter and force my eyes off Katelyn. "I need to hit the bathroom before class."

"Okay." Kim's voice sounds hesitant, as if she might wait for me outside. I flash a smile, making it as genuine as possible. Her suspicious look lightens slightly and she says, "Lunch: you, me and Cass," before heading down the hall toward her first class, her straight black hair hanging down her back.

When she rounds the corner, I pull the mirror out of my purse, a slight shake in my hands, and check the dull red line on my forehead. It's all that's left of the cut I got when my face hit the steering wheel. My old car is a little short in the airbag department. I thought it would take longer to heal, but the doctor said the body gets better faster than we think.

"It'll give you character," he said.

"Have you met my mother? I have enough character."

The doctor also said I'd been through something "traumatic." I looked up the definition on my phone as I waited for Ninny to show up at the hospital. I know what traumatic means, but I wanted to see what the dictionary had to say.

Traumatic (adj.): of, or produced by, a physical trauma or wound; psychologically painful

The hallway empties as I stand in front of Katelyn's paper gravestone. *Boulder's best and brightest.* Except I distinctly remember her getting a C on a chemistry test.

Out of the corner of my eye, I catch a glimpse of a lone girl walking down the hallway, like a shadow creeping up on me. Her purple and gold soccer uniform almost shines in the fluorescent light. My heart rate picks up as I try not to look in

Katelyn's direction. If I ignore her, she'll go away. She always does. I pull in breath after breath, my eyes fixed in front of me, until her brown hair disappears from my peripheral vision.

When she's gone, I use one of my No. 2 pencils to scratch out the word *brightest*.

"You're welcome," I say to her picture before leaving the pencil under the paper gravestone and walking away. I'm sure one of her friends will get mad that I defiled the poster, but there are enough lies floating around in the world. The least I can do is correct one of them.

CHAPTER 2

I'm late for math. The whole class stares at me as I walk in. I swear no one breathes. Mr. Foster looks at my cast and then at me and says, "Oh, it's you. I'll let this one go, considering."

I want to say to Mr. Foster, "Well, if I'd have known that . . ." and walk out of the room, but I don't. Instead, I sit at an empty desk in the back row and slouch down in the seat.

Considering . . .

Hunter Hunter leans over halfway through class and tells me he thinks my blue cast is rad. He's one of those kids who loves his snowboard more than anything and frequently uses adjectives as sentences. *Awesome. Bad-ass. Wicked.* I'm not sure what his parents were thinking when they named him Hunter Hunter. Aspen Yellow-Sunrise Taylor doesn't seem so bad in comparison.

"It itches," I whisper back.

"Sweet," he nods, his shaggy strawberry blond hair bouncing in his eyes. "It's hot."

I can't tell if he means the cast makes me look more attractive or if he means it's hot outside, which explains the itchiness. He just keeps smiling at me and nodding slowly, his neck moving in a wave-like motion.

Later in the morning, Mrs. McNatt lets me leave English five minutes early. "I don't want you penalized by your next teacher because you can't walk as fast as everyone else," she says, her lips pulling down into a frown. People love to give me the pity face: puppy dog eyes and a droopy frown. I get it every time I walk into the grocery store or doctor's office or coffee shop.

Turning down an opportunity to leave class early would probably make people stare even more. What reasonable teenager doesn't want to leave class the moment it's begun? So I shrug and walk out. I don't dare look behind me, even when I can feel an entire classroom of eyes heating my back. Nerves start in my feet and move up to my head; by the time I'm actually out of the classroom, I'm seeing stars and I think I might throw up. The clock on the wall says 11:30. I'm barely halfway through the school day. I shake out my arms, take a deep breath and hobble down the hall. According to the clock next to the art room, it takes approximately a minute and a half for me to get there, so I doodle on my binder until Mrs. Allen opens the door.

Kim, Cass and I walk to Moe's Broadway Bagels for lunch, so Kim can gawk at the college kids from University of Colorado who work there. They're typical college students: greasy, stoned and working for free carbohydrates. Kim loves any boy who will piss off Uma. I continually warn her about the woes of pissing off one's parents with bad sexual decisions, Ninny-style. I've seen the repercussions firsthand and it isn't pretty.

Sometimes I walk around downtown Boulder looking for the other half of my gene pool: a man with Afro-like blond hair and big brown eyes. One time I actually saw someone who fit the description and asked him if he was my dad. He said he was from Texas and as far as he knew he only had three kids but not to tell his wife about the third one. "That was a mistake," he said.

I said, "I'm a mistake, but not one made in Texas," and moved on.

It's not like I've been totally deprived of men in my life. Ninny should've replaced our front door with a revolving one by now for all of the men who've come through it. When I was little, she always had me call them "uncle." Uncle Jake drove a two-seater El Camino. I had to ride around crouched in the back so the cops couldn't see me, which seemed pretty cool when I was three but later I learned about car seat laws. Uncle Toby had a glass eye that never moved in sync with his real eye. Uncle Bill and Uncle Bobby were twin brothers just out of high school; I'm not sure which was creepier. And my favorite, Uncle Tiny Tim: He only lasted a day before Ninny experienced why his nickname was 'tiny.' And now I have to put up with Uncle Toaster.

"Mama like," Kim says as she licks cream cheese from her fingers and points to the guy behind the counter. He's wearing a Vail T-shirt and has big spacers in his ears to stretch out his lobes.

"He's disgusting," Cass says, and throws a napkin at Kim.

"Says the kid with green hair. What is up with you today, Casanova Sawyer? Why the sudden change in apparel?" Kim takes the napkin and wipes her mouth.

"I thought I'd start the year off right." Cass runs his hands over his clean plaid shirt and tucks his long green-brown hair behind his ears. He dyed it last year when he lost a pizza-eating contest against Mitch Laughlin. If Cass won, Mitch owed him a hundred bucks. If Cass lost, he had to dye his hair green, including the stuff around his manly bits. "I'm gonna eat this pizza like it's your mom" were Cass's exact words. Mitch didn't take that lightly.

On the plus side, Marcy Humphrey paid more attention to Cass with green hair and gave him an over-the-pants hand-job after gym class. Still, Cass is growing the green out. Half his head is chestnut brown and the other half's the color of slime. He's dressed well, though, which is weird. I've never seen him in anything but ratty old T-shirts and his favorite jeans with holes in the knees.

"Well, you look like a douche. A douche in a plaid shirt," Kim says.

"I'm sorry, Jasmine. Or should I call you Sabrina, Tonya, Fantasia or Tiffany? I can't keep track. Are you picking these names from the book *101 Trailer-Trash Names,* by Britney Spears?"

"Jerk," Kim huffs and walks over to dump her trash. "Tell him he looks like an asshole, Aspen."

Cass raises a spoon full of yogurt and aims it at my face. "Watch what you say, gimp, or I'll shoot."

I throw up my hands in surrender. "Peace, man. I think you look nice."

"See," Cass gloats at Kim.

I'd be worried about their friendship if I didn't see the way they look at each other sometimes, like their eyes don't notice anyone else in the room. Cass will gaze at Kim when she's not looking, like he's drinking her in from head to toe. And Kim will glare at him sideways, her pointed stare softening for a moment. They might actually be in love. I figure all the fighting is one giant foreplay session. When they finally do have sex, the universe might explode with the second Big Bang.

"Aspen doesn't count," Kim says. "She's been through something 'traumatic' and isn't thinking straight." Kim makes quotation marks with her hands as she mimics the doctor. Now it's my turn to throw my napkin at her. She catches it in midair and smiles at me. "Let's talk about more important things. What are we doing this weekend?"

Cass's mouth falls open. "ExtermiNATION comes out this week. You said you'd go to GameStop with me to get it. You promised." He makes a puppy dog face and looks between Kim and me.

"Those video games promote violence. I'm exercising my right to social resistance in the name of peace." Kim picks at the blue polish on her fingernails.

"They're art," Cass protests.

"You sound like a gaming nerd."

Cass leans forward. "Your new name sounds like a Disney princess who wears too much makeup and thinks misogynistic rap songs are romantic."

"Enough," I yell, and touch Cass's arm. "I'm in. We promised." I glare at Kim across the table.

"Fine. But you better make it quick. No playing every game in the store. Aspen can't stand on her leg that long."

"I'll be fine." I focus on my plate, picking lettuce off my bagel sandwich and tossing it to the side. I've lost my appetite. Kim brings up the accident more and more these days, like making a joke about it makes everything lighter. Or like if she pokes long enough, maybe I'll finally talk to her about it. But no one wants to be caught in her own nightmare. I'm not looking to remember.

"If she gets tired, I'll hold her," Cass says.

"Hold me?" I cock my head to the side.

"Sure. You're like 90 pounds, right?"

"More like 120 with the spore on my leg." I pull apart a piece of the bagel.

Cass comes around to my side of the table and stands in front of me, his eyes scanning my body from head to toe. The look makes me nervous, but before I can protest, Cass lifts me out of my chair and throws my body over his shoulder. "See, I can do it!" he yells as he runs around Moe's.

"Spank her!" Kim hollers, a wide smile on her face, the snarky comments between her and Cass already in the past. Cass taps my butt like it's a drum, as I bob on his shoulder, laughing.

"I've been taking private lessons with Uncle Toaster," he says as he beats out a rhythm.

I dangle upside down, my blood rushing to my head, and giggle like a toddler being tickled. Stars fill the corners of my vision, but I don't care. This moment is so reminiscent of last year. Of how it used to be. I close my eyes and let my brain go cloudy, drinking it in.

"Excuse me, kid," the college student behind the counter says. Cass stops mid-twirl. "You're causing a scene. Can you take your girlfriend outside?"

"We're the only people in here and she's not my girlfriend." Cass glances at Kim.

"Wait, you . . . " The college stoner points at me. "You're that girl."

I push my hair out of my face as Cass sets me down. My bagel sandwich sits in my throat, about to come back up; I swallow hard once, then again.

"What girl?" I try to say it like I have no idea what he's talking about.

"From that accident. No one has hair like that. Shit, man, that was bad. Are you okay?"

I pull on my curls, trying to flatten them out, and cringe. Why does Boulder have to be so small?

"Don't we need to get back to school?" I say to Kim and Cass, my eyes wide and pleading. I grab my purse and walk out of Moe's without another word.

"Peace out!" Kim yells and flashes a peace sign with her fingers. "By the way, love the earrings." She blows the CU student a kiss right before the door closes behind us.

The seating chart is out on Mr. Salmon's desk when I walk into physics. I find my assigned seat, pulling out a pencil and sketchpad to avoid eye contact with anyone, and drift into a food coma. My junior year counselor told me I had to sign up for physics. He said that colleges want to see an array of classes on my transcript. When I told Mr. Crabtree that I don't plan on going to college, he said, "Everyone goes to college." I didn't want to argue, so I let him put it on my schedule. I figure it's better to spend every day sitting in a class I couldn't care less if I fail than sitting in Crabtree's office, which smells like bad breath, sifting through trade-job training brochures.

It's not that I don't like the idea of college. I do. Boulder's a college town, and my house resembles a lot of the fraternities on campus, with its beat-up furniture and revolving front door for Ninny's men. It just that with all of the men come all of Ninny's irrational behaviors.

The worst was back in junior high when Ninny took off for a week of aura cleansing in Taos, New Mexico, with Uncle Steve. She left a wad of cash on the counter with a note saying she needed a "mom break" and she'd be back in a week. At first, I didn't worry. Ninny was right; she had me at such a young age, and she was probably getting pretty tired of taking care of me. And I had never seen so much cash before. It was like Christmas. I went down to Walgreens and bought out the candy section.

But one week turned into two, which turned into three. And after about two days, eating candy lost its charm. Every day, I had to get myself to school and shower and do my homework because the law kind of frowns on an 11-year-old kid being home alone. Keeping up the act was important.

When Ninny finally got back, I screamed at her that moms don't get "mom breaks" and she should have thought about that before she screwed every boy in her grade. Ninny started to cry and hugged me in the middle of my tantrum. She held me in her arms on the couch until we both fell asleep. When we woke up in the morning, she said that she was sorry. Uncle Steve left her in Taos, and she had to hitchhike home, and the whole time she was thinking about me. She promised never to take a "mom break" again. At that point, I was just glad she hadn't been arrested for any of the array of crimes she'd probably committed.

But it took months for Ninny to get off the couch. She'd lost her job before going to Taos, so I encouraged her to go out and find a new one. She just curled up in a ball and smoked a lot of weed. Luckily, we have a small trust fund that Ninny's parents gave her when they up and left her. They weren't pleased that their high school daughter had come home from a concert with not a hangover but a baby. Some parents just aren't zoned for that kind of thing. But at least they left money.

So again, I kept the house clean and got myself to school and showered. I made dinner every night, even though Ninny barely ate anything. She got so skinny, and she was already a rail. I'd never seen her behave like that before. Sure, in the past

27

when things haven't worked out, she'd been sad. But that's usually when she puts on her favorite backless shirt and hits the local Whole Foods to peruse the guys working at the organic meat counter.

At one point after Uncle Steve left her, I was worried she'd never recover. Having Ninny home again was pretty similar to having her gone, except for the added smell of pot. And her eyes were so sad. Eventually, she peeled herself off the couch, cut down on her smoking and found a new job. But seeing what happened after Taos was enough to scare me. If I went off to college, who knows what would happen to Ninny?

Cass keeps saying I should go to Rocky Mountain College of Art and Design and live at home. He thinks that if I just applied for the program, I could be a video game graphic designer because my sketches of people are so realistic.

He's probably right. But lately getting out of bed exhausts me. Forget getting into college.

Looking around the physics room, I find a poster of Sir Isaac Newton. I start replicating it on my piece of paper. I etch the outline of his face and wavy hair, his crooked nose and big, bugged-out eyes. Soon everything fades around me: the noise, the people. I'm looking from the poster to my paper and back again, totally entranced. My hands work without me telling them what to do. With each line, I define the man in the poster until my drawing starts to look like something concrete, something structured, someone real.

"Hi, Aspen."

I blink, hearing a girl's voice somewhere in the back of my head.

Suzy Lions stands in front of me in a colorful maxi dress that hangs down to her ankles, her auburn hair pulled into a high ponytail. I choke at the sight of her, but manage to squeak out a "hi."

"I like your shirt. I hear tie-dye is making a comeback."

I look down at the primary colors swirled in circles on my shirt. "It was my mom's in high school." The words come out smoothly, even though nerves are bubbling in my stomach.

"Vintage, cool. Your mom must have good taste."

"You've never met her boyfriends," I say.

Suzy laughs a little too loud. "Wow, you're really good at drawing. Who's that?" She points at my sketchpad.

"Isaac Newton." I tap my pencil on the sketch and look at the clock. The bell should ring any second.

"Is he your boyfriend?" I point to the poster on the wall, and Suzy knocks the side of her head. "I'm so dumb."

"Don't feel dumb. I have no idea who he is." I force a smile at her.

Suzy cocks her head to the side, like she's thinking hard. "You're kind of funny."

"Thanks," I say, and squirm in my seat, completely uncomfortable with the compliment, especially considering the person it's coming from. "You're kind of funny, too."

Suzy stands in front of me, looking from my sketchbook to my face and back again, like she's searching the paper for something to say. Brown eyeliner rims her green eyes; just the right amount of brown shadow coats her lids. It looks professional.

ASPEN

When Katelyn was still alive, she, Suzy, Olivia Torres, Sophia Mohomedally and Claire Diaz hung out in a pack. They would huddle in the hallway or walk through the school together. People always stopped to watch them. I did, too. I couldn't help myself. They'd walk past me and I'd lean in closer, trying to hear what they were talking about. Inevitably, at least once a week one of the girls would cry, cradled in the arms of her best friends as they plowed down the hallway, not caring who was in their way, because their best friend was upset. Again. Like a walking, talking high school soap opera that no one could turn off.

My leg shakes under the table as I wait for Suzy to leave. She runs her hands through her ponytail and twists her hair, wrapping it around her finger. Inwardly, I pray for the bell to ring and save me from this conversation. It's hard to look at Suzy.

"I'm glad we have class together," she finally says. When Suzy saunters over to her seat, her long maxi dress swishing back and forth, I don't move. I sit in my seat, staring at the chipping paint on the wall by the smart board.

I counted the cracks in the ceiling that night. Lying on the uncomfortable, starched hospital bed, I stared up for what felt like hours, counting the imperfections. At one point, I was convinced the ceiling was going to come tumbling down on top of me. There were so many cracks. So many ways for things to fall apart.

I swallow hard, trying to wet my dry mouth as someone takes the seat next to me. The bell needs to ring *now* to save me from further conversation. I scoot my chair over, the room and all its occupants slowly closing in on me—and then my neighbor's head of messy black hair catches my eye. My stomach drops to the floor.

"Why are you sitting next to me?" I snap.

It's Ben Tyler. *Katelyn's* Ben. His eyebrows are pulled high on his forehead, his eyes wide.

"Taylor and Tyler. I guess Mr. Salmon did the seating chart by last name." Ben says it like I'm interrogating him and he's nervous he might give me the wrong answer.

"Oh." Tingles flood my hands and I shake them out at my side. All around the room, people are looking at me. My cheeks heat with embarrassment. I'd get up and ask Mr. Salmon to change my seat, but then I'd get even more attention. People would start to wonder why I don't want to sit next to Ben Tyler. Hotty Ben. The grieving, perfect boyfriend of the dead Katelyn Ryan. Me getting up is how rumors start. Suzy tells Olivia who tells Sophia who tells Claire that I didn't want to sit next to Ben, and by the end of the week, everyone is talking about it.

I slink down in my seat, wishing I could disappear into the floor. "I hate eyes," I whisper to myself.

"Don't sweat it. I get that a lot, too," Ben whispers out of the corner of his mouth. Only one side of his face curls into a smile, like he can't force himself to pull the other cheek any higher. I feel the same way most days.

Then it hits me. People aren't staring at me; they're staring at *us*.

"I'm sorry." I force a two-cheek smile. "I'm an ass."

Ben huffs out a laugh. A scar runs through his right eyebrow, another across his left cheek. But even with the imperfections on his face, he looks handsome. I count all the colors in his eyes. Yellow, green, brown, flecks of blue.

"Aspen," Ben says. "You don't need to apologize to me."

I saw him at the hospital that night. He was sitting in a chair, his head in his hands, while Mr. and Mrs. Ryan talked to a doctor in purple scrubs with a colorful sleeve tattoo down her right arm. The scrubs looked more like a costume than a uniform. Mrs. Ryan had her hand on Ben's shoulder. Even with a face full of tears, he was beautiful.

At one point, he looked at me from across the emergency room. I was sitting in a bed, waiting for Ninny. My head was bandaged, and my leg was in a splint. I was even wearing one of those terrible gowns that open in the back so everyone can see your ass. As Ben stared at me, I kept seeing him and Katelyn in the halls. The whole school knew when they started dating sophomore year, because all of a sudden Katelyn went from the girl who played soccer really well to the girl who held Ben Tyler's hand in the hallway.

We stared at each other for so long that eventually it got awkward. I asked the nurse to pull the curtain closed.

Ben doesn't say anything else to me during class. Mr. Salmon goes over the syllabus for the year and then says he's retiring in the spring and plans to be sick a lot.

"Nothing's new in physics anyway," Mr. Salmon says. "Gravity is still gravity." He sits down behind his desk, takes a swig of his coffee, and tells us to "read or something." Maybe I won't fail after all.

When the class ends, Ben walks out of the room without another look in my direction.

~~~~~~

"It's a proven fact: People who smoke pot live longer," Ninny says to a customer as she files her nails behind the cash register at Shakedown Street. Pandora's Phish station plays over the speakers. Just walking in the door, smelling the sugar and incense, makes me relax. I smile at the mural Mickey let me paint three years ago when I got the job here. It's a replica of one of my Grateful Dead T-shirts: colorful dancing bears circling around the Earth.

"Just because you wish it to be true does not make it fact." I plop my backpack down behind the counter and grab my apron. It's green with a white peace sign in the middle and SHAKEDOWN STREET printed in block letters over the top. Other than the customer Ninny is trying to convert to "cannabis-ism," the place is dead.

Ninny looks up from her nail file. "My daughter, everyone: the prude."

"Just because I haven't slept with half the dudes in my grade doesn't mean I'm a prude."

"I bet a little sex would put a smile back on that face." Ninny wraps me in a hug and whispers, "Orgasms make you live longer, too."

I push her off of me and laugh, "Then you are going to live forever."

Ninny doesn't know that I've actually had sex. It might be my only secret from her. It happened sophomore year with a boy named Kevin. His family stayed at our house for a few weeks on their way to California. Ninny served them shakes at Shakedown Street and the next thing I knew, I had a boy sleeping in my room every night for three weeks.

We'd stay up and talk about our parents and how he couldn't wait to go into the Army so he could have some discipline in his life. I told him about Taos and how I was worried Ninny would never come home. Then one night we did it. Every now and then, I'll get a letter in the mail from him. They live outside of Berkley now, at some Zen Buddhist camp without electricity. Kevin gave up on the Army when he found psychedelic drugs. Apparently, acid is better than discipline.

"That's the point." She pulls back, smiling at me. "Can I get you something, baby? You look stressed."

"No eating on the job," I say, wagging my finger at her.

Ninny waves her hands through the air. "Whatever. Pick one." She points above the cash register to the brightly colored menu listing shakes with names like Purple Haze, Strawberry Fields and Crystal Blue Persuasion.

"A Sugar Magnolia, please."

"You got it."

Ninny gets to work on my shake while I wipe down the tables and counters. I start in the farthest corner and make my way across the room in a line, one table at a time. It's been my routine since I started working here freshman year. My second day on the job, Ninny came in to visit me wearing one of her summer spaghetti-strap shirts. No bra. Mickey hired her as manager. Said he saw real potential in her "mixology." She'd recently been fired from her job as a bank teller for not adhering to the dress code, so I was just happy she found a place that accepts her for who she is. The probability of her getting fired from Shakedown Street is pretty low.

Ninny places the yellow drink on the table I'm cleaning and says, "Have a beautiful day."

I slam the banana and strawberry shake until my head hurts with brain freeze. Squeezing the bridge of my nose, I say "Delicious" and place the empty glass on the counter. The sweet taste lingers on my tongue. Mickey was right: Ninny does have a knack for making shakes.

We work, serving the random customers who come in the door over the next few hours. At one point, Mickey comes barreling out of the back room carrying a clipboard, his long black dreadlocks pulled into a loose ponytail. He's a dead ringer for Ziggy Marley.

"It's about time you showed up," he says.

"You're the one who told me I wasn't allowed in this joint for a month," I say as I clean glasses in the sink. "Recovery, remember."

"Did I say that? Well, it's good to have you back. Love the shirt by the way."

I wipe my soapy hands on my apron. "I hear tie-dye is making a comeback."

"When did it leave?" Mickey scratches his head with a pencil.

"I think around disco."

He points the pencil at me. "Don't ever say that word in this establishment again."

"I forgot to tell you, baby, your car is ready," Ninny says as she comes up behind me. "Can we bust out of here early, Mick?"

A sinking feeling drops in my stomach. My Rabbit. "We don't need to—" I start, but Ninny stops me with a fingernail in my back.

"Please," she whines. And then Ninny pulls down her shirt so more cleavage pops out. Mickey's eyes travel to her chest. "Aspen's had a long day."

His eyes still on her chest, he says, "Fine. But this is the last time."

Ninny makes an X over her heart and in her sweetest voices says, "I swear."

When Mickey retreats to the back room, I turn to her. "We don't need to leave, Mom. I feel fine."

"This works out perfectly. I need your help making dinner for Toaster. You know I'm no good at cooking. "

I groan. The idea of Uncle Toaster, with his googly eyes and too skinny body, makes my stomach turn. "I change my mind. I feel terrible. You should probably cancel."

Ninny rolls her eyes. "No. At least one person in our house *is* getting laid."

I grab a bucket of soapy water and a rag to wipe down the tables one more time before we leave. Starting in the corner, I follow the path around the room until everything's clean.

For some people, doing my routine over and over would be tedious. But picking up and putting things back the way they were makes me feel comforted.

Stuffing my apron in my backpack, I follow Ninny out of Shakedown Street. The sun is beginning to set over the mountains. As I hobble to the minivan, I glance down at the rotting spore suctioned to my leg and cringe.

I can't believe I'm about to see my car.

CHAPTER 3

Ninny drops me off at Boulder Bump Shop before heading to the grocery store for supplies. I sit in the waiting room, my cast tapping the leg of the chair, making a ticking sound on the metal. It smells like exhaust and engine grease in here.

Ninny and I bought my car together for my sixteenth birthday. She used some of her trust fund money and I had some extra cash from Shakedown Street. Ninny picked it out. She said she always wanted a white Volkswagen Rabbit in high school, but her parents refused, because the car wasn't practical. "I drove a boring Ford Taurus. There's nothing cool about a sedan, except for the large back seat," she said. I stopped her there and accepted the Rabbit as my own. Sometimes, though, I'd catch Ninny secretly driving my car; I'd climb in the front seat in the morning to go to school, the smell of weed would waft out of the vents, and I'd know she had been out the night before joy riding with Uncle Toaster, trying to relive her glory days while I was doing homework or sleeping.

"It's ready," the mechanic says. The nametag on his shirt reads *Bob*.

"Thanks, Bob. How much do I owe you?"

"The Ryans' insurance covered the damage." Bob's voice is soft and kind of sad. The pity voice.

I nod, and swallow the lump forming in the back of my throat. An insurance guy called the house a few weeks after the accident. I couldn't believe what I was hearing on the line.

"We've run the figures and spoken with the Ryans. Together, we think we've found an appropriate estimate on compensation for your pain and suffering," he said. My head hurt just hearing him speak.

"Are you talking about money?" I asked. In response, he rattled off some numbers. His voice was so businesslike and flat. I could hear other people in the room with him; I imagined him sitting at a desk with cat photos and a lame framed picture of him and his girlfriend on a Carnival cruise, posing in their bathing suits with bad raccoon burns from sunglasses. And all around his desk were other insurance workers calling people from similar desks. Occasionally, I would hear a phone ring and someone speaking in Spanish. Halfway through his mumblings, I hung up. I just couldn't take it anymore.

Ninny convinced me to at least let them cover the damage to the car and our medical bills. I told her she could do whatever she wanted as long as I didn't have to hear that guy's voice ever again.

Bob pulls my Rabbit up in front of the body shop. I run my hand over the smooth white hood of the car, not a dent or broken light left. Even the VW sign on the grill is shiny. It looks the way it did the first day I got it. Like the accident never happened.

Sliding into the front seat, my cast heavy on my leg, I pull the seatbelt over my chest. The pinch creeps back up in my sternum, and I try to rub it away. The bruise that was there faded only a few weeks ago.

"Be careful, kid." Bob pats my shoulder through the rolled-down window. I muster a one-cheek smile, even though the space right between my eyes aches with an oncoming headache. "Oh, and I almost forgot. Found this in your car." Bob pulls a phone from the pocket of his shirt. The sight of it makes my stomach fall to the floor.

"Did you look at it?" I ask too forcefully, grabbing it out of his hand.

Bob lets out a nervous laugh, probably because I just treated him like a terrorist. "No. I know better. My kids would kill me if I looked at their phones. Unfortunately, I'm pretty sure it's broken." Bob shoves his hands in the pockets of his greased-up coveralls. "I thought you might want it, though."

"Thanks," I say through gritted teeth. I squeeze my eyes closed, clearing my blurred vision, and put the phone down on the passenger seat. I haven't seen it since the night of the accident. The truth is, I hoped I'd never see it again.

"Take it easy." Bob waves.

I train my eyes on the road as I pull out of Boulder Bump Shop. Because of my cast, I have to press the gas pedal with my left foot. I get angry with Ninny, furious that she's making me pick up the car alone, like it's no big deal.

But she doesn't know any better.

Flipping on the radio, I turn up the music. Sunlight pours through my windshield, and the pounding in my head gets worse, like a heavy drumbeat. I rub my temples and push away the memory of that night. I pray to make it home before Katelyn gets to me, but it's hopeless.

My heart rate spikes as I try not to look at the passenger seat, but Katelyn always demanded attention. She'd walk into chemistry, her long hair swishing behind her, and everyone would stare.

"I told you that I'm sorry." My voice is tight. She doesn't move, the gold in her soccer uniform glinting in the sunlight. She places her hand on top of the phone ever so casually. Even in my delusion, her fingernails are manicured and clean—as opposed to mine, which make me look like a chimney sweep.

"I know why you're doing this, but what's the point?" I say to Katelyn, my voice frantic. "I can't change anything."

Even as I say the words, I know I'm lying. I had my chances to tell the truth. Two, to be exact.

My foot taps so fast in my cast that my toes go numb.

Is there anything you can tell us? Anything we should know?

"I don't remember anything," I lied to Officer Hubert at the hospital, my eyes unable to move off his gun.

When he came back the next day, dressed the same way, and asked the same question, I had another moment in which I could have come clean.

I sat on my hands and didn't move. Officer Hubert had on a beat-up, stained Rockies baseball cap that looked about ten years old. It was oddly out of place with the polished badge on his chest and his starched uniform shirt.

"I don't remember anything," I lied for the second time.

"Well, based on our investigation, it would seem the driver of the other vehicle was to blame." Officer Hubert took off his hat and rubbed the layer of buzz-cut hair on his head. "It was a horrible accident." He touched my leg. "A goddamn shame, really."

I didn't realize police officers could be so nice. I cursed Ninny for playing all her hippie music. How many times can someone listen to Buffalo Springfield before they start fighting the government and burning bras?

Is there anything you can tell us? Anything we should know?

Katelyn's hand doesn't move from the phone. Turning up the radio to blasting levels, I sing along to the Lumineers at the top of my lungs, drowning out my memories. When the light turns green, I grab the phone and throw it out the car window.

It shatters on the road, broken to pieces. When I glance back at the passenger seat, Katelyn is gone.

"This is delicious, baby. What's it called again?" Toaster asks, licking his lips.

I stare at his teeth, all gnarly and crooked. Little pieces of spinach are stuck up by his gums. He looks homeless, dressed in a wrinkled button-down shirt and baggy brown corduroy pants with holes by the back pockets. He smells homeless, too, like greasy scalp.

"I take it you didn't have braces as a kid," I say.

Toaster looks at me from across the table and brushes his dark brown hair out of his face. His eyes are extra bloodshot. How does he afford his weed on his bucket drumming salary?

"Spinach risotto. Aspen made it," Ninny says, walking into the dining room with three bowls of ice cream. She elbows me in the back.

"Ouch! What the hell, Ninny?"

She ignores me and sits down next to Toaster, taking his hand. "And mint chocolate chip ice cream for dessert. I made the ice cream."

"Did you scrape it out of the back of the van?" I ask, crossing my arms over my chest. My head hurts, and watching Ninny and Toaster carry out their disgusting mating ritual is making it worse.

"You look tired, baby," Ninny says.

I shove another spoonful of the risotto I made in my mouth, squishing the spinach up into my teeth and smile. "No. I want to hear more about Salvador's conspiracy theory. What were you saying about gold and silver?"

Toaster opens his mouth to respond, but Ninny shovels a spoonful of ice cream in it before he can. "Delicious," he says through a mouthful of food.

"I'm gonna be sick."

"Maybe you should go lie down." Ninny's eyes bug out of her head as she motions toward the door.

I can take a hint. I push my chair under the table, leaving behind my untouched ice cream.

"It was great to see you, Uncle Toaster. By the way, I can see your balls." I point to a hole in the crotch of his pants, where pink flesh is poking out. "Drink more coffee; you'll shrink those right up."

ASPEN

"Aspen!" Ninny barks.

I stomp up every step to my bedroom. As I close the door, silverware and bowls crash to the dining room floor, followed by laughing, and the sound of unzipping pants. Not that Ninny needs to unzip anything. She could just shove her hand right through Toaster's crotch hole.

I grab my iPod off my desk and plug my ears with headphones. Spinning through the list of artists, I stop on Credence Clearwater Revival. "Fortunate Son" should drown out the sound of Ninny and Toaster doing it on our dining room table. I'm never eating there again.

I press play and stand in front of my sketches in the Grove. All the good moments, frozen in time and plastered to my wall. All the things I want to remember. I let them wash over me, calm my nerves. Toaster will never be good enough to hang in the Grove. And he'll fade soon enough. They always do.

I pull a sketch of Kim and Cass free and examine it more closely. They're lying on my bed, heads touching, and smiling. I managed to catch the exact light coming in the window, shading Kim's black hair to pick up the sunshine. I think back to the day I drew it last year. Even that is starting to become dull in my memory. Turning the sketch over, I read the definition I wrote on the back.

Unity (noun): the state of being joined as a whole.

Smiling, I put the drawing back and pull my dictionary out of my desk. When I was eight, Ninny found it at a yard sale and gave it to me for Christmas. It's old and smells like book mildew, but I love it. It's worn and broken-in like everything in our house. Everything that is Ninny and I. When most kids were reading *Harry Potter*, I was reading the L section. Eventually, I made my way through the whole book. I don't remember the definitions of most words, but I like that I can easily find them out. I guess some people look for meaning in the Bible. I look for it in the dictionary.

Flipping through the A section, I find the word I've spent weeks staring at.

Accident (noun): an unfortunate incident that happens unexpectedly and unintentionally

I've read the definition a thousand times since that night.

When my headache starts to creep back into my temples, I crank up the music and shove my dictionary back in the drawer. Then I text Kim on my new phone. My fingers shake a bit as I press the letters, but I ignore it.

Me: Ninny and Toaster r doing it on the dining room table.

Kim: Burn ur house down.

I laugh. That should satisfy my best friend for the night.

I fall asleep, my ears still plugged with music, and wake up when it stops. Pulling my door open, I check for sex-like noises. The TV is on, the glow from the screen illuminating the downstairs. Then I hear bubbling, followed by something burning, followed by an exhalation. The pungent smell of pot wafts up toward my room.

I shut the door, tearing off my tie-dye shirt, and tossing it in the garbage can. At least Ninny and Toaster are done for the night.

When I go downstairs the next morning, Ninny is feeding Toaster toast in between make out sessions against the kitchen counter. Annoyed, I walk over to the vase of dead daisies and drop the entire thing into the garbage. It shatters into tiny pieces of glass and dead petals.

"What was that for?" Ninny asks.

"The dining room table." I gag myself with my finger as I say it.

"Someone woke up on the wrong side of the bed." Ninny grabs her keys off the counter and turns to Toaster. "You better hit it, baby. Aspen's got her period."

"Have you checked to make sure you've had yours? I'd hate for a drummer baby to be born under a tree," I say through a mouthful of last night's leftovers, and flash Toaster a spinach-filled grin.

"My, aren't we a ball of hormones this morning?" Ninny looks at me with her eyebrows raised.

"I'm a ball of hormones? Who can't keep her pants zipped long enough for her daughter to actually make it upstairs?" I yank open the fridge, grab the orange juice, and slam it on the counter.

"I'm out of here. Too much estrogen for one man to handle." Toaster opens the back door, the sunlight pouring into the kitchen.

"I'll call you later, baby." Ninny kisses him again, with tongue, and places a piece of toast between his teeth. I take a glass and bang it on the counter.

"What is your problem today?" Ninny shuts the door behind Toaster.

"I'm surprised he even knows the word 'estrogen.'"

"Don't be mad at me." She wraps her arms around my waist and squeezes me to her.

I push back. "Don't. I can practically smell sex on you."

But Ninny doesn't let go. She rocks back and forth, putting her mouth to my ear, and says, "I'm gonna do it, so you better prepare yourself."

"Don't." I squirm in her arms.

"You know you can't resist. Don't even try to fight it."

I stomp my foot and grit my teeth. "I can resist you. Your charms only work on homeless men who fancy themselves drummers."

"Shhh," she whispers into my ear, her hand rubbing the center of my back just like she did when I was little and got upset. Ninny knows my sweet spot, right between my shoulder blades. Her hand warms my skin as it moves in a circle, her energy traveling down my back and legs until my whole body feels lighter. Then she sings, "You are my sunshine, my only sunshine. You make me happy when skies are gray." Her sweet voice echoes in the kitchen, and for a second, I forget that she fornicated on the table last night. Ninny nudges me with her hip. "You finish it."

I don't want to. I want to stay mad, to keep my mind focused on the terrible things she did. I shouldn't have to put up with a mom who acts like a college girl. But as her cheek presses against mine, the tension in my shoulders starts to melt, and I sink into my mom like a toddler looking to be soothed. She's too good.

"Please, don't take my sunshine away," I whisper.

"That's my Aspen-tree." Ninny runs her hand over my hair, pulling on a few loose curls and wrapping them around her finger. "You're so beautiful, baby. I knew it the moment I saw you in the yellow sunlight. An angel."

I smile, nuzzling into her chest and holding her tightly around the waist. Sometimes I wish it were still acceptable to curl up in her lap and just lie there.

"Now get your ass to school. And don't forget about Dr. Brenda this afternoon." Ninny taps my butt, unhooking my arms, and walks out the back door. The warmth I felt a moment earlier is gone.

I wash my glass along with the rest of the dishes in the sink and set them to dry in the rack. Wiping the crumbs from Ninny's toast off the counter, I make sure everything is in its proper place. I debate cleaning the dining room table with bleach, but I'm not sure what that would do to the wood. Maybe Kim had it right: I should burn the place down.

On a positive note, Ninny seems to be getting some use out of the toaster Uncle Toaster gave her.

CHAPTER 4

Our principal, Mr. James, calls me down to his office halfway through the day. He sits behind his desk, leaning forward on his elbows. I've never seen his face this close up before. He has acne scars on his cheeks, and his salt and pepper hair has more salt in it than pepper.

"How are you adjusting?"

"Adjusting?" I ask.

"Death is hard, but the death of a young person is even harder. I just want you to know that as a school we're here to support you."

"Okay."

"Anything you need, you come and see me."

I don't respond. Instead, I change the conversation and point to the picture behind his desk, "Are those your kids?"

Mr. James smiles, falling into my trap, and proceeds to tell me about his kids for the next ten minutes.

ASPEN

Mrs. Sapporo, the office attendant who always wears a bun on top of her head and a seasonal puff-painted shirt, writes me a pass back to class. She gives me a half smile and says, "How are you, dear?" She even tilts her head to the side. Today, her shirt is covered in different-colored fall leaves and a scarecrow.

"To every season, turn, turn, turn," I say, grabbing a mint off her desk and popping it in my mouth.

"Pardon?" she says.

"Your sweatshirt." I give her an exaggerated smile.

Mrs. Sapporo doesn't say anything else. I take a handful of mints, clearing out her dish, and stuff them in my pocket. The white and red ones are the best, like little circle candy canes.

I stop in the bathroom on my way to class just to take up more time before I have to go back to the stares and whispers. I enter a stall and stand there, reading stuff people have written on the door. *Jack and Maggie 4ever. FUCK U.*

As I'm about to leave, two girls walk in. I stop still in the stall, holding my breath so they don't hear me, and wait for them to leave.

"Do you have that pink lip gloss?" one voice asks. There's the noise of a girl rummaging around in a purse. "Oh my God, did I ever tell you about the time Katelyn let me borrow her mascara?"

"Oh, my God. No." The other girl sounds disappointed.

"It was *so* sweet. Last year, I was crying over Cam, that asshole, before gym class. Katelyn saw and gave me her mascara, so I didn't have to look like shit the rest of the day."

"She was so nice. You know she lived down the street from me, right?" the other girl says.

"Oh, my God, that's right."

"I used to see her and Ben all the time. Like, *all* the time. They were inseparable."

"They were so in love."

"Totally." One of the girls turns on the faucet. "Holy shit. Do you think she died a virgin?"

The faucet turns off. "No fucking way. She and Ben were totally doing it."

"And poor Aspen. I feel terrible for her."

Shoes click on the ground and the girls' voices fade as they leave the bathroom. When I know they're completely gone, I creep out of the stall and stand in front of the mirror. Bending over, I splash a handful of water on my face.

When I open my eyes, Katelyn is behind me, writing something on the stall door. I jump, my heart rate picking up. But when I turn to see what she's written, she's gone.

"Look at the person sitting next to you. This is your lab partner for the year. Learn to like them. Memorize their smell. Do they use deodorant? An annoying cologne? Get used to it, because I'm not changing your seat," Mr. Salmon says, slamming his physics book down on the desk, his glasses halfway down his nose.

"I guess we're stuck together," Ben says in my direction. "It's a good thing you have nice breath."

"I cleared out Mrs. Sapporo's mint dish." I pass one over to him. "Sorry for being short yesterday."

"I told you, you don't need to be sorry." Ben pops the mint in his mouth. "Thanks, though."

While we wait for Mr. Salmon to proceed with the lesson—he's got his face hidden behind the computer on his desk—Ben pulls Chapstick from his pocket and adds a layer to his lips. He licks them when he's done. There's no way Ben's a virgin.

When he catches me looking, he says, "You want some?"

I sit back, surprised. "Are you trying to share your Chapstick with me, like I shared my mints? Because that is definitely not the same thing."

Ben looks at the tube. "Technically, we're not sharing mints. You gave me one."

I grin. "Do you *share* your Chapstick with all your lab partners, or am I special?"

Ben stifles a laugh. "I've never thought about it."

"Haven't you ever heard of herpes?"

He puts the Chapstick cap back on and grimaces. "Well, now I'm throwing it out."

"Sorry, but it'll probably be awhile before we share Chapstick. We've only been lab partners for a few minutes. I'm not that kind of girl."

"That's okay. I like a challenge." Ben winks.

My cheeks heat. We sit in awkward silence. And then Ben scoots his chair away from me and focuses on the front of the room.

I can't believe I just had a flirty moment with Ben Tyler. And we have to sit next to each other all year. I'm definitely failing physics.

I get a charcoal pencil out of my backpack and start nervously adjusting the already-done picture on the front of my sketchbook. I retrace lines and darken places that don't need to be darkened. Using my middle finger, I smudge the edges of the drawing until my hand is covered in black.

"It's *Steal Your Face*, right?" Ben whispers.

"Yeah. How'd you know?"

"This is Boulder. I think we have more pot dispensaries than Amsterdam."

"Touché." I run my hand over the Grateful Dead album cover replica and push away the curl falling in my face. "They're my favorite band."

"You have . . . " Ben points at my face.

"What?"

"Black on your cheek."

"Shit." I cringe and pull my mirror from my purse. Licking my hand, I try to wipe it away, but it only gets worse, like I put on grey cover-up. When I know it won't come off completely, I put the mirror back and abort the mission.

"You're just going to leave it there?" Ben's staring at my cheek.

"It'll come off eventually. It's not a big deal."

"Doesn't it bother you?" Ben's eyes stay on my dirty cheek, like he's never seen anything like it before. The longer he looks, the more I wish I could melt into the floor.

"Should it bother me?"

"I just thought all girls cared about how they look."

"I guess I'm not like most girls," I mumble.

"Can I ask you something else?" When I nod, Ben says, "Why do you bring a sketchbook to science class?"

"I don't plan on passing."

Ben's eyebrows rise. "I just got nervous about my grade."

"Oh. I guess I could try." I put away my sketchbook.

"I'd appreciate that." Ben smiles, the scars on his cheek and eyebrow creasing.

I dig around in my backpack, looking for paper and a pen. It's overstuffed with my Shakedown Street apron and the new sketches I made for Kim and Cass. Setting my apron on the desk, I dig deeper and grab a few sheets of loose paper at the bottom.

"Can I borrow a pen?" I whisper. Ben nods and pulls one from his back pocket. "Thanks," I say.

"You have a lot of stuff in your bag."

"Doesn't everyone have a lot of baggage?"

Something like a half-laugh escapes Ben's lips, and he nods, "Touché."

We go back to the awkward silence thing. Ben pulls on the neck of his shirt, like he's trying to loosen it, as his leg shakes under the desk. The shirt is a blue button-down with wrinkles around the pocket and armpits. There's even a yellow stain of some sort under the breast pocket.

Mr. Salmon's face is still behind his computer, so I point at Ben's shirt and say, "Mustard?"

He looks down at the stain. "Yeah, I can't seem to get it out."

"Baking soda. I use it on my mom's stuff all the time. She gets the weirdest shit on her clothes."

"You do your mom's laundry?" I nod, and Ben cocks his head to the side. "Don't take this the wrong way, but this is the weirdest conversation I've ever had."

I lean in and whisper, "Don't take this the wrong way, but you look weird in that shirt."

Ben gasps, his colorful eyes getting bigger. "I hate this shirt," he says and un-tucks it.

"Why'd you wear it?"

"I . . . " Ben's mouth fumbles with his words. He squints his eyes at me, like he's looking for something. "It was Katelyn's favorite."

Neither of us moves. Our minty fresh breath mixes together.

"If you two are done talking, we'll get started." Mr. Salmon is standing at the front of the room, arms resting across his huge beer gut. We look forward at the same time. The majority of the class is looking at us. I cringe and slouch back in my seat.

"This is Newton's cradle," Mr. Salmon continues, holding up a contraption with five metal balls hanging from two metal bars. "If this ball on the end is released into the others, the energy travels through the three center balls, forcing the fifth ball to move." Mr. Salmon picks up one end and releases the first ball, causing Newton's cradle to move, the balls on either end rocking back and forth in rhythm. It clicks as he talks. Click, click, click. "Conservation of energy. That's all we are. Balls of energy waiting to smack into someone else's energy. It's why you should always use a condom to protect what's in your balls." Mr. Salmon laughs. "Just a little physics humor."

No one in class moves. I think we're all shocked to hear the word "ball" used so many times in one lesson.

"I hate teenagers," Mr. Salmon says.

At the end of class, I hand Ben his pen. "To borrow. Verb. To accept something with the intention of returning it."

"Keep it." He smiles at me for a moment before tucking in his shirt and meeting his friends in the hallway.

To say that Dr. Brenda's office is cluttered would be an understatement. It verges on hoarder status. Her desk is covered in about a hundred snow globes, each with its own snowy scene: the Eiffel Tower, the Bay Bridge, Times Square. I asked her last week if she'd been to all these places and she said no, that she picks them up in Vegas but hopes to travel more someday. I think it's kind of weird that she displays stuff from places she's never been, but who am I to judge? I see a dead girl.

Dr. Brenda came to see me in the hospital. She said it was standard procedure for her to meet with me before the doctors would let me leave. Then she left her card on the bedside table. Ninny found it and set up six months of appointments. I think Ninny felt so guilty for being late to the hospital that she needed to do something extra "mom-ish," like make me go see a shrink. I do it just to keep Ninny's suspicion down. Most of the time, Dr. Brenda and I talk about the weather and her tchotchke collection.

A couch sits along one wall, a multi-colored afghan spread out on the back. It looks like something Toaster might have in his house, something dumped on the front lawn of a fraternity house after a really long weekend of binge drinking. But it smells okay, so I usually park myself there. Dr. Brenda sits in a large leather chair across from me. Today, she's wearing a red dress that comes to her knees and a neckline that hits at the collarbone. The dress matches her fiery hair. I'd even take Dr. Brenda's straight red hair over my own.

"How are you, Aspen?" Dr. Brenda blows on the top of her coffee cup.

Still seeing a dead girl, I think to myself.

"Fine." I nod and look at the huge landscape painting of the mountains that hangs above her head. "Why does everyone in Colorado insist on decorating their houses like we're all ranchers and cowboys? Did you actually shoot that deer and stuff it?" I point to the deer head above the door.

"No. I took it from my father's house after he passed away."

"Oh. I'm sorry. Is most of this stuff his?"

"Some of it is." Brenda looks around and smiles. "He definitely fell into the rancher category. The house I grew up in had more dead animals on the walls than family pictures."

"So in a way, that deer is kind of a family member. You're lucky your dad didn't hang you on the wall."

"I'm pretty sure he wanted to when I was in high school." Dr. Brenda laughs and sets her coffee down. "But this isn't about me. This is about you and how you're feeling." She squares her shoulders to me, a posture indicating her resolute determination to keep things on point.

"I told you. I feel fine." I stuff my hands in my pockets.

"That's good." Dr. Brenda leans forward on her knees. "Would you like to talk about the accident this week?"

"Have you ever looked up the word 'accident'?" I say. "My dictionary says it's an unfortunate incident that happens unexpectedly and unintentionally. But doesn't that mean that most of life is an accident?"

"Some people feel that way."

"Why do I need to focus on one of the many accidents in my life? Shit, me being born was an accident. I'm like the walking personification of the word."

"Aren't some accidents more important than others?"

"Sure, but they all happen in the past. Why is it important to go back and rehash?"

"Looking at the past has its advantages." Dr. Brenda sips her coffee.

"Like what? When I'm dead, people will make me and my past into whatever they want."

"I think there's a lot we can learn from our past."

"But if most of life is an accident, happening unintentionally and unexpectedly, I have no control at all."

"But we can prepare ourselves for how to deal with the accidents by learning from our experiences." Dr. Brenda sits back in her seat and places her coffee cup down on the table. Putting her hands together in her lap, she says, "Let's say you're a smoker."

"I'm not."

Dr. Brenda cocks her head to the side. "Let's *pretend*," she says. I sit back, my arms hugging my chest. "It's a physical habit. Something you think you need to do to help you get through the day. But it's an illusion. If you're taught the right skills, you can kick the habit."

"I don't get it."

"People have emotional habits, too. They work like physical ones, except we can't see them. We have to talk and learn about them."

"All of this learning seems like a lot of work for moments that may or may not happen," I say.

Dr. Brenda and I sit for a minute in silence. I pick at the yarn coming undone from the afghan and check the clock. Every week these sessions seem to last longer.

"Aspen, can I speak frankly to you?" she finally says.

"Sure, Dr. Brenda."

"You can just call me Brenda."

"If I spent a gazillion years in school to add 'doctor' to the front of my name, I'd insist that people call me that," I say.

"Do you know what a willow tree looks like?" Dr. Brenda sits extra far forward in her seat. Her knee is almost touching mine. The closer she gets, the more uncomfortable I feel.

"Yes."

"It has to bend with the breeze to survive."

"Okay." I shrug my shoulders, which must make me look like an ass, but I don't mean to be one. I'm just sick of her analogies. They make my head hurt.

"What would happen if the willow tree didn't bend?"

"It would snap," I say.

"That's right. The willow tree has to embrace the wind, or it'll break. But no one knows which way the wind will blow. All the tree can do is prepare to move in whatever direction the wind takes it."

Aspen

I stare at Dr. Brenda. The silence between us gets longer. I notice her fingernails are painted hot pink with little yellow flowers etched on the tips. It looks like something Katelyn would have liked. Her nails were always so nicely groomed. Mine are still black from the charcoal.

"Do you want to talk about the accident, Aspen?"

My eyes meet hers. It would be easier if Dr. Brenda looked mad, like she hated spending an hour with me once a week. But she looks kind. Beautiful, actually.

"I told you, I don't remember anything," I say apologetically.

Dr. Brenda nods, taking a sip of her coffee. We chat about Ninny's sex-capades with Toaster for the rest of the session. At one point, Dr. Brenda asks if it's hard for me to have a mom who is so "open." She uses her fingers to put quotes around the word.

"If being open with love is her worst fault, I figure I have it pretty good," I say. "Most parents aren't open about anything."

I turn the topic to Uma and her Kim Jong Il tendencies until the receptionist comes over the intercom and announces that Dr. Brenda's five o'clock is here.

"I like your nail polish," I say as I walk out of her office.

"I'll see you next week, Aspen," Dr. Brenda says, closing her office door behind me.

CHAPTER 5

Kim, Cass and I walk around GameStop in Cherry Creek Mall Saturday morning. Or more accurately, Kim and Cass walk; I hobble. People crowd the store, looking at different video games and testing the gaming systems attached to the walls. Posters for ExtermiNATION, hanging in the windows of the store, show a man dressed in camouflage with guns slung over both shoulders. He's attractive: blond sculpted hair, dirt on his cheek. He stands atop a pile of rubble, a destroyed city blurred out in the background. "Only one man stands between peace and the destruction of all humankind. It's fight or face extermiNATION," is printed over his head.

"I can practically smell the God complexes in this store." Kim leans up against the wall, her hip popped out to the side and a disgusted look on her face.

"And they can smell the overdose of whatever Bath and Body lotion you have on today." Cass plays one of the sample games, his eyes fixed on the screen in front of him.

"I'm not wearing Bath and Body," Kim sneers. "It's Victoria's Secret."

"At least your new Disney name matches your smell, Jasmine."

I laugh and lean back against the wall next to Kim, resting on my good leg. I was at Shakedown Street until late last night. Friday nights are my favorite. Mickey lets me work by myself because the place is so dead. I play the Grateful Dead Pandora station too loud, test out different recipes for shakes and draw.

Mickey gave me a set of keys last year for my birthday. Said he trusted me more than my mom, and if she has a set of keys, why not me?

When Mickey hired me he claimed he'd never seen a more responsible kid wearing irresponsible clothes in his life. I was in a pair of bell-bottoms and one of those Mexican poncho things I picked up at the Crystal Dragon, my favorite store in Boulder. I pointed out that I was fourteen and could no longer be called a kid. He said, "See, you're even responsible with your words. Just promise me you won't trade that in for boat shoes and khaki pants like the rest of the hippies out there." I asked why I would wear boat shoes when we live in the mountains. He laughed, the kind of Santa Claus chuckle that I always envisioned my grandpa having. I couldn't help but smile. In my experience, people who laugh hard, like their laughs are bursting from the bottom of their stomachs up through their chests, make the world a little lighter.

Last night, as I was getting into my sketching zone, Hunter Hunter came in with a group of his snowboarder friends and ordered half of the menu. They leaned on the counter and spoke really slowly and squinted their bloodshot eye. It took ten minutes just for them to pay, all of them fumbling around in their pockets for cash while laughing to themselves. I see this behavior all the time with Ninny. Some mornings I'll come downstairs to a trashcan full of Doritos bags and candy bar wrappers. She'll be passed out on the couch, still in her clothes from the night before, the TV on.

I've only tried pot once. It was when Ninny was in Taos. I got so angry one afternoon, when I came home from school and the house was still empty, that I broke into her stash and smoked. Each time I inhaled, I blamed pot for her leaving me; Ninny clearly loved the stuff more than her daughter. If I was going to be left for a cannabis plant, I wanted to see what all the fuss was about.

I didn't really feel anything at first, which made my blood boil, and then my head started to spin. Eventually, I was face down in the toilet, puking my brains out.

I was late to school the next day, which made the teachers start asking questions, which made me more nervous. In the end, the experience made me hate pot even more.

Hunter and his friends drank their shakes, sucking on the straws like it might be the last food on the planet, and dissected the movie *Inception*.

"This is all a dream, man."

"No, this is a dream within a dream, man."

"Shit, man."

"Real isn't real. Real is really a dream and a dream is really real."

"All of life could be a dream that we never wake up from. We're just dreaming this conversation."

The whole time they were talking, I was dreaming of them getting the hell out of Shakedown Street so I could get back to sketching. After they left, my legs ached from hobbling around in my cast to clean up their mess. If I were dreaming, I'd make sure they put their own cups in the garbage can.

"That guy looks like Tom Ingersol." I point to the poster.

"Don't compare Dex Mayhem to Tom Ingersol." Cass shakes his head.

"Dex Mayhem is his fucking name? He sounds like a porn star." Kim rolls her eyes.

"Did you just say something about porn stars, *Jasmine*?" Cass's eyes are wide on Kim. She slumps back on the wall.

"Whatever. Why do you even like this stuff?"

"Because it's art."

"How is the mass murder of people art?" Kim snaps.

"First of all, this is pretend. Second of all, they aren't people. They're aliens that have taken human form so we can't tell that they're aliens. That's how they're able to take over the world."

"So how do you know who to kill?" I ask.

Cass walks up to one of the TV screens playing the video game and points. "It's in the eyes. If they're green, it's an alien."

"So your job as Dex Mayhem is to kill all the aliens?" I stare at the TV screen, trying to determine which avatars are aliens and which are humans. It's pretty impressive how real they look.

"And have sex."

"You get to have sex in this game?" I ask.

"Only if you save the world. No woman wants to do a loser."

Kim rolls her eyes. "Now I know why you like this. You're having virtual sex."

"We're all having virtual sex, considering none of us is having *real* sex."

I laugh and get even closer to the screen. The people-aliens look so real, their bodies moving in fluid motion. The avatars shift their eyes; they have shadows on their clothes and make facial expressions. Cass is right. Artists must draw them.

"You could do this, by the way." Cass nudges me in the side. "Capturing people is, like, totally your artist thing."

I elbow him back but don't respond. My energy level for a discussion about my future, which I've already decided is too unexpected to worry about, is practically dragging on the ground.

"I like tearing the aliens' heads off," Cass says.

"How do you do that?" I squint at the screen, still mesmerized by how real everything looks.

"You press Y, X, A, B on the controller."

"That sounds like a secret code."

"It is," Cass smiles. "You know you got one if they bleed green."

"I didn't know that about aliens."

"That's because Dex Mayhem is out killing them all, so you don't have to."

"But what if you're wrong?" I ask.

"Wrong about what?"

"What if the person isn't an alien?"

"They bleed red." Cass points to a small puddle of red on the screen. It's getting bigger as we speak.

"So you can kill a human?" I whisper, my eyes focused on the blood. I can't look away.

"Of course. You can always kill a human, but it's an accident. You would never mean to do it. You lose, like, a thousand points. It sucks."

Red pops out on the screen, practically hitting me in the face. The glass on the TV holds my reflection in the color. Why does blood have to be that way?

When I feel like I might throw up, I turn away from the screen. "I think I need a drink," I say to Kim.

"I think Cass needs a life."

"Bring me back a Mountain Dew?" he asks.

I nod, the nausea receding the second Kim and I walk out of the store. People are starting to swarm the mall, bags linked over their arms. As we head over to the food court, we dodge through them like balls in a pinball game, trying to avoid getting hit by a rogue purse or shopping bag. We're about to make it to the food court when I see a few familiar faces in the crowd. Suzy Lions and Claire Diaz are walking straight for Kim and me.

Suzy smiles an oversized grin. Her mouth takes up the entire lower half of her face, which looks kind of weird on such a small body. No wonder she's loud when she cheerleads.

"Hi," she says in a bubbly voice, waving. Kim looks at me sideways, but I ignore her. "We were just talking about you."

"You were?"

Suzy digs into her shopping bag. "Totally. Check it out." She pulls out a tie-dye shirt and holds it up to her slight body. "I just bought it at Forever 21."

Kim glares at it. "Holy shit."

"I know. It's awesome. Aspen totally inspired me." Suzy smiles.

"She did?" Kim says in a flat tone. I nudge her in the side.

"I'm sure it'll look great." I yank on Kim's arm, pulling her away from this awkward encounter, but Suzy stops us before we can make a getaway.

"I'm having a party tonight. You should come."

Kim and I stop still, both of us frozen, gaping at the two most popular girls in our grade.

"Yeah, you should come," Claire repeats less enthusiastically, her face flat, like she has to force the words out.

"Why?" I say.

"Because it's a party and it'll be fun," Suzy says. "Please." She holds out the *e* for a while, making her sound like a five-year-old.

"You want us to come to your party?"

"Yes, silly."

I look at Kim, trying to plead with my eyes for some reason not to go. Talking to Suzy in physics made me uncomfortable enough. The prospect of walking through her house, talking to her friends and drinking her alcohol makes my stomach hurt again.

Once Kim shrugs like she isn't totally against the idea, I'm stuck. I can't say no. It'll make me suspect. Why wouldn't

Aspen

I want to go to Suzy's party, with booze and boys and bad decisions? It's the teenage trifecta of awesome.

"Sure," I squeak out.

Suzy claps and jumps up and down, excited. "We'll see you tonight then." She stuffs her tie-dye shirt back in the bag before she and Claire take off down the mall. Before they turn into Anthropologie, Suzy turns around and yells, "Just leave your boyfriend, Isaac, at home!" and winks at me.

Kim and I don't move. I glance at her out of the corner of my eye. Her jaw has fallen slack. "What the fuck just happened?" she asks.

"We agreed to go to a party at Suzy's house."

"I know that." She hits my arm. "I mean, why were we invited?"

"Because we're cool?"

"There are two kinds of cool: people who are obviously cool, and people who are secretly cool because they know it's totally lame to actually say you're cool. Suzy is the first. We're the second. The two cools don't mix."

"I have a feeling there will be a lot of things mixing at the party."

"We're really gonna go?"

I pull in a deep breath. My skin feels tight around me. Malls aren't natural places; with all the doors that only open inside, it's like we're trapped in shopping hell and there's no way out.

"Why not? It's our senior year."

Kim nods at my declaration. "Why not. It's our fucking senior year."

Ninny and I stare at each other over pizza as I wait for Kim and Cass to show up. Incense burns in the kitchen, and Ninny has lit candles instead of using the lights, to save energy. Our dinner would look romantic if a Domino's box weren't sitting between us.

I pick at the pizza, digging each black olive out of the cheese and eating it individually. Ninny looks at me sideways. In response, I pass my glass of milk over to her.

"Why do I have to drink this?" she says. "You're not eating anything healthy either, baby."

"Technically, olives are a fruit." I smile at her. "And osteoporosis is a real problem in older women."

"I'm not an older woman," she says. "And I'm not the one who looks like she spent the day being tumble- dried. You're practically falling into your pizza. Do I need to tell Mickey to give you more time off?"

"No." I answer quickly. "It's just tiring to walk with this cast on."

Ninny narrows her eyes like she doesn't believe me. I shove the piece of pizza in my mouth to prove that I'm hungry and eating and not worn out. She leans forward, resting her elbows on the table.

"Well, your cast comes off next week, and we can be done with all of this." Ninny smiles, pulling the cheese off her pizza and blotting the tomato sauce clean with a napkin.

ASPEN

We sit for a minute in the dull light of the house. It's quiet. I stare down at my plate and pull the crust of my pizza into little bite-sized pieces.

"Would you call me a mistake or an accident?" I ask.

"What?" I look up as Ninny sits forward in her seat, putting her pizza down.

"You didn't mean to have me. So am I a mistake or an accident?"

"What's the difference?"

"The definition of a mistake is 'an action or judgment that was misguided or wrong.' An accident is something unintentional and unexpected," I say.

"If you're asking me whether I think it was wrong to have sex in high school, the answer is no. Sex is natural and beautiful. But I'd be lying if I said I wasn't sloppy on the whole birth control thing. And you were definitely unexpected." Ninny takes a bite of her bare pizza, eyes squinting in thought. "I guess you're an accidental mistake, which is not to be confused with a mistaken accident."

"What's the difference?"

"I don't really know. I like leading with the word I like best. Accidental mistake sounds poetic. Like I didn't mean to do it, but my mistake produced something beautiful."

"But this beautiful accidental mistake ruined your relationship with your parents. Seems like maybe I'm more of a mistaken accident," I say.

When I was little and Ninny told me about her trust fund, she said her dad left her a note on the day her parents moved away from Boulder. The note said something like, "Our high school daughter left on a trip to Winter Park and a stranger came back. We donate to poor strangers, but we don't live with them." Even thinking about reading something like that makes my heart hurt.

"Aspen, baby, I *made* an accidental mistake. *You* are not that. You are a human being with a soul. Not a grouping of words."

I nod. Ninny takes another sip of my milk.

"Tell me about school," she says, changing the subject.

"It's a brick building with lots of horny teenagers roaming the halls."

"Aspen," Ninny barks. "Tell me something I don't know."

"People treat me differently," I say, spinning my plate around on the table.

"Are they bullying you?" Ninny's back gets straight. "Because I'll march my ass down to that school and bitch the shit out of that principal."

"Nice, Mom. You managed to use almost every curse word but 'fuck' in that sentence."

"Fuck," Ninny says and smiles. "Seriously though, what do you mean differently?"

I stack Ninny's dirty plate on mine and carry them to the kitchen. She follows behind me with the milk glass and sets it down on the counter. I scrub everything clean, debating whether or not to tell her that Hunter Hunter talks to me every day. He's upgraded to two-word sentences. "Rad T-shirt." "Smokin' Birkenstocks." "Homework sucks." And he never came into Shakedown Street before yesterday.

Also, Josephine Cusack asked me how I get my skin to be so clear. People say hi to me all the time and wave and smile. It's like I'm the most popular person in school, which makes me want to cry.

"Mom," I whisper as I stack the dishes in the drying rack. "I think I've made an accidental mistake. Maybe a mistaken accident."

"What, baby? I can't hear you over the faucet." Ninny turns off the water.

"I think . . . maybe . . . " A figure moves by the kitchen window. A flash of brown hair. I drop the plate in the sink. The porcelain rattles and Ninny and I jump. "Damn it," I say, picking up the plate and setting it to dry.

Before Ninny can say anything, Kim and Cass burst through the front door.

"Ninny!" Cass yells, almost tripping on the doormat. "Shit, it's dark in here."

"Casanova!" Ninny flicks on the lights and runs from the kitchen to greet my friends. She wraps her arms around Cass, giving him a proper hug. I watch, my nerves still frayed.

I grab the sponge to clean the table, and internally wipe away the words I was going to say a moment ago.

"If you and I went to high school at the same time . . . " Ninny's looking Cass up and down.

"Mom!" I yell.

"No, keep going," Cass smiles.

"I'm ready to get drunk. Let's blow this joint." Kim gives Ninny a high-five.

"Don't bring up blowing a joint around Ninny. You'll put thoughts in her head." I wipe the crumbs from the table into my hand and carry them to the sink.

"Ha. Ha. Very funny. And yet, a great point," Ninny says, "So, what are you kids doing tonight?"

"We're teenagers, not kids," I correct her.

"Party at some popular girl's house. Aspen got us invited. It's like she's famous or something. I'm hoping for naked chicks." Cass nabs a slice of pizza from the open box and stuffs it in his mouth.

"Real sensitive, Cass," Kim says.

"You love me." He smiles, his mouth full of food.

I glance at Ninny. Her head is cocked to the side, and her eyes look like they're working overtime to appraise the level of sexual tension between my two best friends. Her mouth cracks open, ready to say something, and her eyes turn sparkly the way they always do before she talks about sex. I cut her off before she can get a word out.

"We're out of here," I say, pulling the fringe on Kim's brown suede jacket. She grabs Cass' arm.

"Great to see you, Ninny," he yells.

"Don't drink and drive," Ninny offers as we're walking out the front door.

"Don't worry," I say. "We're walking. It's a nice night."

"Aspen." Ninny stops me before I shut the door. I poke my head back in. "Did you want to tell me something?"

I pause and take in the innocent look on Ninny's face. In the house, the candles flicker. "Just that I'm sorry I called you old."

ASPEN

"Be careful tonight. If anybody does something you don't like, kick them in the crotch with your cast. That way it'll be good for something after all. " Ninny smiles, and I can't help but love her. Even if she's not the most on-time person in a crisis and screws her boyfriend on the dining room table.

CHAPTER 6

Suzy's huge white colonial house sits on a hill and has a yard that takes up half the block. Two swings hang from a big tree in her backyard, alongside a bubbling fountain with a statue of a naked boy in the middle. Teenagers gather in the backyard, laughing loudly as a group of guys down shots. I see Tom Ingersol's sculpted hair from the bottom of the driveway. It makes me nervous. And not the excited, itchy nervous that tells you something wonderful is about to happen. A creepy-crawly nervous.

As we walk up, the heavy beat of a rap song emanates from inside Suzy's house. My feet drag on the ground; the uncomfortable feeling in my stomach holds me back. I glance around, worried Katelyn is hiding in the trees, waiting to pop out at me, utterly pissed that I'm invading her world.

"High school kids have the worst fucking taste in music," Kim groans, adjusting her hot pink nose ring.

"You *are* a high school kid," Cass says.

"This is a façade." She points to her face. "Inside I'm a sixty-year-old rap-hating hippie."

"It's a hot facade." Cass smiles in the twilight and Kim blushes, her cheeks practically matching her nose ring.

My eyes skim the trees and shadows. Distracted, I hug my chest.

"Are you okay?" Kim touches my arm.

"We need an escape plan," I say quickly. Kim and Cass look at me, surprised. "If this party sucks," I try to say casually, forcing myself to relax, "let's use a code word to leave."

"Vagina," Cass offers.

"How are we supposed to casually drop that into conversation?" Kim asks.

"Exactly. The code word can't be something like beer or red plastic cup. It needs to be something we rarely say. Like the medical term for your lady bits. Vagina is perfect."

"You say 'vagina' all the time," Kim says.

"No. I think about vaginas all the time. I don't usually talk about them."

"I agree with Kim. The fact that we're even here is weird enough," I say. "We don't need to be shouting about vaginas."

"How about olives?" Kim says.

"Olives?" Cass rolls his eyes. "Vagina is so much better."

"'Olives' is perfect. 'I hate *olives*, don't you?' 'Aspen, didn't you have *olives* on your pizza tonight?' See, plenty of excuses, but not a word people usually use in everyday conversation."

"Perfect." I smile, relieved.

"I still like plain old vagina better, but since we've said it a few times in this conversation, I'm satisfied." Cass runs his hands through his long green-brown hair. "Can we really do this?"

"It's our senior year. We're getting drunk tonight." Kim pats him on the back and links her arm through mine, pulling me toward Suzy's house.

We walk to the backyard, three in a row. I fidget with my hair, tucking it behind my ears, untucking it, and then retucking it. Frustrated with myself, I pull it into a ponytail.

"Maybe this was a bad—" I begin to say, but I get cut off by a flailing Suzy, charging at us full steam, cigarette in hand.

"Oh, my GOD. You made it," she slurs, spilling a bit of whatever's in her red plastic cup on my sandals. "I'm so happy." She hugs me, stumbling to the side.

"Isaac is still a little bummed he wasn't invited." I pat her back.

"Well, if he didn't look like such a narc . . . " Suzy wags her cigarette.

"You know Cass and Kim," I say, helping Suzy balance, while trying to avoid getting burned.

"Sure." Suzy extends the word for two syllables too long and then looks at me, leaning in too close to my face. Her breath smells like cigarettes, sugar and alcohol. "We need to capture this moment. You mind?" She hands Cass her phone to take a picture of us. Then Suzy pulls me into her side until we're cheek to cheek, like we've been friends for years, and smiles. "Just don't get the cigarette. My parents would kill me."

"Say cheese." Cass takes the picture. I'm not sure I'm actually smiling when it flashes. I might look like a deer in the headlights. That's what this moment feels like.

"I'm totally gonna Instagram this." She smiles down at the picture. "You guys don't mind if I steal her for a while, right? I have to pee."

"Can I come?" Cass asks. Suzy squints her eyes at him.

"You're cute. I heard about you and Marcy Humphrey. She's not the only girl with that talent." And then she blows Cass a kiss. His eyes grow three sizes.

"We're getting a drink," Kim says, violently pulling him away from Suzy by the arm. And then it's just Katelyn's best friend and I.

Suzy squashes her cigarette out on the ground. I fidget with my hands, unsure of what to do, and she yanks on my shirt. "Come on. I need to piss like a race horse."

Inside the house, Suzy stumbles toward the stairs. I glance around, checking out the living space. A long wooden table that seats about twenty fills a white dining room, where a gigantic chandelier with what look like real crystals hangs from the ceiling. Ninny and Toaster wouldn't know what to do with all the open table space. White furniture decorates the living room. Silver candlesticks stand over the huge fireplace, and hanging above them is a framed professional photo of Suzy, her brother and her parents posed in a field of wildflowers, the whole family smiling widely. A shiny black baby grand piano sits in the corner, not a speck of dust on it.

Once we're upstairs in Suzy's room, she slams the door behind me.

"You have a bathroom in your room?" I ask. The room smells like flowery perfume and face powder.

"Make yourself at home." Suzy checks her reflection in the mirror hanging over her large wooden dresser, fixing her lipstick, and proceeds to the bathroom. I wait for her to shut the door behind her, but she doesn't. Suzy pulls down her pants and plops herself onto the toilet seat, making an "ahh" sound as she pees. "I had to break the seal," she explains. "My bladder was about to explode."

She sits with her pants around her ankles on the toilet as I walk around the room like a caged animal. It was easier to be outside at the party. I could hide on the fringe and pretend all this wasn't really happening. But being in Suzy's room is like entering the fifth dimension of popularity.

I look through the makeup sitting out on her dresser. She has every color of eye shadow in the rainbow. I pick up a pink lipstick and hold it to my face. Then I notice the picture stuffed into the corner of the mirror.

Katelyn sits next to Suzy, her head resting on Suzy's shoulder, a smile on her face. Not a big smile, just a closed-mouthed one, the kind people who hate their teeth make. Katelyn's knees are pulled up to her chest; she's wearing dark jeans and a Boulder soccer shirt. Suzy's leaning her head on Katelyn's. They look like models from *Seventeen* magazine. Ninny's never even shown me how to put on Chapstick. Unable to stop myself, I pick up the picture.

"She was beautiful." Suzy rests her elbows on her bare knees as she sits on the toilet.

I nod, my eyes unable to move from the picture. Katelyn looks so alive.

"What was she like?" I ask. As I hold the picture, my stomach gets tight.

Suzy washes her hands and says, "She could be . . . I don't know . . . like really fun. Like the best drunk of your life." She dries them on one of the pristine white towels in the bathroom. She stumbles toward me and looks down at the picture in my hand. "That's my favorite," she says, pointing at their faces. "We both look hot in it."

I nod, once again fixated on the girl in the picture. I try to see the fun.

"It's still strange that I'll never see her again." Suzy sways to the side. "My parents keep saying that I'll see her when I get to heaven. Do you believe in heaven?"

"I don't know."

"I think my parents are full of shit. They just want to make me feel better."

"That's probably true."

She takes a sip out of her cup. "Katelyn's not in heaven."

"Was she a virgin?" I bite my lip, pissed I let the words slip. Suzy's feet stop, but her body moves forward a bit, like she might fall over.

"What?"

"I just overheard some girls . . . " I stumble over the words in my head. "Never mind. I shouldn't have asked."

"No, wait." Suzy grabs my arm. "What did you hear?"

"Nothing."

Just then the door flies open and Olivia Torres stumbles into Suzy's room.

"There you are." Olivia holds onto the door. Her long black hair falls over her shoulders, resting against the royal blue sleeveless shirt she's wearing. Her brown eyes are glazed over as she looks at Suzy and then me. "What are you doing here?"

"Suzy invited me," I say, quickly. My stomach turns in on itself as I stand in Suzy's room with Katelyn's two best friends.

"Oh," Olivia says, still keeping herself steady on the doorknob. "I was coming to tell Suzy that we're gonna do a shot for Katelyn."

Suzy's seriousness melts in an instant, and she says, "I love shots."

"Katelyn loved shots." Olivia's voice wobbles and her bottom lip quivers, but her eyes don't leave me. It's almost like she can sense the guilt seeping out of my pores.

"Don't start, Liv, or I'll start." Suzy meets her at the door, wrapping her arms around Olivia's neck. They both start crying.

"I just can't believe she's not here," Olivia says into Suzy's shoulder.

I look down at the picture in my hand. Katelyn belongs here, with her pretty face and shiny hair and shots, with her best friends. Tears prickle my eyes and the picture in my hand starts to shake. When it falls to the ground, a word comes out of my mouth without me thinking.

"Olives."

"What?" Olivia asks, through her tears.

Aspen

"I had olives on my pizza tonight."

"I love olives," Suzy says, lifting her head off of Olivia's shoulder.

And then I walk out of Suzy's room, down her grand staircase, through the dining room with the huge chandelier, and out the back door, mumbling "olives" the entire time. I look for Cass and Kim in the crowd of people, but my vision blurs, mixing everyone together.

This is Katelyn's party. For the first time, I actually try to find her in the crowd. She used to throw her head back and laugh whenever Jeremy Christman hit on her in chemistry.

"Aspen?" a voice says.

Are there stars on your panties? Because your ass is out of this world, Jeremy would say. Katelyn would laugh and say that "panties" was her most-hated word.

"Aspen, you're shaking." Someone grabs my hand. My eyes snap into focus, and I choke back the tears collecting in them.

Ben Tyler stands in front of me.

CHAPTER 7

"Are you okay?" Ben asks, his eyes serious.

"Everyone keeps asking me that." I pull my hand out of his.

"I'll try to stop."

"It's nice coming from you," I say, and instantly wish I could put the words back in my mouth.

Ben stuffs his hands in the pockets of his gray hooded sweatshirt. "What are you doing here?"

"You don't think I should be here either?"

"No. Did someone say that to you?" Ben's eyebrows pull tight. "I only meant a party like this seems a little pedestrian for a girl like you."

"A girl like me?"

"That's not what I mean. I just—" Ben runs his hands through his black hair. "What is wrong with me?"

I cover my mouth to stifle my giggles.

"Now you're laughing at me."

"Did you just use the word 'pedestrian'?"

"You make me nervous," he says.

"I make you nervous?"

"Did you just call me out for saying 'pedestrian'?"

"I did," I say.

"What's wrong with that word?"

"Nothing." I shrug. It was on our English vocabulary list this past week.

We stand, silent, both of us looking around Suzy's yard, avoiding eye contact.

"Do you want some?" Ben holds out his red plastic cup, but before I can grab it, he pulls back. "What about herpes?"

"You wouldn't dare." I squint my eyes at him and snatch the cup, slugging down a huge gulp. "Beer?"

"I can get you something else."

"No. I like beer." I drink down the rest, fast. A bit drips down my chin, and Ben wipes it up with his sweatshirt. My eyes get wide as I realize: He just touched me. I hand him the cup and take a step back.

"I think I need to walk," I say. When neither of us moves, I add, "You want to come?"

Ben looks over his shoulder at the group of guys standing on the lawn, laughing. I recognize Tom's voice.

"I should probably . . . " He glances back and forth between the guys and me, and then he says, "What the hell. A walk would be a nice change." His tone is flat and I can't tell if he really wants to come or if he's just doing it because I had a minor freak-out moments ago. But as we head down Suzy's driveway, away from the party, I find I don't care.

I fill my lungs and push everything out. The nights are turning cold now. I look up through the trees to the cloudless sky. All the leaves are starting to change to yellow and orange. When I take a step into the street, Ben grabs my arm. "Where are you going?"

"To the middle of the street."

He stares at me for a moment. "That's not safe."

"Life isn't safe." I pull my arm from Ben's hand and go to lie down in the middle of the road. Getting a clear view of the sky, I make a wish on the first star I see. *Star light, star bright, first star I see tonight. I wish I may, I wish I might, have this wish I wish tonight: I wish I had straight hair.* It's the same wish I've had my whole life. I know it won't come true, but that's the thing with wishes. The whole point of wishes is to try to make the impossible possible.

Ben stands on the curb, the tips of his shoes hanging off the edge, like he's deciding whether or not to jump. I spread my arms and legs out wide, making my body into a human star. Wind blows up the bell-bottoms of my jeans, chilling my legs.

"Isn't it weird to think that everyone in the world is breathing the same air?" I roll my head to face Ben. He's still perched on the side of the curb, looking down at his feet.

"That's a lot of bad breath," he says.

"The air the one thing the entire world touches."

Ben lifts his leg out past the curb and dangles his foot over the street. He pauses, his shoe inches off the ground, and then, like he's sick of fighting gravity, he steps towards me and lets himself fall.

"What are we doing here?" Ben says as he lies down next to me, his arms and legs extended like mine.

"I haven't decided yet. Maybe we should see what happens." I take in Ben's jeans, his black and white checkered Vans. "By the way, you look better tonight. More comfortable."

"Someone once told me that no one in high school is comfortable," Ben says, his eyes staring up at the sky.

"That's genius."

"Actually, she wasn't that smart." Ben's cheeks fall slack and I know he's talking about Katelyn.

"Do you miss her?" I ask and then roll my eyes at my stupid question. Of course he misses her. "You don't have to answer that."

"I do," Ben pauses, his eyes still focused above him. "Miss her."

"I think a lot of people miss her."

"What makes you say that?"

"She just seems to be all anyone talks about lately."

Ben sits up on his elbows. "What are people saying?" His voice has an edge to it I've never heard before. It's not cutting—more like a parent protecting a child.

"Just that she was kind of perfect," I qualify.

He eases back onto the cement.

We lie silently for a long while, not looking at each other. As the silence goes longer and longer, I wonder what the hell I was thinking, asking him to come with me. Now I'm stuck in the middle of the road with Katelyn's boyfriend and the wind up my pants.

"Want to play a game?" I say.

"What's the game?"

I sit up and cross my legs. "You have to say the first thing that pops into your head."

"That's not a game."

"Yes it is. The definition of 'game' is an amusing activity. This is an *activity*."

"How do you know the definition?"

"They're my specialty." I wave my hand through the air. "But whatever, are you in or out?"

Ben sits up in the road, crossing his legs underneath him. "This might be embarrassing."

"Even better." I resituate myself on the ground, finding a more comfortable position. "Okay, favorite band." Ben takes a few seconds, his eyes searching the space around us for the answer. "You're taking too long," I snap.

"Okay, okay. Vampire Weekend."

"Favorite color."

"Purple."

"Purple? You're right. You should be embarrassed."

"What? Boys can like purple. We're supposed to be honest, right? And you're wearing Jesus sandals." Ben points at my one Birkenstock-covered foot.

"Fine. Favorite food?"

"Tacos."

"Favorite song?"

"Anything by Vampire Weekend."

"That's cheating but I'll let it slide. Favorite sport?"

"Soccer." Ben smiles. The air seems to lighten around us as we talk. "This is kind of fun."

"Sweet or salty?" I ask.

"Salty."

"Swim or ski?"

"Swim."

"Movies or video games?"

"Movies."

"Boxers or briefs?"

"Boxers."

"Worst thing that happened to you today?"

"I remembered that Katelyn's dead." Ben stares at me as the words fall out of his mouth. Neither of us can move. "I'm sorry, Aspen. That just slipped out."

I swallow hard. "That's the point," I say. "You can't help but be honest. Ninny got me to tell her about my first kiss this way."

"Ninny?"

"My mom."

Ben pauses, picking up a loose piece of gravel and tossing it into the air. "I keep waiting for it to get better. I know it's probably wrong, but I kind of want to forget about everything that happened, so I don't have to feel so shitty all the time. You know what I mean?"

"I do. I know what you mean," I whisper.

"Can I tell you something else?"

I nod at Ben. I swear at this moment I'd do anything to take the pain in his eyes away.

"I know I don't really know you, but this is the best I've felt in weeks," he says. "That's pretty fucked up, isn't it? Considering . . . "

I lie back down on the ground and stare up at the speckled night sky. "Isn't it weird that it takes millions of years for the light of a star to actually travel to Earth? So the ones we see right now may have already burned out," I say.

"It is weird." Ben lies back down next to me. When I turn my head away from the sky, his eyes are on me. "Did something happen to you at the party?" he asks.

"No." I lie too easily.

And then, for too many seconds in this unexpected and unintentional moment we stare at each other.

When Ben finally opens his mouth to say something, he gets cut off by one word.

"OLIVES!" Cass comes screaming out of the house, a line of burly guys following him. "I HATE OLIVES!"

"I'm going to kill you, pizza boy!" one of the guys yells.

"She wanted it!" Cass yells over his shoulder. "I can't help that the bottle landed on me! Her tongue went down my throat!"

"Shut the fuck up and run, Casanova!" Kim screams, following close behind Cass.

"Shit," I get up off the ground. "Were you gonna say something?"

Ben shakes his head. "No."

"Thanks for not letting me lie in the street alone." I take off down the road, hobbling on my one good foot. When I glance back, Ben has his knees pulled up to his chest, and he's resting his chin on them.

In the moment before I turn away, I swear he smiles.

I'm lying in bed when my phone flickers brightly on top of the dictionary on my desk. I get up and pick it up, checking the screen.

It's not the right phone.

"I threw you away," I say, dropping it to the ground. But the light keeps getting brighter and brighter. I scramble back against the wall and bump into something. Turning, I see Katelyn, her bright blue eyes alive, her skin clear and beautiful.

"I'm sorry," I say to her. "It was an accident."

Katelyn says nothing. Instead, she turns to the blank wall. All my sketches are gone. The Grove is dead. Katelyn raises her hand and writes the word "liar." It drips down to the carpet, like paint. Or blood.

That's when I open my mouth and scream.

I hear the piercing shriek in my dream before I realize it's not a dream. It's me in my bed, yelling like a baby. I sit up quickly, and grab my throat just to make sure it's actually coming from me. The moonlight streaming in my window catches the faint outline of a girl wearing a soccer uniform, crouched in the corner of the room, her long brown hair hanging straight over her shoulders. I clamp my hands over my mouth, as Ninny bursts in the door. She flicks on the light and Katelyn disappears.

"What is it, Aspen-tree?" Ninny's wearing nothing but Toaster's beat up University of Colorado T-shirt. He runs in behind her in tighty whities, and I cringe.

"It's nothing," I say, wiping sweat from my forehead.

"Honey."

"Just a bad dream, Mom." I try to get my breath under control and snuggle back down into my sweat-soaked sheets.

"Are you sure?" Ninny's brow is pinched, her eyes scanning my face. I nod and force a smile. The hardest smile I've ever had to give someone. Worse than when she walked into the hospital that night, carrying the daisies, and apologized for being late.

Ninny kisses my cheek. "Do you want me to check for the boogeyman under your bed?"

Shivers cover my skin as I search for Katelyn, but I keep cool, making my voice even. I answer her the same way she used to answer me when I was little and asked her that question. "If a man's gonna be in someone's bed, it better be mine," I say.

Ninny laughs. "Remember, dreams can't hurt you, baby," she says and shuts the door.

"I know," I say, even though I know that the small things are sometimes the deadliest.

Chapter 8

The week after the party, my cast finally comes off. My calf is half the size it used to be, and so dry I think I might have leg dandruff for the rest of my life.

"Let's makes a deal," the doctor says. "I never want to see you again." He hands me the orange Sharpie I stuffed down the cast to itch my leg.

My eyes bug out of my head, shocked at his words because his voice is so flat and doctor-ish that he sounds serious. Then he half smiles and it dawns on me that he's making a joke. A really bad doctor joke.

"I'll watch out for accidents," I say, even though you can't watch out for accidents because they're unexpected.

After my dream, sleep becomes scarce. The boogeyman Ninny used to stare away seems to be tucked tightly in the corner of my room. But staying awake helps. Most nights, I draw until my hands and eyes get so tired, I'm forced to sleep. I even picked up a tube of cover-up. Every morning, I dab a cream colored blob of concealer over the blue shadows collecting under my eyes. The bags disappear in seconds.

My hands start to go numb at random times, too, like when I'm in the car or when Olivia and I exchange glances in the halls. She never smiles at me. Her cheeks will go from perky to deflated with one look in my direction. Her shoulders even slump, and I'll want to throw up because she's so sad. Usually when that happens, I focus on a crack in the wall or hum a song that I heard on the radio until the feeling returns to my hands.

Walking helps, too. I've started wandering my neighborhood at night, which I know may not be the safest decision, but it's safer than my bedroom and safer than sleep. I just walk and stare at the stars. For the first time in my life, I'm glad Ninny has a date with dope every night that puts her into a sleeping coma. It's that or she's sleeping at Toaster's, which makes leaving the house even easier. I even walk to school some days. I figure a little bit of exercise can't hurt.

Some nights, I'll feel Katelyn behind me, like a shadow creeping closer and closer. When that happens, I pick up the pace to a jog. I usually end up running full speed until I can't breathe any more and I have to hunch over, my sides splitting from cramps.

One afternoon, I catch her sitting at a table in Shakedown Street. It scares me so badly I drop the shake I'm making. When I go to clean up the glass on the floor, I don't notice it's chipped. It slices my hand.

Aspen

The shake mixes with my blood and I mutter, "I think I'm bleeding a rainbow."

Ninny freaks when she sees the colorful mess, screaming at me, "What happened? What happened?" over and over. But I can't say I just saw a dead person, so I just stand there.

She carts me down to the urgent care clinic. The glass only sliced my hand a little. It just looked like a lot of blood because of the liquid from the shake. The nurse puts one of those butterfly bandages on my hand.

"I hope I never see you again," I say as we leave. By the look on her face, she doesn't get the joke. "I guess it's a doctor thing."

By the time Ninny and I make it home, my head is swimming so badly, I go up to my room and stuff my head under my pillow until the pounding subsides.

When I go to see Dr. Brenda the next day, she asks what happened to my hand.

"I broke a glass."

"How?"

I stumble over my words, and for a moment I debate telling her. I stare into Dr. Brenda's brown eyes, as she leans forward, barely blinking.

"I saw something."

"You saw something?" Dr. Brenda makes a note in her notebook. It's a new addition to our sessions, always there on her lap, ready to collect the things I say. Like she's a detective searching for clues and one day she'll be able to piece together what happened that night based on the little things I say.

"Never mind." I sit back in my seat and stare at the deer head hanging over the door.

"Energy can be neither created nor destroyed. It simply moves from one place to another," Mr. Salmon says. Ben's asleep next to me, resting his chin on his palm, the littlest bit of drool escaping the corner of his mouth. I laugh when his face slips off his palm and almost hits the desk. Mr. Salmon glares at me. "Mass-energy equivalence. Write it down."

I scribble the words in my notebook as heat creeps up in my cheeks. A few people in class look at me, and I slouch lower in my seat.

At one point in the lesson, Mr. Salmon tells us that energy can become mass and mass can become energy, and then he notices that half the students are sleeping and says, "I can't believe it's only October." He starts a countdown at the top of the board and sits down at his desk. 135 DAYS UNTIL THE LAST DAY OF SCHOOL.

I steal a glance at Ben. He makes sleeping look so easy. So peaceful. I don't know how he stays calm amidst all this commotion. The rumors are getting out of control. All anyone talks about is Katelyn and Ben. How people used to see them kissing on the soccer field. How someone overheard Ben say once that he wanted to marry Katelyn. How *perfect* they were. How *perfect* she was.

I can't seem to shake the feeling that I need to know her, so a few days ago I looked up the definition of *perfect*.

ASPEN

Perfect (adj): 1) having all the required or desirable elements, qualities or characteristics.

The definition is so clinical. Suzy described Katelyn as the "best drunk of your life."

Yesterday, I corrected a girl when she said that Katelyn was so awesome and so good at soccer and so perfect.

"Katelyn was actually the best drunk," I said.

The girl crunched her nose up at me and said, "What?"

"Never mind," I said and quickly walked away.

Today, I heard a rumor that I got drunk with Katelyn once.

The loudspeaker blares a few minutes before the end of class and shocks Ben out of his sleep. He sits up quickly, wiping the drool from his mouth. One of his cheeks is red with the imprint of his palm. He rubs it and yawns, arching back in his chair. I pull a red and white mint from my purse and pass it over to him.

"In lieu of a toothbrush," I whisper.

Ben cups his hand over his mouth and smells his breath. "Thanks." He smiles as he unwraps the mint.

"It's that time again," the cheery voice of Ella Vega, our student council president, says over the speaker. "The votes have been tallied, and I have the nominees for this year's homecoming court. Final voting will take place next week, and king and queen will be announced at the homecoming game."

I pull my sketchpad and a charcoal pencil out of my backpack and work on the picture of Dex Mayhem that I started last night. Since Cass said I should be a video game designer, I thought I'd try my hand at it.

"The nominees for queen are Olivia Torres . . . " Ella's voice continues.

I smudge the lines around Dex's sculpted face, giving him a chiseled, dirty yet sexy I-kill-aliens look.

" . . . Claire Diaz, Suzy Lions, Sophia Mohomedally . . . "

I'm fading into my drawing trance when someone in the classroom says my name. Wiping my hair out of my face, I ignore the sound until Ben's elbow knocks my side.

"I let you sleep," I bark in a whisper. "You can let me draw."

"Aspen."

"What?" Ben's face is covered in shock, his eyes bulging out of his head. I sit up quickly. "What is it?"

"You're nominated."

"What?"

"For homecoming court."

"Very funny." But then I feel it. Eyes. Every set in the classroom on me. My body comes to attention like I'm a caged animal looking to get out of a maze. Suzy's face is almost exploding in a grin. "This is a joke, right?"

"Ella said your name."

"Well, she can take it back. I don't want to be on homecoming court. I don't even believe in monarchies. Queens always get their heads chopped off, and I like my head. Other than my hair."

"I like your hair."

"You like my hair?" We stare at each other. I fumble with the words inside my head. Finally I manage in say in a whisper, "I can't be nominated."

Ben reaches up and brushes my cheek with his fingertips. "You have black on your cheek again," he says.

"See, I can't even keep my face clean." My cheek heats to a fiery level just as Suzy flops into the seat in front of us.

"We need to celebrate. This is amazing," she squeals, clapping her hands together. "Let's go shopping."

Ben stuffs his physics book in his backpack. A sinking feeling settles in my stomach. He doesn't look at me as he leaves the room.

"We need to go to the Cherry Creek Mall. They have the best stores," Suzy continues. "Hello, Aspen, are you listening to me?"

"What?" I snap back to Suzy.

"Cherry Creek Mall."

"I hate malls. Too many doors that only open inside."

"No girl hates malls," Suzy says as we walk out of the class together.

"Look, I've gotta do a thing down this way," I say, pointing in the opposite direction from Suzy's locker. "I'll see you later."

"Cherry Creek, Monday after school."

"Whatever," I say as I walk away, lost in a zone.

It takes five hardy bangs before the principal's door opens. I try to calm down, but my jaw is tight and my foot won't stop tapping on the ground.

"Aspen," Mr. James says as he opens the door. I'm beginning to hate the sound of my name. "Can I help you?"

"You said I could come to you with anything."

"Yes."

I try to keep my voice even when I say, "I don't want to be on homecoming court."

"Why not?" Even Mr. James has pity voice and pity eyes, the kind that pull down on the side all sad-like.

"I just . . . I don't think . . . " I can't find the words to say what's in my head. The truth that, if said out loud, would make me seem ungrateful and selfish: I'm only nominated because of the accident with Katelyn. And I can't accept that.

"What is it?" Mr. James touches my arm.

I take a deep breath, my resolve fading. "Never mind."

"People want to support you, Aspen. Consider this their way of showing it."

"Great," I say with emphasis and I give him two thumbs up, even though everything in my body hangs down about to splatter on the floor.

Kim waits by my locker, a pensive look on her face. My nerves pick up.

The picture Suzy took of us at her party got a gazillion "likes" on Instagram. I'm pretty sure the entire school saw it. People commented on how pretty I looked and how awesome Suzy's tie-dye shirt was. I know it's all supposed to make me feel better, like Mr. James said, and I don't want to be ungrateful, but it just makes me feel shittier. Like I'm on some bad reality TV show that makes me famous because I have five kids with five different guys. And I'm pretty sure, by the way Kim's face is contorted into a sour expression, that it makes her feel shitty, too.

Before Kim can say anything, Cass comes screaming down the hall. "Hail, Queen Aspen!" He runs up to me, and lifts me off the ground. "Do you think we'll be able to see your crown through your 'fro-hair?"

I smack the top of his head. "I haven't won yet."

He sets me down, his tall figure towering over me. "You got this in the bag."

"I don't want to be in a bag or a dress or a crown." I elbow him in the side and look at Kim. She's biting her bottom lip, more like chewing on it, her eyebrows pulled tight. "Say something snarky and make me feel better."

"I have a date to the dance," Kim says.

"What?" Cass bites.

"To homecoming. I have a date."

"Who?" Cass asks. There's tension in his throat like the words hurts.

"Jason Park."

"What?" he yells. "Is this some *Jasmine* thing? An alternate person who's taken over your brain? You said he was a douche."

I cringe. Jason is the only other Korean in our grade and Uma's dream guy for Kim. Cass can't compete with that.

"My exact words were 'he's a douche with a bad Asian mustache,' but I changed my mind. He's nice."

"Nice," Cass mocks. "I hope no girl ever calls me *nice*. That's code for 'I'm never gonna touch her boobs.'"

"Maybe Jason will touch my—"

I cut Kim off. "Then will you go with me, Cass? Pretty please." His eyes are still shooting daggers at Kim. "If I'm going to kowtow to this archaic high school ritual, I need a date to give me a corsage. Plus, every queen needs a king, right?"

Cass's shoulders fall and he huffs. "Of course, I'll go with you. But I'm pretty sure Ben Tyler will be your king."

"What?"

I hadn't thought about a king. Of course, it'll be Ben, for the same reason I'm nominated. That and he's just plain hot. Everyone likes a hot king. Thinking about him makes my stomach tight.

"Have you ever noticed how long his eyelashes are?" Cass says.

"He does have nice eyelashes." Kim leans back against the lockers.

"Are we seriously talking about his eyelashes?" I ask, a confused anger coming over me. I don't *want* to know Ben's eyelashes, and yet I do, so well. His eyelashes are kind of like Snuffleupagus's on Sesame Street, all long and accentuating his colorful eyes.

I grab books out of my locker, shoving them in my backpack without looking to see if they're actually the ones I need for my homework.

"Can I have a ride?" Kim asks me.

"I walked today."

"You walked when you have a car?"

"Exercise is good for you."

"That's propaganda sold to you by the American government. Exercise is overrated. Asian people never exercise and we're, like, the skinniest race."

"That's because half the population is starving," Cass interjects.

"Shut up."

"You shut up."

"Will you both shut up?" I yell and rub my temples. Kim and Cass look at me.

"My mom's picking me up, anyway. Dentist appointment." Cass stuffs his hands in his pockets, rocking back on his heels. He pauses for a second and stares at Kim, as if he's holding back words. But Kim doesn't say anything, just wrinkles her nose and looks at the wall. "I'll see you guys tomorrow."

Cass leaves, his head hanging low over hunched shoulders.

"Will you go to Common Threads with me to get a dress?" Kim asks when Cass is out of earshot.

"Why did you do that to him?"

"Do what?"

"And why the sudden school spirit?"

"We're seniors," Kim says. "We need to do this stuff. We never went to a party at Suzy's before, but we did it."

"Cass almost got his ass kicked by Brian Fontaine."

"Whatever. He shouldn't have French-kissed Lily."

"Are you jealous?"

Kim adjusts her backpack, shifting her weight from side to side. She looks at me with resolute eyes. "Will you go shopping with me or what?"

I say yes, but as we walk out of school, I can't stop thinking about the love the two of them ignore. Don't they know we're all one accident away from death? There might not be a tomorrow for them to love each other.

The next day, Hunter Hunter shows up at Shakedown Street, riding his skateboard up to the counter. He flings his head off to the side to move the hair falling in his face.

"Do you get free shakes?"

"Sometimes."

"Cool. Is that the Dead?" He points at my mural.

"It is."

"Cool. Do you have a date to homecoming?"

"I do."

"Cool. Maybe we could dance together?"

"Sure."

He leans down on the counter. "Your scar is totally bad ass."

"Cool," I say. He's rubbing off on me.

Hunter smiles. Ninny walks out of the back room and gives him a suspicious look, but not a "mom" suspicious look of "what the hell do you want with my daughter?" It's an intrigued suspicious look, as if the second he walks out the door she's going to ask me if we've made out.

"I better hit it." Hunter jumps on his skateboard. "I totally voted for you," he says over his shoulder as he rides out the door.

"Voted for you?" Ninny taps my butt.

"Ugh, homecoming court." I go back to cutting strawberries.

"Oh, my God! You are, like, so cool!"

"Shut up, Ninny. Don't make it worse."

"I think I need to do a cartwheel. This is so exciting." Ninny walks to the middle of Shakedown Street and flings herself forward, looking like a five year old. She jumps up, her hair in her face. "I've still got it," she says a little out of breath.

"You just flashed Pearl Street."

"Whatever." She adjusts her shirt.

Mickey comes in the back door with two huge grocery bags in his arms. "Who just flashed Pearl Street?"

"Ninny," I say, my head down, focused on the strawberries.

"Damn." Mickey sets down the bags and snaps his fingers.

"That's because Aspen-tree is on homecoming court," Ninny squeals.

He groans, putting a bunch of kale in the refrigerator. "I thought I taught you to fight against conformists, not join them."

I help Mickey unload the other bag. "I'm not joining anybody. But I can't turn down the nomination."

"Nor should she," Ninny interjects, sitting back in a chair and putting her feet up on the table. "My baby deserves to win."

"I don't deserve anything. And get your feet off the table. I just cleaned it."

"So turn it down." Mickey puts his hands on his hips.

I look from Ninny to Mickey, like the devil and the angel sitting on my shoulders fighting about what to do. Except I'm not sure which one is the demon and which is the voice of reason.

"You know as well as I do, Mick: If you go against the tide, you're asking to drown. I just want to get through this year alive."

The statement hits them at the same time, like a rock to the face. Pain surfaces in their eyes. Real pain, not the pity I get at school, and I wish I could reverse time and take it back.

Ninny shakes it off first. "You're gonna look great in a crown."

"Just promise me you'll both be at the football game," I say, going back to cut more strawberries.

Ninny comes around the counter and hugs my shoulders. "I wouldn't miss it."

"Me neither." Mickey smiles.

I keep my head down and cut, stroke after stroke. Homecoming is a moment. And then it'll be gone. Like everything else.

And there are worse things than wearing a crown.

CHAPTER 9

Later that week, Tom Ingersol congratulates me on my nomination. We're standing at my locker, and he's got his faux-hawk in perfect position. "I voted for you," he says.

"Thanks, Dex," I say and then realize my mistake.

"Who's Dex?"

"Nobody."

Tom gives me a sideways grin and says, "Do you have a date?"

"I do."

He runs his hands over his slick hair. "Then I'll see you later, locker buddy." Tom winks at me. It should give me a good kind of butterflies, because Tom is actually really hot if you shave his head, but it just makes me slouch lower in my shoes.

On Friday, Kim and I are about to get in my car when someone yells my name across the school parking lot. We look up at the same time, and see Ben in his soccer uniform, running like a madman toward us, his cleats clomping on the ground.

"Aspen," he says, out of breath and bending over, clutching his side. "Shit, I have a cramp."

"Put your hands over your head," Kim says, and Ben does it. He looks cute in his shin guards and shorts with little beads of sweat coming off his forehead. For a second, I imagine what's under the shorts. He said he wears boxers.

"Aspen," Ben says. That's when I realize I'm staring at his crotch.

"Yes." My eyes snap to his face.

"I slept through class like three times this week, and we have a test on Monday," he says, panting, arms stretched up to the sky. "Will you study with me?" When he notices Kim raising her eyebrows at him, he qualifies, "Because we're lab partners."

"I don't know. You're not really keeping up your end of the bargain."

"Please, I'm begging you. If I fail physics, I'll lose my scholarship." Ben grabs my hand. I steal another glance at his shorts.

"Let go of her hand," Kim says, annoyed. We both look at her, our hands dropping to our sides.

I choke and squeal out, "Can you come to my house?"

"I'll go wherever you want me to go."

"When do you want to shop?" I ask Kim.

"Sunday. Kim Jong Uma's got me on lockdown tomorrow. College prep."

"Tomorrow then."

Ben nods. "I promise, I won't sleep as much." He walks away, and I go to get into the car, but Kim doesn't move. She just stands there, arms across her chest.

"What the fuck?" she says.

"What?"

"What the hell was that?"

"Ben asked me to study with him."

"You say that like it's normal for Ben Tyler to do that." Kim says the words in a flat tone. I can't tell if she's happy or sad or mad. "Something's going on."

"Whatever, Jasmine." I get in my car, and turn up the radio. Kim slides into the passenger seat. We don't say a word as I take her home.

The next morning, Ninny and I sit at the dining room table, eating cereal. I had to endure another evening with Uncle Toaster and his smacking lips while he ate the mushroom ravioli that I cooked. At one point I asked him if he was a cow. He looked at me, confused, and said, "No, why would I be a cow?"

"You sure do like grass." I pointed at his bloodshot eyes. "And you smack your lips like you were raised in a barn."

At that point, Ninny sent me to my room. I didn't mind. I had a pounding headache anyway. I fell asleep for a few hours here and there, until the sun came up.

I poke at my cereal with my spoon. "Do you love Toaster?" I ask Ninny.

"I dunno. Define it."

"Love: an intense feeling of deep affection or romantic sexual attachment."

Ninny scratches her head. "The second part, but minus the romance. I love the way he loves on me."

"That's gross." I plop my spoon in my cereal, now finished eating. "Have you ever been in love?"

"Aspen, baby, you know I don't put a lot of weight on emotions like that. People who believe in love and marriage and forever tend to break promises." Ninny sits back in her chair.

"Is that what happened with Uncle Steve in Taos?"

"Taos was different." Ninny's eyes get serious.

"How?"

She sits back in her chair. For a moment, Ninny doesn't answer my question, and then she says, "You want to know what I believe in? When you meet someone and you're drawn to that person for a moment in time. But that's it. It fades like everything else. And there's nothing wrong with that. I'd rather spread my love."

"I'm ready for your love to fade with Toaster." I get up and rinse my bowl out in the sink, slightly annoyed that Ninny didn't answer my question. She comes up behind me and wraps her arms around my waist.

"Now, the love between a mother and her child," she says, petting my head. "That is forever."

"What's the difference?"

"I don't know. It just is. Some things can't be defined."

I smile and lean my head back to meet hers, my annoyance fading. Her patchouli oil fills my nose, and it's so familiar. It's crazy how a smell can cause the world to spin differently. It can bring you back in time or move you forward or pause the moment so you can live in everything that smell means.

When Ninny was in Taos and I wasn't sure if or when she was coming back, I curled up in her clothes every night after school and slept there. I was worried that one day the clothes would stop smelling like her and then I'd really be alone.

"But what about your parents?" I ask.

Ninny's arms and back stiffen. "My parents are an anomaly, which can be defined as 'assholes.'"

"Do you ever miss them?"

Ninny plays with one of my curls. "Do you want me to braid your hair today, baby?" She whispers in my ear, and I nod. Then we sit down, and she strokes my hair, separating it into two ponytails. Her soft touch on my head makes me sleepy and calm. Ninny lets out a long breath. "My mom taught me how to braid. We used to practice on my dolls. She would say every respectable girl knows how to braid."

"You never taught me."

"I couldn't care less if you're respectable." Ninny ties a rubber band around the end of one braid. "I care that you're you."

"Your parents didn't want that for you?"

Ninny doesn't say anything for a few seconds. Her hand just holds the end of my braid. The only other time she's spoken this much about her parents is when she told me about her trust fund and the note her parents left. "My parents didn't want a lot of things." Her voice sounds distant and soft; then, as if snapping out of it, Ninny says, "They left. I have you. I prefer the latter. That's all that matters."

Ninny finishes the braid on the other side and goes into the kitchen for another cup of coffee.

"Do you ever think about them?" I ask.

"Why would I want to think about the worst moment in my life? It won't change the fact that they're assholes." Ninny sips her coffee and stares down at the mug in her hand. I don't press it further. This is one of the very few times I understand Ninny completely.

At that moment, there's a knock at the door.

"Who's that?" Ninny sets her mug down.

"That's probably Ben."

"Who's Ben? Is he your boyfriend?"

"No," I snap. "He's my lab partner."

"Is he hot?"

"Is that really appropriate?"

"When have I ever been appropriate? Do you want to make out with him?" My cheeks heat at the thought as I picture Ben's round "I'm not a virgin" lips. "Oh, my God, you do!" Ninny yells.

"Please don't do another cartwheel."

"I've gotta see this boy." Ninny nudges me out of the way and sprints to the front door.

"Don't even think about it," I yell after her, but I'm too late.

She flings open the door. "May I help you?" she asks in a mature voice that isn't her own.

"Um, I'm here to study with Aspen," I hear Ben say, as I hide, cringing.

Ninny takes a second, and then her voice returns to normal. "Studying, huh? I used to *study* a lot with boys. You look like you've *studied* with a few girls before."

"What?" Ben's voice is a mixture of fear and confusion.

I pull the door back and yank Ninny away. "Ninny's kidding," I say. "Well, not about the sex thing."

"I thought we were talking about studying."

"Boys and their *study* habits," Ninny says to herself. "I bet you *study* by yourself every morning before school." She rolls her eyes as she grabs her purse off the coat rack.

Ben walks in the door, looking half terrified, half intrigued. "I've heard a lot about you, Mrs. Taylor." He seems hesitant as he looks around the house, like something or someone might jump out and bite him.

"No 'Mrs.' Marriage is a misogynistic invention created by men who wanted to squelch the innate power of women, who had no security in their own sexuality and felt the need to control a woman's. I am a free being, living without the constraints of a prefix to my name. Please, call me Ninny." She holds out her hand to shake.

"Ninny, it's nice to meet you." Ben takes her hand, and like my mom is still in high school, she blushes.

"I've heard a lot about you, Ben."

"That's enough of that." I grab onto his backpack and yank him toward my room.

"Leave the door open!" Ninny yells after us. I turn around and squint at her. "I'm kidding. That was so unnatural. I'm heading to Shakedown Street, Aspen-tree. I'll be back by dinner." And then Ninny points to Ben and makes out with her hand.

"Bye, Mom," I say through gritted teeth. Once we're in my room, I slam the door shut. "Sorry about that."

"Ninny," Ben says, his eyes fixed on the door. "Now, I understand."

"Why I'm so weird?"

"You're not weird. You're honest." Ben sets his backpack on my bed and starts to wander around, picking up knick-knacks and pictures. I push down the guilt that creeps up at the word "honest." "Did you do all these?" he asks, pointing to the Grove.

"I did."

"Which one is your favorite?" Ben reaches out to take the one of Kim and Cass off the wall. I swat his hand away.

"That's like asking a parent which kid they like best. I love them all equally."

"Parents always lie." Ben pulls on one of my braids. "They totally have favorites." And then he winks at me. My stomach gets tight just seeing his eyelashes.

I sit down on my bed and wipe my sweaty hands on my quilt. "I will admit, every time I do a drawing, I think I like it the best, but then I hang it up with the rest and it becomes a piece of something bigger and better."

"That's poetic." Ben sits next to me, his leg inches from mine. I can practically feel the heat of his body.

I grab my physics book. "Where should we start? Newton's first law or the big bang theory?"

Ben lies back on my bed and then flips over onto his stomach, like he's been here a million times before. He kicks off his Vans. He's wearing white athletic socks. One has a hole in the heel.

"So do you have a date?" he asks.

"What?" I pull my eyes off his socks.

"A homecoming date."

I flip a page of the book and pretend to look for something. "Yeah, I'm going with Cass Sawyer. You?"

Ben cradles his head in his arm. "I don't plan on having a date to anything for a very long time." He plays with a string coming off my quilt, wrapping it around his finger until his skin turns blue.

"Cass is my best friend."

"That's nice."

"That's why we're going together. As friends."

"Friends are good." Ben's eyes are still fixed on the string.

I flip through my notes and find the page of definitions. Ben finally pulls the string loose from my quilt, snapping it free.

"I like Ninny," he says.

I roll my eyes. "Everyone likes Ninny. And she likes them back, a little too much."

Ben chuckles, making the bed move. My eyes strain not to look down the length of his body. Down his back to his butt and to his legs. He's wearing an old red T-shirt with a few holes in the neckline, and jeans. It might be my favorite outfit ever.

"The big bang theory: the current model of galactic evolution in which the universe was created from an intense and brilliant explosion of a primeval fireball," I read aloud.

"Primeval Fireball would be an awesome name for a band." Ben rolls onto his side.

"A band?"

"They'd be a mix of Metallica and Adam Lambert. Hardcore rock with makeup."

"Can we stick to definitions?"

Ben yawns. "Definitions are boring."

"Definitions are not boring. They're comforting."

"Comforting?"

"Yes. There are no surprises. You know exactly what a word means. You just have to memorize it."

"You don't like surprises?"

I grunt and snap my book closed. "You're the one who asked for this study session. If you don't want to do it, then why are you here?"

Ben looks at me with wide eyes. "I'm sorry," he says, and cracks a grin.

"Now you're laughing at me."

"No, I'm not." Ben hides his smile with his hand. I pick up one of my pillows and whack him over the head with it. He grabs it from my hands and does the same back, knocking one of my braids loose.

"You wrecked my hair." I laugh, checking my reflection in the mirror. One of my braids is loose, so I pull both free, returning my hair to 'fro status.

"I thought you didn't care about things like that." Ben hugs the pillow to his chest.

I tie my hair in a bun on top of my head. "It's not that I don't care. I just know I'll never be perfect." I use the word intentionally.

"No one is perfect."

"People say Katelyn was."

Ben's eyes focus on my pillow.

When he doesn't respond, I ask, "What was she like?" I ask. My stomach rumbles with nerves the moment the question comes out of my mouth.

It takes a second for him to respond. Then Ben says, "Complicated."

"Everyone is complicated."

"Then she was like everyone." He doesn't say anything else.

I pretend to check my reflection in the mirror one more time, but really, I steal a glance at Ben. His head hangs low. It makes all my nerves turn sour.

"Beta Particle," I say.

"What?"

I move to sit back down on the bed. "That would be the name of my techno band of geeks, and their groupies would be called 'electrons.'"

Ben's one cheek pulls up into a half-smile and he finally looks at me. "Can I be an electron?"

"No way. Electrons love definitions."

"I can love definitions."

"You just said they're boring."

116

"I take it back."

"For someone who loves definitions, you can't seem to make up your mind."

"I love definitions." Ben grabs my hand and places it on his heart. "I swear."

My breath catches in my throat. I grab the pillow away from him and hit him in the shoulder with it. "I don't know. You probably can't even define beta particle."

"That's why I'm here." Ben walks over to my stereo. "But we need music." Before I can stop him, he presses play on my iPod. As guitar chords come through the speakers, I stuff my face into the pillow, embarrassed. "Vampire Weekend?" he asks.

I peek one eye out. "I thought I'd see what's so great about them."

"And?"

"They're pretty good." I set the pillow back down. "But not as good as Beta Particle."

"Duh. It's impossible to be better than Beta Particle."

"Spoken like a true electron."

Ben scoots back on my bed and lies down. "By the way, I'm glad you're going to homecoming with a friend," he says, yawning and closing his eyes. I can't tell if he means it's nice I can go to a dance with my friend, or if he's happy I don't have a real date. And like so many other things in my life, I'm not sure I want to know.

ASPEN

I remember Ben falling asleep multiple pages of definitions into studying. I remember thinking I might rest my eyes, too. And then I woke up, my face plastered to my notebook, and now there's a small puddle of drool on the paper. The music has stopped. I sit up quickly. For a second I have no idea where I am. It's the hardest I've slept in weeks. I rub my eyes, checking the corners of my room for any hint of the brown-haired girl that lurks in the shadows. Nothing.

Ben sleeps next to me, his face resting on my quilt. He breathes evenly and slowly. For just one moment, I stare at his back rising up and down.

When I finally do get up, I stand in front of the Grove, staring at the empty spaces. The only noise in my room is Ben's deep breathing. I go to my desk and grab my sketchpad, excited to capture this moment with Ben lying on my bed, so I can add him to my wall forever. My charcoal pencil sits poised on top of the paper . . . and then I set the sketchpad down. I inwardly wish Katelyn to be alive.

"I fell asleep," Ben whispers as he pushes himself up on the bed.

My cheeks get hot at the sound of his voice. "Me, too."

"You have pen on your face."

"I do?" I check my reflection in the mirror. There are blue faded words on my cheek. I lick my hand and start to rub them away.

"That seems to be a pattern with you." Ben looks at me through the reflection in the mirror, his eyes clouded with sleep. He stretches his arms over his head, revealing a sliver of skin right above his jeans. I divert my gaze to the ground.

Ben doesn't seem to notice. He packs up his things and says, "Sorry I totally crashed. It's just that I have a hard time sleeping at night. I start thinking about everything and . . . " He trails off.

"Me, too," I admit.

A look of relief comes over Ben. "You, too?"

I nod, and he smiles. "Well, I guess I should get out of your hair," he says, tapping the matted bun on my head.

"Are you making a hair joke? Because it's not funny."

Ben smiles. "Do you want to come with me?"

"Where?"

"Wherever."

I pause and then ask, "Can we walk . . . wherever?"

"We can do whatever you want."

"Do you like free stuff?"

A moment later, Ben and I are headed out the door and into the cool fall air.

Ninny's face lights up when we walk into Shakedown Street. "Done *studying*?" She winks at Ben.

"Control your hormones, Ninny. We just want a shake," I say.

"You both work here?" Ben whispers to me.

"How do you know I work here?"

"I saw your apron in your backpack."

Ninny leans on the counter, her eyes moving up and down Ben's clothes. "One shake with two straws? I don't know. His clothes look pretty wrinkled."

"They're always wrinkled."

"Hey." Ben nudges me.

I elbow him back. "You're the one who called me honest."

"You guys are too cute," Ninny says, leaning even further over the counter, a goofy grin on her face. She looks like a twelve-year-old kid. "*Studying* suits you Aspen, baby. I haven't seen you look this good in weeks. I told you orgasms make you live longer."

"Ninny!" I yell, but a laugh bursts out of Ben's lips.

"We just fell asleep," he says. "I promise. I'm not that kind of guy."

"You look like that kind of guy." Ninny smiles.

"Can you get us two Strawberry Fields? Please?" Free food might be awesome, but it's not worth this torture. "We're gonna sit outside, away from you. And you should clean the tables before Mickey sees."

Ninny salutes me and pinches my cheek. Ben and I take a seat at one of the few wire chairs and tables in front of Shakedown Street on the Pearl Street Mall. It's the kind of mall I like: the outdoor kind that's really just a pedestrian street with shops and people walking with coffees, all bundled in scarves. And every store door opens directly outside.

"Is it weird that you work together?" Ben asks, sitting down.

"Sometimes." I zip up my fleece jacket to block the cooler fall air. "But usually I'm just glad she has a job."

"I like Ninny. She's not like my parents at all."

"She's not like anyone's parents. I'm sure yours are normal."

"What's normal?"

I pull out my phone to look up the definition. "Normal: usual, average or typical."

"Nope. My parents definitely aren't normal."

"What's not normal about them?"

"For starters, that sentence is plural and I only have one." Ben leans back in his seat, hugging his arms over his chest to protect himself against the chill. "My mom died after my sister was born."

"How?"

"Cancer." Ben doesn't look at me when he says it.

"How old is your sister?"

"Sam's ten," he says.

I sit back in my seat letting the information sink in. Ben's mom has been dead for ten years. Ninny's trip to Taos doesn't seem so bad. And at least I never knew my dad, so I can't really miss *him*. I just miss the idea of him. But Ben must remember what his mom looked like, how she sounded and smelled.

"What about your dad?" I ask.

"Still trying to get over it." Ben's voice is deep as he looks off at the people walking down the street. "So am I officially an electron or what?"

"I don't know," I say. "You did fall asleep."

Ben finally looks back at me. "So did you."

"Define kinetic energy."

"Energy that a body possesses by virtue of being in motion."

"Radiant energy?"

"Energy that is transmitted in the form of electromagnetic radiation."

"Potential energy?"

"Energy possessed by a body by virtue of its position relative to others." Ben leans in across the table, a sly grin on his face. "I told you I love definitions."

I stumble over the next word in my head. Luckily, Ninny comes out with two drinks and sets them down in front of us, breaking up the moment.

"Have a beautiful day," she says, and winks at Ben.

"Thanks, Ninny." He takes a sip.

"Speaking of beautiful, my daughter's not bad to look at."

I choke, and some of my red shake comes out my nose. "What is wrong with you?"

"Aspen's not like anyone else I know, that's for sure," Ben says.

"What does that mean?" I set my cup down and lean toward Ben.

"I just mean that you're not like anyone else. You leave dirt on your face. You wear Jesus sandals." Ben's voice wobbles as he speaks.

"It wasn't dirt. It was charcoal," I say through clenched teeth.

"I just mean you're unique." Ben stumbles over his words. "Shit. You lie down in the middle of the road." He looks at Ninny and back at me.

"That's my cue," Ninny says, and exits quickly.

"I'm not saying this right," Ben says.

"That seems to be a theme with you," I mumble.

"It's because you make me nervous."

I ignore the disappointed feeling in my stomach and focus on the people walking up and down the street. You can find every different kind of person on Pearl Street. Rich, poor, college students, four-piece string bands, homeless bucket drummers by the name of Toaster.

"Aspen, look at me."

I blink, noticing someone in the crowd. Two people actually.

"Don't be mad," Ben says.

My breath picks up as they walk towards us. One—with long brown hair down her back and the hips of a goddess. The other—his hips shift awkwardly, weighed down by the gun and handcuffs clipped to his thick belt.

"I'm not—" but I can't get the rest of the words out. The closer Officer Hubert and Katelyn get to our table, the blurrier my eyes get, until I think I might pass out. I clasp my hands in my lap when I notice they're shaking.

"Aspen, it's good to see you," Officer Hubert says with a smile. But she just stands there. Silent.

I tap my finger on my leg, focusing on the beat. "Hi," I choke out, breathless.

"How are you?"

"I'm fine." I force the corners of my mouth upward.

"That's good. You look good. No more cast."

"All healed up." My voice practically squeaks as I hold out my leg, my finger tapping faster. But I don't let my eyes shift to her.

"I've thought about you a lot," Officer Hubert says with genuine concern. He tips his Rockies baseball cap to Ben. The same one he wore that night. "Take care," he says over his shoulder as he makes his way down the street. Katelyn follows and soon she's lost in the crowd.

"Not a fan of cops?" Ben asks.

"Ninny taught me to be wary of authority."

"Aspen, what's wrong?"

"Why do you think something's wrong?"

The corners of Ben's eyes are pulled down, and he looks pale. He glances at my busy hands. "I can just tell."

I press my hands against my legs.

"That was the police officer—" Ben starts to say, but I cut him off.

"I'm freezing. It's too cold to eat this outside." I stand up and throw my shake out.

Ben doesn't say a word, just follows suit. He doesn't bring up Beta Particle or his parents or how I make him nervous again.

Chapter 10

Kim and I go shopping on Sunday. I walk around Common Threads, my eyes hanging at half-mast, as I clutch a large chocolate macchiato.

I couldn't sleep again last night. Officer Hubert's voice kept ringing in my head. When I couldn't take it anymore, I looked up Ben's address on the Internet and walked over to his house. It's only a few miles from mine. I stood across the street from the one-story box house and waited to see if any lights turned on or if I could see him moving around in the darkness. It's not like I would have knocked on his door or anything. It just would have been nice to know I wasn't the only one awake in the darkness.

My legs started to hurt from standing, so I sat down next to a pile of leaves. I'd pick up a handful and crumple them to bits and let them drift off my palm into the wind. After awhile, I ran home and crept back into my house, tiptoeing past a snoring Ninny, asleep on the couch. A joint rested in an ashtray on the coffee table.

"Are you okay?" Kim looks at me sideways as I limp around the store. "You look extra gimp-ish today. Does your leg still hurt?"

The run home in my Birkenstocks caused little blisters to form on my feet. I had to put a bandage on every toe. This morning, I found an old pair of sneakers in the back of my closet. I haven't put them on since gym class freshman year. "Time for new Birkenstocks." I shrug.

"Are you sure that's it?"

I hold up a baby blue puff-sleeved dress. "This one is totally you."

"If it'll keep Jason Park away from my boobs, I'll take it." Kim skims a rack of dresses. "Uma's *way* too proud of this moment. I need to do something disappointing ASAP."

"You could tell her you're going to community college," I offer.

"Jesus, you sadist, I don't want to give her a heart attack." Kim and I both laugh.

In the end, we find two dresses, a long, pale pink off-the-shoulder number for me, and a mustard yellow muumuu for Kim.

"If Jason thinks I'm sexy in this, he's delusional." Kim gives the cashier ten dollars for her $8.99, male-repellant homecoming frock.

That next day, at my appointment, Dr. Brenda sits in front of me, her trusty notebook on her lap, a new snow globe on her desk. This one has the Seattle Space Needle inside.

"Did you go to Vegas again?" I ask.

"No, that one is actually from Seattle. I spent the weekend at a conference." Dr. Brenda sips her coffee.

"A head-shrinker conference? Aren't you worried everyone is psychoanalyzing you?"

"I know they are," Dr. Brenda laughs and sets her coffee down. "It's not that different from high school."

"It's all a fishbowl."

"A fishbowl?"

"You know, like the ones at the doctor's office that kids press their noses against and tap on. Have you ever thought about how the fish feel, being stared at all the time?" I pick at the loose fabric on the couch.

"Do you feel that way?" Dr. Brenda asks.

"Sometimes."

"How does it make you feel?"

"Like a fish in a fishbowl." I sound like an ass.

Dr. Brenda makes a note in her notebook, and I cringe. I shouldn't have said anything. I gaze up at the dead deer head hanging over the door.

"Why can't we just let go of the dead?" I ask.

"What?" Dr. Brenda sets her pen down.

"That deer. I'm sure if it could talk, it would say, 'Take me down. I'm sick of sitting up on this pedestal for people to look at.'"

"But it means something to me."

"So you keep this dead thing around because you can't bear to let it go? Or maybe you want to admire its perfection. But I'm sure the deer wasn't perfect. I'm sure it had dirt on its face and bad hair days, too. And I get that it's complicated and all that. But what does complicated mean? Why can't we just take the deer off the wall and let it rest in peace?"

I yell the last part. It shocks Dr. Brenda so much that she sits back in her seat and sets down the notebook. It even shocks me. "Sorry. I don't know what I'm saying. I'm nervous about my physics test."

"Aspen, this isn't about my father's taxidermy," Dr. Brenda says. "This is about you grappling with the fact that a young person was killed in a car accident that involved you."

"You know what this is about?" I sit forward in my seat. "This is about how one accident has become *the* accident. My life has been punctuated with a proper moment. But we've already established that life is filled with accidents. Hundreds and thousands of moments that I have no control over, because they're unexpected. And yet, we keep going back to one. Like maybe I can change something or do something different. But I can't. So what's the point?"

"Our past and our present can be very firmly linked. Our memories have a way of creeping up on us."

"Not if we don't let them." I stand up and sling my backpack over my shoulder. "Mind if I leave early? I need to study."

"For your physics test?"

"Yeah."

Dr. Brenda nods as I walk to the door. Before I can close it, she stops me and says, "If life is totally out of our control, Aspen, why study for a test? Think about it."

Mr. Salmon hands a Scantron sheet to each student who walks through the door, announcing we have 45 minutes to answer 200 multiple choice questions. "If you think I'm grading an essay my last year of teaching, you're crazy." Then he sits down behind his desk and reads *The Denver Post*.

Ben looks up at me as I walk to our joint desk. He doesn't say a word, but pushes a folded piece of paper towards me. I open it and find a hand-drawn picture of an emblem: a bunch of red and blue circles clustered together, and two circles jumping out of the back. It reads: *Official Electron for Beta Particle: Let the radioactive revolution begin.*

"Did you draw this?"

Ben nods, a sly grin on his face. "Sorry for being a jerk."

I stare down at the poorly drawn picture and smile back. Taking a mint from my purse, I hand it to Ben under the desk. He pops it in his mouth as Mr. Salmon begins to pass out the test.

After class, as I'm taping the picture to the inside of my locker door, Suzy comes up behind me.

"Beta Particle. What's that?"

"It's a joke," I say, practically caressing the picture.

"Do you want to take my car or yours?"

"Take your car where?" I close my locker door.

"Dress shopping, silly."

"I already have a dress," I say as a vague memory pops into my head: me, agreeing to go shopping with Suzy, even though

I'm not sure I actually agreed. I think I grunted and walked away. "And I can't—" But Suzy cuts me off.

"I already told Twitter we're going." She looks so excited; she's practically bouncing on her toes.

"I forgot to tell my boss I can't work." But the bouncing doesn't stop. "I guess I could get a new shirt. Can we swing by Shakedown Street?"

Suzy claps and grabs my backpack, dragging me out the doors of the school.

We drive in her black SUV over to Shakedown Street. When we walk in the door, Suzy's jaw falls open and she says, "This place is rad."

I leave her to look around, and find Ninny in the back storage room. She gives me a wad of cash and tells me to buy something pretty. I count the money, and realize it's a bunch of one-dollar bills. Ten one-dollar bills, to be exact. I stuff the money in my pocket, thanking Ninny for any type of donation.

Suzy and I search rack after rack of clothes at Nordstrom in Cherry Creek Mall. I peel through the clothes, unsure what I'm supposed to be looking for. I already have a dress for the dance.

"So do you know where you're going next year?" Suzy asks, looking through a stack of black dresses.

"I'm going somewhere?" I say.

"College, silly." She adds a short black strapless number to the pile of dresses slumped over her arm.

"I'm not going to college."

Suzy stops in her tracks. "Everyone goes to college."

"Not everyone. Starving teenagers in Africa don't go to college. The majority of India doesn't go to college. I'm pretty sure this whole college push is an American thing."

"But you're American," Suzy whispers like it's a secret. "I thought for sure you'd be off to art school in New York or something."

"Nothing's ever for sure," I mumble to myself as I examine a rack of designer jeans. "Are you ready to try those on?" I ask.

In the dressing room, I take a seat on a bench next to a full-length mirror. Suzy locks herself in one of the stalls with all her potential dresses and shuffles around behind the closed door. All I can see is her feet as she takes off her pants and slips on dress after dress. She finally comes out in a super short black silk dress. It looks more like lingerie. She walks over to the mirror to investigate.

"So I'm going to the dance with Aiden," Suzy says, twisting and turning to see every angle of her body. "And I like him, but I don't like-like him. He's just a friend. What do you think?"

"I think he's going to like-like you in that dress."

Suzy frowns at herself in the mirror. A few minutes later, she comes out in a dress not very different from the black one. Short, shimmery and uncomfortable looking.

"What do you think?" she asks.

"It's purple."

Suzy assesses herself and sticks out her tongue. "Bleh."

She disappears back into the dressing room. The sound of clanging hangers and rustling clothes follows. I stick my finger in the hole of my jeans and feel the scaly skin where my cast was.

"Was Katelyn perfect?" I ask.

"What?" Suzy pokes her head out.

"It's just . . . that's what everyone keeps saying."

Suzy comes out of the dressing room in an aqua strapless number and sits next to me. She looks around the Nordstrom like people might be spying on us.

"I think people just want to remember Katelyn how *they* want to remember her," Suzy says.

"But what was she really like?"

"Does it matter?" Suzy cocks her head at me. "And, anyway, it's complicated."

"Ben said the same thing."

Suzy sits up straighter. "When did he tell you that?"

"When we studied together for the physics test."

"Did he say anything else?" Suzy shifts in her seat, like her dress is uncomfortable.

"Just that he's not into dating right now."

"Wait." Suzy's mouth falls slack. "You *studied* together?" Her voice is loud and surprised.

"You make it sound like we had sex," I whisper.

"Did you?" I cock my head at her. "Do you like him?"

"No," I say, too emphatically.

"You like him," Suzy mocks like a third grader. I get up and start pacing the dressing room. "Aspen, it's okay if you do."

I stop, unable to hold back anymore. "How is it okay?"

Suzy looks down at her feet but doesn't say a word. I tap my foot on the ground, waiting. She stands up, pushing down the wrinkles in her dress.

"How do I look?"

"Not bleh. Beautiful, really," I say.

"Great." Suzy's usual sparkle returns fully to her eyes. "Let's take a pic."

She wraps her arm around my neck and holds the phone out in front of her. She makes a pouty face into the camera, her butt popped out behind her. When I laugh, Suzy snaps the picture. She types the caption "Shopping with Aspen," followed by seventeen hash tags, and posts it on Instagram.

We find a new shirt to for me to wear to the homecoming game. It's a white peasant blouse with red, blue, and orange flowers embroidered around the neckline.

"Hippie chic," Suzy calls it. "It's totally you."

Ninny's ten dollars covers about one sleeve of the shirt, but it's better than nothing.

At one point on the drive back to Boulder, Suzy turns to me and says, "Just because someone is dead, doesn't mean that they're gone. I think after death might just be the time when we're most alive to people." She looks back at the road.

"Maybe."

"You know you can talk to me about what happened. That's what friends are for," Suzy says.

I turn toward the window, unable to look Suzy in the eye, and play with the hole in the knee of my jeans. "I know."

CHAPTER 11

The night of the game, I pace around my room practicing the smile I'll need to produce if I win queen. I'm pretty sure I look like I'm struggling with a bad case of gas. Pulling on the bags under my eyes, I examine the scar on my forehead. A straight faded pink line that will never go away.

When the pacing verges on manic, I sit down in front of my computer and flip through the pictures of Katelyn on her Facebook page. After she died, her parents memorialized it. People posted pictures and notes and condolences to the family. Her face was a constant in my newsfeed. It was enough to drive me not to log onto Facebook. That and Facebook is officially archaic. But after shopping with Suzy, I pulled up Katelyn's page again and went through the pictures like a hundred times trying to see what everyone else sees.

I pause on a picture and click to see the comments.
She's so beautiful!

OMG, I can't believe she's gone.

¡Te queremos!

The world lost an angel.

We'll miss you forever.

I look for a comment made by Suzy but can't find one. I lean into the screen, examining it closely. I try to see a beautiful angel. Putting my finger on the computer, I touch Katelyn's blue eyes.

Her blue eyes.

A chill goes up my spine as something flashes in my peripheral vision. I turn my computer off quickly and glance around for Katelyn; she's here somewhere, even if I can't find her.

"It's just a crown," I say to her. "Don't be so superficial."

Ninny and Toaster are waiting on the couch when I walk downstairs. Ninny makes me twirl in a circle to show off my outfit. I'm in my bell-bottoms and the "hippie chic" shirt Suzy helped me find. I put cover-up under my eyes and some pink cheek dye I picked up at Walgreens and my hair is pulled half back in two braids Ninny helped me do earlier, with a few loose curls around my face.

"Beautiful, baby," Ninny says.

I smile. I don't care how often Ninny says it; I'll never get sick of my mom calling me beautiful.

"Like mother, like daughter," Toaster says, wrapping his lanky arm around her shoulder. I roll my eyes. I still hate him.

Kim and Cass meet at my house, and we all pile into Ninny's van. Cass sits on the floor, picking chocolate chunks out of the melted mint chocolate chip ice cream stain on the upholstery, and Kim and I take the back seat. It's starting to smell. I bite back the urge to yell at Ninny and tell her to clean her damn car.

Uncle Toaster sits shotgun and gives Ninny a neck massage with his gross long fingers the entire drive. I gag, and Kim giggles into her sleeve.

We park at the football field parking lot. At the gate, Cass gives me a big hug, spinning me around in a circle.

"Don't forget us when you're queen," he says.

"Don't forget to smile," Kim adds.

"And wave." Cass imitates a Miss America wave.

"You look stupid." Kim knocks his arm.

"You look Asian, *Kim*."

I walk away as they both start singing, "Bye-bye, Miss American Pie, drove my Chevy to the levee, but the levee was dry." Ninny and Toaster join in, laughing.

"It's just a crown," I say to myself.

I walk through the crowd to the spot where Ella instructed us to meet on the opposite side of the field. Football players run up and down the field, knees high, doing warm-ups. The band plays as people take their seats in the stadium, the lights bright on the field. Most of the trees are bare now, their gold and red leaves scattering on the ground. An icy chill fills the air. I pull in a cold breath and shake my hands out at my sides.

A huddle of people stands at the exact spot Ella Vega told us to go. The scents of expensive perfume and powder fill the air.

My stomach growls. I didn't eat anything before we left.

"Hey," Ben says, coming up behind me.

"Your ugly shirt." I point to the blue button-down he's wearing, the one from the beginning of the school year.

"I thought you said it looked weird, not ugly."

"It's the same thing. And I thought you said you hated it."

We stand quiet for a moment, neither of us moving toward the crowd.

"I got the stain out," Ben says.

"Baking soda?"

"Worked like a charm." He winks. And we wait. "Well, *you* look nice tonight."

"I didn't say *you* look ugly. I said *that shirt* is ugly."

"And weird."

"Yes."

"Aspen!" Suzy yells, and bounds over to us, her cheerleading skirt flying up as she bounces. "And Ben." Suzy gives my arm a squeeze and smiles a naughty grin.

"Suzy," Ben says and takes a step back.

"Well, now that we've all announced ourselves," I say, and walk over to the group of nominees. Olivia gives me a sideways glance and says something to Claire in Spanish. The only second language Ninny ever taught me was stoner lingo.

Don't Bogart my can, man.

I need an ounce, not an eighth.

Can you roll me a fatty?

Judging by the snarled look on Olivia's face when Ben stands next to me, whatever she's is saying isn't all peace, love and happiness.

"I'm putting you next to the person you'll walk down the field with!" Ella yells over the commotion like a drill sergeant. She walks down the line, shifting people like chess pieces. When she grabs my shoulders, I move to stand next to Tom Ingersol. He's dressed in his purple and gold football uniform. In his pads he looks about seven feet tall. Even more like a video game avatar.

"First down the field is freshman court, followed by sophomores and then juniors," Ella says. She hands roses to each of the girls. "Seniors will be announced one couple at a time. When you hear your name, walk down the fifty yard line and stop halfway."

Across the field, people shuffle to their seats in the bleachers, filling the entire "home" section. I look for Ninny in the crowd, but everyone blends together into colorful blobs.

"I guess we've gone from locker buddies to a couple," Tom says out of the corner of his mouth. "A step in the right direction."

"Don't tell my boyfriend," I say.

"You have a boyfriend?"

"No. I was making a joke."

"Oh." Tom forces out a fake laugh.

"No laughing," Ella yells. "This is serious."

Tom buttons his lips closed. I can't help but chuckle.

"When Mr. James announces the king and queen, those two people will come to the center of the group to get their crowns. Smile and wave, you got it?"

The group nods in unison.

"Let's do this," Ella says.

She sends the underclassmen down the field two at a time until all that's left are the seniors. I look down the line at Ben. He's paired with Claire and they're holding hands. I get the urge to hit her in the forehead with a giant spitball. When he catches me staring, I stand up straight, eyes trained down the field.

"Aspen Taylor and Tom Ingersol." Our names echo around the stadium.

"That's us." Tom offers me his arm. As we walk, the noise from the crowd becomes muted in my ears, like I'm swimming underwater. I sing "American Pie" in my head.

We stand in a line, in front of hundreds of people who live in my town, who until this past summer probably didn't know my name. Now, all eyes are on me.

I find a good-looking family sitting in the front row of the bleachers. The little boy has popcorn.

My stomach turns. I should have eaten.

Ninny used to take me to drum circles on Pearl Street when I was little. But no football games. And Uncle Jose took me to the rodeo once. I fell off a horse.

The little boy offers his dad some popcorn. The dad takes a handful and passes it down the line to the mom. She shakes her head.

"This year's homecoming king is—" Mr. James takes a dramatic pause.

The mom holds the bag of popcorn in her lap. She doesn't offer it to the girl sitting at her side.

"Ben Tyler."

I stare blankly at Katelyn sitting with her family in the bleachers. She's crying.

I cough to clear the lump in my throat. The lights on the field are so bright. I blink three times in a row.

"God, can someone turn down the wattage?" I mutter.

Katelyn doesn't go away. She doesn't stop crying.

"What?" Tom whispers.

White spots fill the corners of my vision. "No wonder we suck at football. How can you see anything with all these lights?"

"Suck at football?" His voice gets louder.

I rub my temples and close my eyes. "Yes. But it's not your fault. It's these damn lights."

"And this year's homecoming queen is . . . "

I can hear her crying. Tears from her blue eyes.

"Aspen Taylor."

I look up to the evening sky as I get pushed down the line. I stumble over my feet. I can't breathe.

"Aspen, look at me." Ben's voice sounds in my ears. I squint my eyes at him.

"It's so bright."

He grabs my hand. It's balled in a ninja-tight grip at my side. Like I'm ready to punch someone. Claire, maybe. But I can't feel anything in my hands.

Ben peels each of my fingers open. One at a time. My pale white skin flushing back to life. Until my palm is free. He slides his hand into mine.

"Just breathe," he says.

I look back at the crowd. Katelyn is gone. And finally someone turns down the lights.

"Smile and wave," Ella says, pushing a plastic tiara onto my head. It pinches as it presses through my hair and into my skull. An underclassman snaps a few pictures for the yearbook.

"Are you okay?" Ben asks through his smile.

"I didn't eat anything."

"Are you sure that's it?"

I pull my hand free from Ben's and nod.

Ella ushers us off the field as people congratulate us. Ninny runs over, Cass and Kim following close behind. She flings her arms around my neck, squeezing to near-suffocation levels. "You did it, baby!" she yells.

"Is that real?" Cass touches the tiara on my head; I swat his hand away, but Kim doesn't say anything. She looks from me to Ben and back again, a discerning look on her face. I try to ignore it.

Ninny goes right up to Ben and plants a kiss on his lips. "You can *study* with Aspen anytime, Benny."

"Thanks." He laughs uncomfortably as Ninny steps back. "Aspen, I need to talk to you." He pulls me away from the group of people, drawing me over to a corner next to the bleachers. People still stare at us, but Ben doesn't seem to care. "What the hell just happened?" He leans into me as he speaks.

"I didn't eat."

"I know that. What else?"

I close my eyes and for a second I hear her again. "I just thought . . ."

When I look back at Ben, his eyes get big and the blood drains from his cheeks. He takes a step back as a woman approaches us.

"I wanted to congratulate you." Katelyn's mom wraps her arms around Ben, giving him a hug. Not a strong hug, but the kind when people lightly tap your back.

"Thanks," Ben says into her ear.

Mrs. Ryan brushes Ben's shoulder off like she's dusting a mantel, and then leaves her hand, resting there. He looks frozen. "You're wearing the shirt Katelyn gave you. She always loved you in that," Mrs. Ryan says. "I'm only sad it couldn't have been Katelyn standing next to you."

Ben nods slowly.

And then Mrs. Ryan turns to me. "You look very nice, Aspen. That's an interesting shirt." Her gaze is blank. "Why don't you come and sit with the family for the game?" she says to Ben.

"I don't—"

But Mrs. Ryan cuts him off. "It's only right we should be together, don't you think? For Katelyn. You know I truly believe that she can still see us. I bet it would make her smile, knowing we're all together."

I stare at Mrs. Ryan's hand, perched on Ben's shoulder.

"I'll see you later, Aspen," Ben says to me before walking away.

I don't move. All I can feel is the tiara on my head. Ninny comes over a second later. "Mickey said free shakes at Shakedown Street," she whispers in my ear.

"What?" I turn to her, my head cloudy.

Ninny scans my face as if she's trying to read my mind. "You're pale, baby."

"Did you say something about food? I need food."

"Then let's get out of here." Ninny wraps her arm around me.

As we're walking out of the stadium, I can't help but glance over my shoulder one more time at Ben. Mrs. Ryan's hand hasn't left Ben's shoulder. Like a bird clawing on a tree branch. And as if Ben can sense me looking, he finds me in the crowd. For a moment, our eyes lock.

Then he turns back away and tucks in his shirt, like he did at the beginning of the school year. He straightens, pulling his shoulders back. Like a proper king.

Chapter 12

Ninny cooks for Kim, Cass, Jason and me before the homecoming dance. She spends all day in the kitchen, making weird noises and cursing. At one point it sounds like a symphony of pots and pans, and I ask Ninny if Toaster is over. When it gets so bad that a mini fire breaks out, she gives up and runs to the grocery store for frozen pizza.

"Frozen is at least fancier than Domino's," she yells.

Kim drags her yellow muumuu up the stairs to my room like she's marching to a funeral. I play with different hairstyles, trying to tame my bird's nest of curls. But I'm distracted by last night. The way Mrs. Ryan held onto Ben. How I want to know what Olivia said to Claire. How I want to burn the shirt Katelyn gave Ben. Which means I might actually be turning into the devil.

When Kim is done adding seven layers of black eyeliner and dark purple lipstick to her face, she lies on my bed, propping herself up on her elbow. "That was crazy last night," she says.

"I know. I can't believe Olivia didn't win. She was, like, totally robbed." I say it in my best valley girl voice, all bouncy and airy, as I pull my hair back.

"That's not what I mean and you know it. I'm talking about you and Ben. What the fuck is going on?"

I play with my curls, tucking a few strands into the loose bun at the back of my head. "Nothing."

"Shopping with Suzy is not nothing. Whispering in corners with Ben is not nothing. Getting crowned homecoming queen is not nothing." Kim sits up on the bed, her back taut. "Come on, tell me. I'm your best friend. That is, unless Suzy has replaced me."

"No one could ever replace you."

Kim gets off the bed and puts my crown on her head. Looking at our reflection in the mirror, I can't believe we're almost eighteen. I can see who she'll be next year: college Kim, passing out flyers for the monthly women's march on some prestigious campus, making out with an English major who has long hair and Converse shoes. But that guy will never be Cass. And the guy she marries will never be Cass, because the first person you fall in love with is always the first.

"You've never told me what happened that night," Kim says, looking at me in the reflection.

"What night?"

"Aspen." Kim pops her hip out.

I turn from the mirror and put on my dress. "Remember the first time you and Cass slept over?" I say.

Kim nods, adjusting the tiara to sit right on top of her head.

"I buried Paul," she says in perfect imitation.

We stayed up all night listening to "Strawberry Fields Forever" by the Beatles over and over, just to hear the part at the end when John Lennon says, "I buried Paul." Every time it happened, we'd scream like little kids in a haunted house. Then we fell asleep in my bed still fully clothed, three in a row. Ninny made at least a thousand jokes about me having a boy in my bed at age nine. But I never saw Cass as someone different from me, no matter the body parts. He's always been my kindred spirit. Penis and all.

"What's going to happen next year?" I ask.

Kim's stance shifts. For the first time, I see fear in her eyes.

"I don't know." Kim puts the tiara back. "But I better have sex." I elbow her and we both crack a smile. "You'd tell me if something is going on, right?" she asks, her eyes pleading. I don't hesitate to nod. That fact makes my stomach sour.

"I still have the song, you know." I scroll through the Beatles playlist on my iPod. Then Kim and I lie down on my bed, our heads touching. As the flute comes through the speakers and the Beatles' voices spread across my room, it's as if Kim and I are transported back to that night. Back to when a voice in a song was the scariest thing in the world and a boy and two girls sleeping in the same bed was innocent.

Right before Cass shows up, Ninny knocks on my door to check our progress.

"Is everybody decent?"

"When have you ever cared about that?" I smile at my mom.

"Aspen-tree, you look beautiful." Ninny looks at Kim. "Kim, baby, you look like a mustard bottle."

"Or a gothic banana." I add.

Kim blushes, running her hands down the front of her yellow muumuu. "You guys are the best."

"I almost forgot, baby. I made this for you." Ninny holds out a bunch of baby's breath flowers, their stems woven together to make a wreath. "Thought you might want to put it in your hair."

"Thanks, Mom."

When Ninny's done fastening the wreath to my curls, she says, "There. Your look is complete, flower child."

I run my fingers over the flowers. Tucked amongst so many curls, they almost get lost.

"My hair kind of resembles an untended garden," I say.

"Flowers are meant to be wild, not pruned." Ninny kisses my forehead and taps my butt. "Now will you two please help me with the pizza? If I burn it, we're screwed."

Cass shows up in a navy blue suit, two sizes too small. The pants land right above his ankles and the jacket sleeves are three-quarters length. The only thing that fits is the white button-down underneath and his red tie. His long hair is pulled back in a loose ponytail that hangs down his back.

"I had to borrow my dad's stuff." He shrugs.

"I like it. But where's my corsage?"

"Shit. I forgot."

"Well, now I really don't have to put out for you."

Once Jason shows up, Ninny snaps a few pictures with my phone before returning to the kitchen to watch the pizza. She takes it out a few minutes early so it doesn't burn, leaving the crust a bit gummy. No one seems to care, especially not after Ninny sets out a bottle of red wine and tells us to "have at it."

Cass stays mute for most of the dinner, taking big gulps of wine until his teeth are stained red. The only time he talks is when Jason gets sauce on his face.

"Dude, you have pizza sauce on your mustache." Cass points at Jason's upper lip.

"I don't have a mustache." Jason wipes his face with a napkin.

"That's not what Kim said." Cass smiles behind his glass.

"I'm about to go Dex Mayhem on your ass," Kim bites back.

"What's going on?" Jason asks, looking between the two of them.

"Nothing," Kim and Cass respond together.

The conversation ends there. Ninny drives us all to the dance in her van, claiming she draws the line at drinking and driving.

"I was unaware you had a line," I mock as we all climb into the car. Kim and I sit in the back on an actual seat, while Cass and Jason take the floor. Ninny looks like a proper chauffer with no one in shotgun next to her.

"What the hell is this?" Jason asks, pointing to the green stain in the upholstery.

"Dessert," I say, my eyes fixed forward.

Colorful strobe lights keep the beat to the rap song playing inside the gym. It seeps past the door into the hallway. I grab Cass's hand.

"Is it too early to leave?" I whisper.

"I don't trust that douche." Cass points at Jason, who's bobbing his head to the beat. Jason puts his arm around Kim. She takes his hand off her shoulder.

"Touch me again and die." She squints at him with her black-rimmed eyes and he backs up. "I need a drink of water."

"I'll wait for you in there, baby," Jason yells. Without losing the beat, he bobs into the gym to shake it by himself.

"Baby? That guy's an asshole," Cass says.

My ears go fuzzy trying to adjust to the loud music in the gym. I look from person to person. All the pretty dresses and done-up hair.

"You wanna dance?" Cass yells, arms open wide.

"With you? Always." Cass wraps his arms around me, like a ballroom dancer. "But it's a fast song," I say.

"My dad only taught me how to slow dance."

"You smell good." I stuff my nose in his shirt.

"All for you, *baby*." Cass twirls me in circles, my dress billowing out around me, and then pulls me tight to him again.

"I'm still not putting out," I say in his ear. Cass laughs as he moves me back and forth.

I rest my head on his shoulder and zone out. My gaze floats among the ruffles and ties and fancy hair. I find a boy dressed in brown corduroys and an un-tucked yellow collared shirt. No blue shirt. Ben even has his black and white Vans on. I pick my head up and rest my chin on Cass's shoulder to watch Ben. He's laughing next to Tom and Aiden. I smile and laugh along with him. And at this moment, it hits me that I need him.

"Aspen," Cass says.

I need him like I need a shower every morning or sleep every night.

"Aspen, you're biting me."

"Huh?" I dislodge my teeth from Cass's shoulder.

"Don't get me wrong, that was kind of kinky, but my dad would kill me if I got spit on this suit."

As I laugh, Hunter emerges from the crowd. His strawberry-blond hair flops into his lightly bloodshot eyes. He runs his hand through it, pulling it free, but the strands fall back into place, sticking in his eyelashes. "Mind if I cut in?" he asks Cass.

"Fair warning: She bites," Cass says and I nudge him in the side.

"Awesome." Hunter grins.

I grit a smile as Hunter whips me around the floor. He gives me a spin before pulling me against his chest. We bump together too hard and he steps on my feet.

"Sorry," he says. "I'm clumsy."

A subject and predicate? We're making progress.

"That's okay," I yell over the music.

"You look hot." Hunter's voice sounds rehearsed, like he was planning to say that to me no matter how I looked. I grab Hunter's hand, which is lurking dangerously close to my ass, and place it higher on my side.

The song changes to a faster tempo and Hunter picks up the beat, swinging his hips. I follow his lead. When he starts shaking his head from side to side and up and down, I do the same. The movement makes everything cloudy, the strobe lights a blurred rainbow on my vision. I close my eyes, letting the fuzz block my mind. I flail my arms over my head to the beat, until they tingle.

"This isn't a drum circle, Aspen. It's homecoming." I open my eyes as Suzy bumps my hip. She fumbles to the side from the contact.

I smile at her honesty. "Thank you," I say, and stop dancing.

"You have flowers in your hair. How pretty." She pets my head.

"How many drinks have you had?"

She huff and holds up all her fingers. "I don't know. A lot."

"Cool," Hunter says. "Got anything on you?"

Suzy looks down at her slim fitting aqua dress. "I can't even wear a bra. Where would I put a drink?"

"Bra," Hunter laughs.

Suzy squints at him. "Are you in Special Ed?"

"What?"

I yank Suzy away from Hunter, walking to the back of the gym. She stumbles from side to side. I hold her up and smile as we walk past Mrs. Calhoun, one of the chaperones, trying to give the illusion that Suzy isn't completely wasted.

"Are you okay?" I whisper. Suzy's breath stinks like rum and she looks pale.

"I don't know. Everything's kind of spinning."

Before we can get to the bathroom, Tom Ingersol runs up to us.

"Hey gorgeous," he says. He's dressed in a navy blue suit, his faux-hawk unmoving. Tom's clearly not sober either, because never once has anyone called me gorgeous. Plus his lips are curved into a goofy, sloppy grin.

"I hope you left your boyfriend at home. We are a couple, after all."

"He knows about Isaac, too?" Suzy asks.

"Wait. Who's Isaac?"

Suzy slumps closer to the ground. I yank her up. "Isaac Newton. We're going to the bathroom."

"Isaac Newton? Is he new?" Tom asks.

"No, he's old. Very, very old," I say.

In the bathroom, Suzy leans up against the sink, staring at herself in the mirror. Her eyes are wobbly, the lids hanging at half-mast. "Yep, I'm gonna throw up."

She rushes into the stall and hangs her head in the toilet. I grab her hair, and close the door so no one can see Suzy having an extremely drunk moment that might get her suspended. When everything seems to have come out of her stomach, she sits down on the bathroom floor, her knees pulled up to her chest, showing her underwear.

"Did I ruin my dress?" she asks.

Other than a few wrinkles, it's clean. "Just your dinner."

"Thanks for holding my hair." Suzy wipes her hand over her mouth.

"What are friends for?"

"I told you we would be friends." Suzy grabs me around the neck in a hug, and I hold her back.

"Can we get off the floor now?" I ask after a few long seconds.

When we walk back into the gym, Ella is standing on the DJ stage, microphone in hand.

"Oh, God," I say, and stop still.

"Can I have the king and queen up here?" Ella says into the squeaky mic.

"That's you!" Suzy squeals, dragging me through the gym to the steps of the stage, which isn't really a stage. It's a platform holding the DJ's setup, and it wobbles. Suzy gives me a push in the back.

"It's time for our king and queen to dance," Ella yells too emphatically into the microphone. People clap. I look out at the sea of teenagers, their hands smacking together, some enthusiastically, some not so much, like this is the stupidest thing to clap for.

Ella puts her hand over the mic and whispers, "Smile, for God's sake. You're queen."

My lips part and I force my cheeks up. I'm pretty sure an "I have gas" smile is stuck on my face.

Ben meets me on stage and stands on the other side of Ella, his hands tucked firmly in his pockets, as the DJ starts a slow song.

"Act like you like each other. That shouldn't be too hard." Ella gives us an exaggerated, fake smile that makes me uncomfortable, and she puts the microphone down.

Ben seems to brush it off. "You heard the woman," he says, pulling his hands free and extending one out to me.

"Don't step on my feet." I say as he leads me to an empty space on the dance floor.

ASPEN

One of his hands wraps around my back; his other stays firmly locked in mine. And then he pulls me to him, his chest pressed against me. I look down at our sandwiched bodies.

"I think they say it's better to look up."

"What?" I ask.

"For dancing. You're supposed to look at the person."

I force my eyes up to Ben's face. An overwhelming sense that I desperately need to kiss his eyelids comes over me.

Ben steps back and forth, his eyes searching the gym over my head. If he bats his eyelashes one more time, I might start biting things again. I gnaw on my lip.

"You know what this dance is missing?" Ben asks.

"What?"

"Beta Particle. I haven't heard them played all night."

"That's because homecoming is way too pedestrian for them."

"Pedestrian: lacking inspiration or excitement." Ben leans into me. "I've been studying my definitions." He presses his hand into the small of my back. My heart pounds and I pull back a bit. "What's wrong?" he asks.

"Nothing," I choke out. Ben cocks his head to the side. "I was just wondering . . ." I pause. "What are the Ryans like?"

Ben stops dancing. My urge to bite things goes away. "They're clean. Why?"

"Clean? What does that mean?" I ask.

Ben's arm falls from my side. When that happens, I regret asking the question. "Mrs. Ryan was always picking up after Katelyn." Ben's voice is flat.

"That sounds kind of nice. Ninny never picks up after me."

Ben wraps his arms around me again and leans down to my ear. "It wasn't that nice." Ben's breath hits my ear. "Sometimes it's good to be dirty."

I swallow hard, my teeth clenching down.

"The flower crown suits you better," he whispers.

I close my eyes and the people and music melt away. At this moment, if Ben asked me to clip his toenails, I would. Or give him a calf rub while he's wearing his sweaty shin guards.

But when I look up, Olivia and Claire are staring at us, whispering. Olivia narrows her eyes on me like a girl aiming at a target. And she's not the only one. The majority of the school has stopped dancing to watch the girl who lived dance with the perfect dead girl's boyfriend.

Everything stops. The music. The dancing. The mingling heartbeats.

Before Ben can say anything, I leave him on the dance floor and run into the bathroom, locking the stall door. I can't breathe. My head collapses on my knees, my eyes blurry, my body wanting to give out and fall on the floor.

When I look up, Katelyn is standing in front of me.

"Go away," I whisper to her. But she doesn't. She just stands, her mouth hanging open like she's about to scream.

A fire burns so low in my stomach. I look Katelyn square in the eyes and say, "Fuck off." I swing the stall door open. "By the way, Suzy just puked in there."

CHAPTER 13

I text Kim and Cass to meet me outside. I stand in the cold, pacing. I can't go back in there.

"Holy hot dancing," Cass says when he and Kim come out of the school. "Did you bite Ben, too?"

"I need to rip some aliens' heads off," I say.

"Nothing's going on?" Kim pops her hip out to the side, her face scrunched up like she smells something rotten. "That's not nothing. You were practically making out for the whole school to see."

"Can we just get out of here?" I snap.

I stalk off as it starts to drizzle. They catch up to me. I can't bring myself to say anything, so the three of us walk to Cass's house in silence. I stomp my feet on the pavement. Every few feet, a flower falls out of my hair to the ground, wet and matted. Kim gives me suspicious looks the whole way, but doesn't say anything else. She stops still at one point and says,

"Shit. I totally forgot about Jason." Then she shrugs. "He's a fucking douche anyway."

"A douche with a bad Asian mustache," Cass corrects.

I open my mouth and let some rain fall on my tongue. It's cold with the oncoming winter.

By the time we get to Cass's, my feet are freezing and all the flowers have fallen out of my hair.

We stay up until four in the morning playing ExtermiNATION. I get pretty good at telling the aliens from the humans, and I even manage to rip a few heads off. After Cass falls asleep on the couch, controller in his hand, and Uma has picked up Kim, I slip out the back door and walk home as the sun comes up. Then I plop down on my bed and pass out in my dress.

When Ninny walks into the room the next afternoon, my head hurts. She tiptoes over to the bed and lies down next to me.

"You're lucky I'm not a mom who cares about curfew," she says.

"You're lucky I'm not a teenager who cares—" I groan and roll over, "Do you really want me to finish that sentence?"

Ninny laughs, playing the drums on my ass. "The sun is up. The sky is blue. And there's a cute boy downstairs for you," she sings.

"What?" I sit up, my brains meeting my skull. Even my eyes hurt.

"That rhymes. I'm impressed with myself."

"Focus, Ninny. Is someone here?"

"You should brush your hair."

"That's not an answer."

She gets up. "Maybe we should try dreadlocks on you? I could have Mickey do it."

"That's not an answer!" I yell.

She just smiles and closes the door.

I check my reflection in the mirror. My hair is a mess: On one side, the curls are sticking out everywhere, and on the other, they're matted to my head. "Oh God," I mutter. I grab a pick and start pulling it through my hair, but it's hopeless.

Sighing, I touch my sunken cheeks and pale skin. The circles under my eyes sag lower. I pinch my cheeks, hoping to bring some life back to them. Nothing. Grabbing a ponytail holder, I twist my hair into a curly bun on my head, running downstairs, still in my dress.

Ben sits on the couch next to Ninny, chatting. I stop in my tracks halfway down the stairs.

"What are you doing here?"

"Aspen," Ninny barks. "I taught you to be more polite than that."

"No, you didn't."

Ninny rolls her eyes as Ben looks me up and down. "You're still wearing your dress," he says.

"Why are you here?" I ask.

"Why are you still in your dress?"

"You never answer my questions." I put my hands on my hips.

Ninny looks from Ben to me and back. "I think I'll go to Salvador's. It's always good to see you, Benny." She kisses him on the cheek.

"Good to see you, too."

Ninny slips on her jacket and grabs the pot stashed in the kitchen before disappearing out the back door. Ben sits still on the couch, staring at his hands in his lap. "You left without saying anything last night. I was worried."

"Well, I didn't want to tell you this, but you're a bad dancer."

"I am?"

"No." I press my fingers into my temples, trying to massage out my headache.

Ben walks into my kitchen like it's his and fills a glass of water.

"Thanks." I down half, and some water dribbles out of the corner of my mouth. Ben wipes it away with his sleeve. Yep, I still want to read him poetry on a bearskin rug.

Ben takes me in from head to toe. "You didn't have to get so dressed up for me," he says.

"I wasn't expecting company."

"I can go."

"No," I say quickly. "Just let me get changed."

He nods and sits back down on the couch, both arms extended out on the cushions, feet up on the coffee table. I stare at him for a second.

"What are you looking at?"

"Your shoes are wet." I point at the watermarks on the coffee table.

"Shit." Ben sits up and wipes them with his sleeve.

I can't help but giggle. "Ninny bought that at a dead woman's estate sale for five dollars."

"So you're saying it's an antique." He smiles and slips off his shoes. Today, he's wearing two different colored socks, one black and the other navy blue. No holes. I can't take my eyes off them. And I bet they don't even smell. I resist the urge to bend down and test the theory. "Weren't you gonna change?" he asks.

I nod, running upstairs to my closet. Picking the first things I find, I throw on holey jeans and a red hooded sweatshirt. But when it comes to my socks, I stand in front of the drawer, debating which pair I should put on. What would tell him I feel the same way he does? I settle on socks with little pockets for each toe, like gloves. Then I splash some water on my face and brush my teeth before coming back downstairs.

Ben hasn't moved from the couch. He sits, his feet up, playing on his phone.

"What are you doing?" I ask as I sit down next to him, peering over his shoulder.

"You changed quick." He almost jumps, clutching the phone to his chest.

"Don't get too excited. I didn't shower or anything." I set my feet up on the table next to his, displaying my socks. I even wiggle my toes. "You know, you're wearing two different colored socks."

"I am?" Ben pulls his feet up to get a better view. "Holy shit. I am. Are those glove socks?" He points at my feet.

I cross my legs, stuffing my feet under myself. "Maybe."

"Let me see." Ben grabs my leg, but I fight against him. "Are you ticklish?"

"No," I lie, and scoot away.

"You are." Ben's eyes sparkle with deviousness. And then he dives towards me full speed, knocking me on my back on the couch. He grabs for my feet and my sides, his fingers finding all my weak spots. I laugh uncontrollably. This might be better than poetry on a bearskin rug. I can't stop giggling and wiggling and feeling like I might explode with happiness.

"Stop," I laugh. "Stop."

Ben freezes on top of me. His lips are inches from mine. He stares into my eyes as the weight of his body presses on me.

Ben looks at my lips and moves an inch closer. My breath hitches in my throat—and then he sits back quickly on the couch, releasing me. I follow suit, pulling down my sweatshirt and tucking loose curls behind my ears.

"Sorry," he whispers.

"It's okay." I say the words, even though it's not okay.

Ben picks up his phone. "I was actually looking up the definition of a word."

"You were?"

"I think I have Addictive Definition Disorder."

"I hear ADD is going around." I smile.

"It's more contagious than herpes," he says, a forced smile on his face. My stomach drops at the sight of it.

"What word?" I choke out.

"What?"

"You looked up the word 'what'?" I say, attempting to bring the mood back to where it was a moment ago.

"Sorry."

"Sorry, that was a bad joke?"

"'Sorry' is the word I looked up," Ben says.

I sit back. "Why?"

"Because I owe you an apology. I'm sorry about last night."

"For what?" I say, trying not to let disappointment seep into my voice.

Ben looks down at his hands. "I'm still not over everything that happened. It's so complicated, Aspen."

"Do you want to talk about it?"

"I do. I really do." Ben wrings his fingers together and then stands up abruptly. "But I can't." He leans over to put his shoes on and picks up one of Ninny's yoga magazines, which is lying on the ground. "Here."

He hands it to me.

"Sorry about the mess," I say.

I grab the magazine from Ben. An ache covers his eyes and I want to cry right here, right now. "I told you before, don't be sorry."

Ben walks out the front door without a look back in my direction.

My head falls to my chest as I breathe away the tears collecting in my eyes. Bending down, I rip the socks from my feet and throw them across the room.

And then all that's left in the house is the sound of silence.

CHAPTER 14

I go back to normal. Or whatever my life was before Ben. Before visions of toenail clipping and bearskin rugs. It's all I can do. Kim and I get coffee and listen to music and dissect every college kid behind the counter at Moe's. She asks me to pierce her bellybutton, which I refuse in the name of both regret and staph infections. I even sit in Dr. Brenda's office and talk about my lack of motivation and let her tell me that going to college is important.

"You're smart, Aspen."

"Who knows what will happen by next year?" I say. "The future is unexpected and unintentional."

"That doesn't mean *you* have to be unexpected and unintentional."

I nod, even though hearing her talk in her psychobabble way is as painful as slowly poking my eardrums with a sharp toothpick. But it's better this way. That's what I tell myself.

ASPEN

Olivia only accosts me once in the bathroom after homecoming, asking me what it feels like to replace a dead girl.

"What?" I ask.

She rests her butt against the sink. "Doesn't it bother you?"

I stumble on my words and instinctually want to punch Olivia right in her big beautiful, brown eyes.

When I don't answer, Olivia leaves, tossing her hair over her shoulder. I take it as a slap in the face, considering I can't toss my hair anywhere. It just bounces.

On the bright side, Kim doesn't give me any more suspicious looks, and a few weeks after homecoming, the rumors at school about me and Ben dating or banging (depending on whether you ask a boy or a girl) actually die down.

Not having Ben so prominently in my life doesn't hurt so badly, I find. It's kind of like losing a kidney. If I can learn to function without it, I'll be fine. Who needs both kidneys, anyway?

The only time it gets hard is in physics when Ben is physically next to me. I'll stare down at his calves and wonder what they'd feel like in my hands, or remember that he told me he wears boxers, which makes my eyes drift up his legs to his—and then I have to stop myself.

One afternoon during lab, Ben asks if he can borrow a piece of paper.

"No," I say, rolling one of the toy cars Mr. Salmon gave us back and forth across the desk.

"Okay. Sorry."

I rip a sheet free from my spiral notebook. "You can *have* a piece of paper. I don't want it back."

Ben cracks a small smile. "I should know better," he says. "Since I have ADD and all."

It takes everything in me not to ask him to define a word. Next thing you know, I'll ask if he wants to have babies.

To further the torture of my life, I have to endure a Thanksgiving with Uncle Toaster. He brings over a bag full of dented cans of cranberry sauce that he found discarded behind the grocery store.

"I've decided to become a freegan," he says, setting them down on the counter.

"What the hell is that?" I ask as I mash potatoes on the stove.

"I won't be defined by the consumerist structures set up by the wasteful American government. There are people starving all over the world, yet we discard a can for being dented." Toaster picks one up and pets it. "It's not the can's fault that someone didn't take proper care of it."

"So you're finally admitting you're a Dumpster-diver?"

"Aspen," Ninny barks. She's pretending to watch football on the couch so that she doesn't have to help cook.

"I prefer freegan."

"Well, I think you're 'freegan' insane." I go back to mashing the potatoes.

Not even Ninny touches the cranberry sauce at dinner.

Later, in my room, I'm flipping through pictures of Katelyn on Facebook. I've looked through at least 100 photos, reading the comments on all of them. I'm not exactly sure what I'm even looking for. But I am *absolutely* sure I've become a stalker.

My computer dings with a chat notification.

Suzy Lions: I miss u

Aspen Taylor: u saw me a few days ago

Suzy Lions: school doesn't count

Suzy Lions: we need 2 do something

Aspen Taylor: ok

Suzy Lions: shopping next week. i need a new tie-dye.

I hesitate, unsure if I should type something back. It's been more than a month since Suzy and I hung out, and the truth is I miss her, too. She's oddly loyal and fun.

I scan the comments below the picture of Katelyn pulled up on my screen and look for Suzy's name. There's a comment from Ben, but Suzy hasn't written anything. I click to the next one. No Suzy. I go through 15 pictures, searching for a comment made my Suzy about Katelyn. She hasn't left a single one.

The Grove rustles like a breeze is coming in my window, but it's closed. And an odd smell wafts into my room. I turn and see Katelyn standing with one of my sketches in her hand. It's one of Ninny sitting in our backyard, wearing a huge sunhat.

"Put that down," I say. Katelyn shakes her head. "Put it down."

She rips it to shreds. I run to stop her but she disappears and I fall into the wall, knocking my head. When I stand up, the sketch is back in its place.

I tell Suzy that I'd like to go shopping with her.

Suzy Lions: GREAT!

I stay up half the night, rubbing the small bump on my head and trying to find a single comment Suzy has made on Katelyn's memorial page. I come up empty.

"Where should we go?" Suzy asks, looping her arm through mine as we walk out of physics. "I need an authentic tie-dye, not one I bought at Forever 21. I want it to smell like pot, not cheap perfume."

"There's this one place, but I'm not sure you can handle it," I say.

"Oh, I can handle it." Suzy bounces up and down.

We walk out to her black SUV, and I stand at the door, holding the handle. It's cold in my palm. The vision of Katelyn ripping my sketch to shreds makes me hesitate.

"It's open," Suzy says, snapping me out of my trance.

Gritting my teeth, I slide into the passenger seat. When Suzy starts the car, I roll down the window.

"It's freezing," she says.

"You want a new shirt, right?" I glare at Suzy. She rolls her eyes and zips her coat all the way up to her neck.

We drive, Suzy shivering in the driver's seat. She turns up the heat and holds her hands over the vent. I hang my arm out the window, resting my face in the breeze.

We park at the Crystal Dragon, a small boutique with tapestries hanging in the window. Just walking in the door reminds me of being little. The strong smell of lavender and patchouli oil hasn't changed. I walk up to a shirt and press it to my face. All the clothes smell like the store. You have to wash something at least ten times before you stop smelling like a Phish concert.

Along the wall is a glass case filled with colorful pipes and bongs. On top sits dangly jewelry. Clothing racks are spread around the store, and tapestries cover the walls. The far back room is filled with posters.

"This is perfect," Suzy squeals, already flipping through a rack of shirts.

"I bought my first Grateful Dead shirt here," I say, holding a turquoise necklace to my neck.

"How do you even know about this place?"

"When I was little, Ninny liked their black-light room."

"Your mom?" I nod. Suzy holds up a shirt to her small body. And then she asks, "What's a black-light room?"

I put the turquoise necklace back. "I'm not exactly sure, but Ninny always came out of it very happy." I lean my hip against the case of bongs. "It got shut down a few years ago."

"My parents would never!" Suzy's eyes get big as she shakes her head.

"Ninny never says never."

A small round woman wearing a flowing dress and an anklet that jangles as she walks comes out of the back of the store, carrying a box of clothes.

"Can I help you?" She sets the box down on the counter.

"I need the perfect tie-dye," Suzy says.

The woman smiles warmly. She looks like an aunt. Or what I envision an aunt looking like. Someone who squishes you into her soft exterior and smells like cookies and always has gum. "You've come to the right place," she says.

Suzy and the woman walk around the store, looking at each shirt, dissecting Suzy's personality. At one point, the woman says she sees people in colors.

"Like an aura?" Suzy asks, intrigued.

"Kind of." Suzy's color is blue, she says. "Not a baby blue. Ocean blue." The woman waves her hand in the air like she's drawing the color on Suzy's body.

"I have a color?" Suzy gets even more excited.

The woman touches her arm and smiles. "Everyone has a color, baby. It's just most people don't know what it is."

They scan the racks for a tie-dye with Suzy's "color". I go to the back room and flip through the posters, scanning the faces I know so well. Uncle John Lennon. Uncle Jethro Tull. Uncles Simon and Garfunkel. I know them better than any man who's walked through my front door. Uncles Crosby, Still, Nash and Young got me through the three weeks Ninny was away in Taos. I'd cry at night as I listened to "Teach Your Children," because the song isn't really about parents teaching kids, it's about kids teaching parents. And I hated that I needed to teach Ninny that the people who love you don't leave.

When I get through all the posters, I walk back to the front to find Suzy.

"What do you think?" she asks, pulling a short-sleeved pastel-colored tie-dye from her bag. Her ocean blue color is speckled down the center in a large swirl.

"It's great."

Suzy presses the shirt to her nose. "And I got you this." She digs to the bottom of the bag and pulls out a blue, pink and purple string-braided bracelet, like the kind kids make at summer camp. "A friendship bracelet. One for you and one for me." Suzy grabs my wrist and ties it on me. Then she shows me her wrist, wrapped with an identical one.

"Thank you." I smile.

"Friends." Suzy taps her wrist against mine. Then she turns back to the counter and says, "Leona, what's Aspen's color?"

Leona puts her finger on her chin, scanning my body. When her brow knits and her eyes turn serious, I want to hide behind the counter.

"I can't believe this."

"What?" I ask.

Leona comes over to us, her anklet jangling as she walks, and grabs my shoulders. "Is everything okay, honey?" Her eyes search my face, concerned. I step back from her.

"Yes."

"What is it, Leona?" Suzy asks, looking between the two of us.

"You have two colors. Yellow and grey. But not a light grey, a stormy grey."

"What does that mean?" Suzy leans into me, her eyes big.

"There's someone else here, too." Leona looks around the store.

"Okay, thanks." I grab Suzy's arm, dragging her toward the exit.

Leona snaps out of her trance when the door dings. She smiles, a distant look on her face, and says, "Peace out."

In the parking lot, Suzy stops, confused. "I didn't see anybody else in there."

"I think Leona spent too much time in the black light room," I say.

"That is the coolest store I've ever been in." Suzy takes her shirt out of the bag to admire it one more time. "It even smells real. I'm never washing this."

I laugh half-heartedly. My eyes keep glancing back at the store, waiting for Katelyn to appear and show her stormy grey color. Or rip another one of my sketches.

"Want to get coffee?" Suzy asks.

"I should probably head home."

"Please," Suzy begs. "It's been, like, forever since we hung out." She flashes her wrist with the friendship bracelet.

"Sure." I nod. But even in Suzy's car on the way to the Unseen Bean, I can't stop thinking about how Leona could tell someone is following me. Or maybe she was just high.

We order two chocolate macchiatos with whipped cream and Suzy pays. "I have a new favorite store, thanks to you."

We take a seat and sip our drinks while Suzy asks me question after question about the Crystal Dragon and the Grateful Dead and how I know so much. I tell her about Ninny and the Widespread Panic concert, and how I've had so many uncles in my life that I've lost count, and how Jerry Garcia died too young and too brilliant and we miss him every day.

"Like the Ben and Jerry's ice cream flavor guy?"

"That's Cherry Garcia. It was named after Jerry, the lead singer in the Grateful Dead."

Suzy sits back in her seat, taking a long sip of her drink and licking whipped cream off the top. "I can't believe you were born at a rock concert. That is so rad. Being born in a hospital is so boring."

"But safer. Can I ask you something?" I say and lean in, making sure to display my friendship bracelet on the table. When Suzy nods enthusiastically, I say, "What did you really think of Katelyn?"

Suzy sits back in her seat, her eyes on her drink. "Why do you ask?"

"I'm just curious, I guess."

Suzy eyes fill with water, like she might cry. I want to take the question back.

"Some days, I'm so mad that she's dead." Suzy sets her drink on the table. "That she left me."

"But it was an accident," I say, repeating Officer Hubert's words. And I swear it was.

Suzy nods slowly, her lips in a tight frown. "Right."

I sit back in my seat, having officially killed the mood. "Do you want to hear about the summer Ninny and I lived out of the back of her van and followed Rusted Root around the country?"

That perks Suzy up. Her cheeks brighten almost instantly. She leans in across the table, but stops halfway. "Oh, my God," she says and kicks me under the table.

"Ouch." I grab my shin.

"Sorry," Suzy whispers.

"What is it?" I look over my shoulder. There, standing at the counter ordering, is Ben. As if he can sense us staring, he looks in our direction. Suzy waves her arm like a madwoman, motioning for him to come over.

"What are you doing here?" Suzy asks, when Ben gets to our table.

"Getting coffee." Ben lifts his drink. "What are you doing here?" He says in the same tone.

"Aspen took me shopping for a new tie-dye. Do you want to sit down?" Suzy pulls out the chair between us. Ben doesn't move. "We don't bite."

"I wouldn't exactly say that," I mumble to myself. I slump lower in my chair.

Ben looks around the coffee shop and then takes the seat.

Suzy get her shirt out of the bag and lays it on the table. "So, what do you think? This lady at the shop—her name's Leona—she's so rad—says my color is blue, but not a baby blue, ocean blue."

"It's cool. I hear tie-dye is all the rage." Ben sits back and sips his coffee. Then he turns to me. Our eyes meet, and the need to know what socks he's wearing is back. "What did you get?"

"Nothing," I say.

"Leona says Aspen has two colors. Yellow and grey, but not a light grey, a stormy grey." Suzy leans her elbows on the table.

"Two colors? Are you that special?"

"More like that weird," I say.

"I prefer the word 'unique,'" Ben smiles.

Suzy eyes us and then says, "I need to go to the bathroom. Aspen, will you come with me?"

"What?"

Suzy comes around to my side of the table and yanks me up by the arm. "Come on. It's not like we've never peed together before." She pats Ben on the shoulder. "Don't leave before we get back."

Ben sits back in his seat, coffee in hand, and settles into a comfortable position. Suzy drags me across the Unseen Bean and into the bathroom. Once we're safely inside, she goes up to the sink and turns on the water.

"I thought you had to pee," I say.

Suzy doesn't wash her hands, but rests her butt up against the sink. "Enough is enough."

"Of what?"

"You and Ben. I want you to get out there and finally admit you like him." I fumble over what to say to Suzy. "He makes you happy. I can see it."

"So what?"

Suzy huffs and turns toward the sink. She runs her hands under the water and grabs a paper towel.

"You know what I'm really mad at Katelyn for? I'm mad at her for not living. Happiness isn't a given in life. And when you're happy, you should hold onto it." Suzy's hands twist tight around the paper towel.

"So Katelyn wasn't happy?"

Suzy doesn't answer. She tosses the towel into the garbage can. "Just get out there and make it happen." She sounds like a coach giving a pep talk, and I laugh in spite of myself.

When we get back to the table, Suzy doesn't sit down. Instead, she grabs her shopping bag and says, "I forgot I have this thing. Ben, you don't mind taking Aspen home, right?"

He glances at me, confused. "Sure."

"Thanks." Suzy gives me a quick hug and a wink. Then she leaves, swinging her bag behind her.

I sit back in my seat and stare at the almost empty coffee cup in front of me.

"How was the bathroom?" he asks.

"Informative."

Ben raises his eyebrows. "Do tell."

"What happens in the ladies' room stays in the ladies' room."

Ben laughs and pulls out a colorful hacky sack from his pocket. He tosses it into the air and catches it on the backside of his palm.

"You don't have to take me home. I can walk," I say.

"No. I want to," he says quickly. And then Ben looks around the coffee shop. "You want to get out of here?"

A few leftover fallen leaves scatter the street as cars drive past us on the road. Snow will be here soon. Maybe even tomorrow.

Zipping up my fleece jacket, I hug my chest for warmth. Ben doesn't move, just throws the hacky sack into the air again.

"You want to play?" he asks.

"Are you sure? I'm pretty damn good. I'd hate to beat you."

"You realize I play varsity soccer. And I'm going to college on a *soccer* scholarship."

"You realize I was raised by Ninny. I've had more drum circles in my backyard than Red Rocks."

"You asked for it." Ben smiles.

ASPEN

We find an open space under a bare tree on the outdoor pedestrian mall of Pearl Street. Only a few people walk around us, clasping their shopping bags. Down the block a four-piece string band plays average bluegrass music, a hat placed before them for donations.

Ben kicks the hacky sack in my direction. I catch it with my knee, bouncing it high and then volleying it back to him.

"So you have a soccer scholarship?" I ask.

"To University of Colorado."

"You're staying in Boulder?" I pause for a second, surprised, and snap out of it when the hacky sack flies towards my face. I duck the moment before it would have hit me in the nose. Ben laughs loudly and then clasps his hand over his mouth.

"Shit. Sorry."

I snatch the hacky sack off the ground. Then I kick it high in the air with my heel.

"Why University of Colorado?" I ask.

"There's no way my dad can afford college without the scholarship. I don't really have a choice." Ben volleys the ball with both knees, his eyes focused. He kicks it high and catches it with his head.

"Impressive." I clap. He bows, catching the hacky sack as it rolls off. "Do you wish you had a choice?"

"Sometimes. But I'm glad I can be here for Sam, since my mom isn't."

"Do you miss her?"

Ben rolls the hacky sack around in his hand. I bite my bottom lip, worried I shouldn't have asked that question. It takes him a second, but then he nods. "What about you? No dad?"

"You know Ninny. There's a list of potential people. It gets longer the older I get."

He makes a fake shocked face. "I can't believe Ninny *studied* with that many people in high school." Ben kicks the hacky sack in my direction. I knock it with the outer edge of my foot, sending it over my shoulder, where I catch it on the opposite knee.

"Most people *study* with someone in high school. It's just that no one talks about it." I pause. "Unless you're Ninny."

"So you've . . . *studied* with someone?" Ben asks.

I volley the ball back to Ben. "Maybe." He misses the hacky sack and I giggle. "You?"

Ben picks it up off the ground and takes a seat under the tree. I move to sit next to him. "Maybe." Ben rolls the ball around in his hand. "Don't ever tell me the guy's name, okay?" Ben's voice sounds serious and anxious. "It's only one guy, right?"

"Only one guy," I say. "And he doesn't live here."

"Thank God." Ben pushes out a long breath.

"And you? Only one girl?" Ben nods slowly, both of us acknowledging who we're talking about. "Were you in love with Katelyn?" I ask.

"I don't know," he says, picking up a leaf and spinning it around in his hand. "Some days, I thought I was." The terrible side of me is glad he just used past tense. "What about you? Were you in love?"

"God, no. I just wanted to do it."

A deep laugh bursts from Ben. The sound makes me smile. "How come this is so easy?" he asks.

"Are you calling me easy?" I nudge him in the shoulder.

"I'm not sure if you're easy. I'll have to find out." He leans into me.

I smile, but as soon as it's there, it falls away. "It is kind of messed up," I say, unable to meet Ben's eyes. "That this is easy."

"But everything seems so hard most of the time. I'm just so tired of it."

And I think I might be tired too. Exhausted, really. "Did you just say easy and hard in the same conversation?"

"I'm a teenage boy. What do you want from me?" Ben nudges me again.

We sit quietly for a while, Ben playing with his leaf, me reveling in how good it feels to have my kidney back. And then Ben says, "So what about you? College."

I shake my head. "The future is too unexpected and unintentional for me to make any decisions at this point."

"Fair enough." Ben pulls his knees up to his chest. The wind on Pearl Street makes pieces of the trash dance in the air, spinning around one another.

"How did you get those?" I say, and point to the two scars on his face.

"This one," Ben touches the one on his cheek, "I fell out of a tree and caught a branch with my face."

"Gross."

"And this one," Ben touches the one over his eyebrow, "I got kicked in the head with a soccer cleat."

"I bet that hurt."

"What about you? Any hidden scars?"

I pull my jeans up to my knee. A thick scar lines the center of my kneecap. "Kim and I snuck into her neighbor's hot tub and they caught us. My knee got cut on the fence running away." Ben laughs, skimming the length of the scar with his finger. My leg feels like it's covered in shivers. Embarrassed, I roll down my pants and point to my forehead. "And you know how I got this."

Ben's eyes travel from my knee to my face. They land on my scar and stay there.

"It'll never go away, will it?" Ben asks. By the sad tone of his voice, I get the feeling that Ben isn't talking about my scar.

"I don't think so," I say.

Ben stands up, wiping dirt from the back of his pants. "I better get you home." And then he holds out his hand to me, to lift me off the ground. We walk over to a parking lot behind the Unseen Bean, where he points to a tow truck. "That's me."

"Side job?"

Ben laughs. "Loan from my dad."

"Your dad's a tow truck driver?"

"Technically, he manages a towing company." Ben runs his hands through his hair. "Un-technically, he's a tow truck driver."

"Un-technically isn't a word."

"Well, it should be."

"Kind of like Beta Particle should be a band."

"Exactly," Ben says. He stops at the driver's side door and turns to face me. "My dad's the one who called me that night."

179

"What?"

"He was working the night of the . . . "

I freeze, everything inside of me turning cold.

"Did he see . . . " I don't finish the question before Ben nods. I stare at the back of the truck, at the crane and the hook and the levers that must have lifted Katelyn's broken car from the ground. I almost trip over my own feet as I stumble backwards. "You know what, Shakedown Street's just around the corner. I'll catch a ride with Ninny."

"I can take you." Ben reaches for my hand, but I pull away. "It's okay. Really."

I speed across the parking lot, my breath coming faster and faster. At the corner, I duck into the alley. I brace myself against the wall, but my knees buckle and I slump to the ground. Footsteps sound on the pavement.

"I told you, Ben. Ninny can drive me." But when I look up it isn't Ben in the alley with me. Katelyn stands in the shadows. The darkness casts an odd mark on her face. And the smell is back. I cradle my head in my hands. It's starting to hurt.

I sit nestled against the wall until it's completely dark out.

When I creep out from behind the building, I check the parking lot for Ben. The tow truck is gone. All that's left are leaves and pieces of trash, dancing in the late fall wind.

CHAPTER 15

Ninny is upside down on a yoga mat when I walk in the door. Fresh incense burns in the kitchen and Bob Dylan plays over the stereo. The lights are dimmed, and candles flicker over the unlit fireplace.

"What are you doing?" I whisper, afraid I'll mess up whatever aura-cleansing, Zen-yoga thing Ninny's trying this week.

"Feeling the earth beneath my feet."

I bend down to look at Ninny's face, all bright red and sweaty. "But your feet are up in the air."

She comes down from her pose. "Come here, Aspen-tree." Ninny pulls me down beside her. It must be the yoga mat, because I sit up straighter. I even cross my legs. "Now close your eyes," she whispers.

"Why do I need to close my eyes?" I ask in a hushed voice.

"Just do it." Ninny puts my hands in a prayer position right in front of my heart. "Let the earth hold you."

I peek out of one eye. "But the floor is holding me."

"Semantics."

"You know that word?"

Ninny knocks my arm. "Deep breath in and out."

"Are you going to make me say om?"

"Just feel the energy."

"What energy?"

"Your energy."

I shift my butt on the hard ground, trying to get comfortable. It's better to do what Ninny says. When she gets determined, she'll just beg you until you say yes. I follow her breathing, sucking deep breaths in and out through my nose.

The longer I sit there, the more tired I get, and the more my stomach growls. When Ninny seems consumed in meditation, I tiptoe into the kitchen and grab a container of leftover macaroni and cheese and pop it in the microwave. Then I plop myself down on the couch.

Ninny takes a deep breath, pushing everything out of her lungs, and opens her eyes. "You could at least try, Aspen-tree," she says, getting off the mat to pour a glass of wine. I watch her, noting that she barely looks old enough to drink legally. Not a single wrinkle marks her face.

"What were your parents like?" I ask, poking my food with a fork.

She peers around from the kitchen. "Why?"

"I don't know. Just wondering."

"Who cares what they were like?"

"I care."

"Well, they don't deserve your care."

"Don't you ever wonder if they've changed?"

"They haven't."

"You don't know that."

"I don't want to talk about this anymore," Ninny snaps. I stab at my macaroni and cheese. She comes to sit next to me and pets my hair. "It's in the past, baby. There's no use looking back."

I put my empty container on the coffee table and settle in next to Ninny. "I went to the Crystal Dragon today."

Ninny cups her wine glass in her hand. "I miss their black-light room every day."

Pulling the blanket off the back of the couch, I lay it over the two of us. "Where does your energy go when you die, Mom?" I ask.

"I don't know, baby."

"Mr. Salmon says that energy can't be created or destroyed, so it must go somewhere."

Ninny takes another sip of wine, tipping her head back against the cushion. "Well, Mr. Bob Dylan said the answer is blowing in the wind."

I close my eyes and listen to the music, to the song playing over and over. Uncle Bob Dylan might be right. Maybe the only thing left after we die is the air we breathed when we were alive, carried in the wind.

"Bob Dylan is a genius," I say.

"That's my girl."

I smile and stuff my face into her shirt, breathing in her earthy scent. We fall asleep together until morning, Bob Dylan playing on repeat. It's the first night I've slept straight through in months.

"Cass and I have a very important question for you," Kim leans on the counter at Shakedown Street, her round sunglasses still on her face.

"Is it true that if a girl jumps up and down after sex, she can't get pregnant?" Cass asks.

"No!" Ninny's voice booms from the back room.

I throw a strawberry at Cass's head. He dodges it a second before it smacks him right between the eyes. "What? I'm just trying to be safe."

"Who are you having sex with?" Kim snarls her lip at him.

"Who am I *not* having sex with once I get to college is a better question."

"Is 'olives' still our escape word, because I'd like to get out of this conversation," I say, interrupting the fight that I know is about to take place.

"We have a surprise for you. A birthday present." Kim's face lights up.

"My birthday isn't until the summer," I say, looking over my shoulder as I turn on the blender.

"Well, it's not a surprise if it happens on your birthday. Duh," Cass yells over the noise. He nudges Kim. "Tell her."

"Deadly Grateful is playing the Boulder Theater this weekend." Kim pulls three tickets out of her purse and fans herself with them. "Do you want to go?"

I snatch them from her, excited, and check to see if she's for real. Printed across the top of the tickets is DEADLY GRATEFUL, all in capital letters. My mouth practically drops to the floor. It's the name of the greatest Grateful Dead cover band to ever walk the earth. If I can't see Jerry Garcia live, may he rest in peace, Deadly Grateful is the next best thing.

"Is that even a question?"

"Lately, I haven't been so sure with you." Kim hides her frown behind her shake. I come bounding around the counter and grab my best friend in a bear hug. She exhales into my ear, holding onto me tightly. When she pulls back, she says, "I get this for free now. Right?"

I roll my eyes but nod. Kim and Cass hang out, sitting at a table in the corner while I work, Kim studying and Cass playing a game on his phone. In between customers, I stare at a blank page in my sketchbook, my mind distant, and tap my charcoal pencil on the edge of the counter. My fingers are black with soot. Nothing gets drawn on the page.

Later, the door dings with another customer. Suzy's voice echoes through the room. "This place is so cool."

I stand up, shocked. She's dressed in Boulder High sweatpants and her new tie-dye. "What are you doing here?" I ask.

"I thought I'd get a shake, silly." She leans on the counter, a broad smile on her face. "Plus we need to discuss what happened yesterday. So . . . "

I look at Kim, who stands up at the question, and I cringe inwardly. "What happened yesterday?" Kim asks, coming up to us. "And why do you smell like the Crystal Dragon?"

"Aspen and I went shopping." Suzy says, and smiles. "When we were at the Unseen Bean afterward, Ben showed up. He gave Aspen a ride home."

"Aspen is having sex with Ben?" Cass yells, still looking at the game on his phone.

"What?" Ninny comes careening out of the back room.

"I am not having sex with Ben," I say through clenched teeth.

"You went shopping with Suzy at the Crystal Dragon? That's our store." Kim's eyes look beyond hurt. "I thought you were done with these people."

"These people?" Suzy takes a step back.

"Aspen, are you having sex with Ben?" Ninny grabs my arm. "If so, we need to talk about protection."

"Why didn't you tell me?" Kim whispers.

I try to formulate answers to all the questions flying around me, but my mind just spins helplessly. What I want to say would only produce more questions—that the accident might be the best-worst thing that ever happened to me, and I deserve all the terrible-wonderful feelings that come with it.

"Nice bracelet, by the way." Suzy puts her wrist next to mine, flashing our matching friendship bracelets.

Kim grabs her backpack in a huff. "I'm going home." She grabs Cass's arm and yanks him out of Shakedown Street. He barely looks up from his game to wave as the door shuts.

I slump down on my elbows on the counter, disappointed in myself.

"Maybe we should get you on the pill, just in case?" Ninny pats my back and then disappears into the back room.

"Did I say something wrong?" Suzy asks.

I shake my head and think, *I'm* wrong. All wrong. And the only person who makes it better also makes it so much worse.

Chapter 16

On Friday after physics, Ben sidles up next to me in the hallway.

"So what are you doing this weekend?" he asks, walking in time with me.

I glance around the hallway, surprised he wants to be seen with me with so many people are around. Judging by his casual stance, Ben doesn't seem to care.

"Going to a concert."

"Beta Particle?"

"I wish. It's impossible to get tickets to see them."

Ben's arm swings next to mine.

"You?" I ask.

"Tom made us promise to go to the basketball game." He rolls his eyes. "So who are . . . " But Ben gets cut off when Olivia comes up behind us.

"The king and queen, together again?" She wraps her arm around Ben's waist. "You make a nice couple. I'm sure Katelyn would be happy for you two." Her voice is coated in disdain.

"We're not a couple." Ben takes Olivia's hand off his waist. "And you knew Katelyn about as well as everyone else in this school. It's a joke." All the ease in Ben's voice moments ago is gone, and a weight seems to hang on his shoulders. "Sorry, Aspen."

He leaves us in the hall, the air tense and weighted.

"Sorry for what?" Olivia says mockingly.

I appraise her nice clothes and shiny hair. For once, I'm glad I look nothing like her. "I think he was apologizing for you being such a bitch."

I walk away from Olivia, a sour feeling sitting in my stomach, but a smile on my face. It felt good to finally admit the truth.

Kim and Cass come over the night of the Deadly Grateful concert. Kim walks in my front door, hesitant, and I grab her. "I'm sorry I took Suzy to the Crystal Dragon and didn't tell you about it," I say, hugging her. She pushes back on me.

"And that you saw Ben and didn't tell me."

"And that, too."

Kim narrows her eyes at me. "It's just weird for you to hide things from me."

"Technically, I didn't *hide* anything. I just forgot to tell you."

"Is that anything else you 'forgot' to tell me?" Kim asks.

I rub the scar on my forehead. It aches from a bad night's sleep. "No," I say, my voice not wholly convincing.

"This is so fucking exciting," Kim finally squeals, grabbing my shoulders, shaking me. And for the moment, it feels like everything from the past few days is washed away.

Kim gives me a brown scarf she picked up at Common Threads as a birthday present. When Cass hands me a pack of condoms, he says, "The gift of staying STD-free. It's the greatest gift one can give." I punch him in the arm and run upstairs to put the pack in my nightstand.

Ninny drops us off at the Boulder Theater, a sad look on her face. "So many memories," she mumbles as we get out of the car, and then she yells, "Don't eat any apples!"

The entire concert hall smells exactly like my house, with the faint scent of pot and patchouli oil filling the room. Kim holds on to my hand, yanking it every few seconds and repeating, "I'm so fucking excited!" in a squeal. We dodge in between people buying T-shirts and concessions and walk down toward the stage, staking our claim on a small portion of floor where we can dance.

The stage crew adjusts microphones and guitar stands as people wait for the band to come out. There's a static buzz, energy in the air.

"Check, check," a crew guy says into the microphone and taps on it. "Check, check."

A woman picks up a guitar and plugs it into an amp. She plays a few chords of the song "Touch of Grey."

Hearing it makes my throat dry and I cough. She plays some more. I plug one ear, trying to be nonchalant.

"Are you okay?" Kim nudges me.

"Is it loud in here?"

"It's a fucking concert. Of course, it's loud."

My fingertips start to tingle. "I think I need some water."

Out in the hall, I shake my hands out at my side. A headache starts to poke the back of my skull.

That song.

I try to rub my headache away.

"Hey, tree-girl." I look up to find Hunter standing in front of me, a goofy grin on his face. He's in his big ski cap, wearing a Phish shirt.

"Hey, gun-wielding-camouflage-boy."

"What?"

"Your name's Hunter."

He laughs so loud the hallway practically vibrates. It makes my head hurt more. "You're funny."

"Thanks." I start to walk away, but Hunter grabs my arm.

"You want some?" He holds out his hand. A brownie rests in his palm. Ninny has been making these brownies since before I was born. The kind that most likely taste like shit because they're stuffed with twigs and seeds.

He leans in and whispers, "It's got hash inside."

The dessert-turned-drug looks so innocent, so delicious resting in Hunter's palm. "Fuck it." Grabbing the brownie, I eat the whole thing.

"Cool." Hunter wraps his an arm around my neck and walks me back into the ballroom. When the lead singer of Deadly Grateful comes on stage, the hall erupts into loud screaming and clapping. My brain melts with the noise. And

ASPEN

before the band can play the first note of their first song, I'm as high as the rafters.

CHAPTER 17

Ninny is right. Being high is awesome. It's like my shoulders are feathers floating above me, and my brain is filled with air. The most wonderful air I've ever breathed, because every breath releases the tension I've held in my chest for months.

I walk around, listening to Deadly Grateful and singing the songs at the top of my lungs. I spin in circles, waving my arms like a bird that wants to fly away from the nest it's been trapped in. Being high is much better than caring.

Cass eventually finds me. I drape myself over him and wrap my arm around his neck, which is hard to do, considering his height. "Kim thinks I'm hiding things."

"Are you high? I want some."

"Do you?" I poke him in the nose.

"Yes, where's the pot?"

"No." I shake my head. "Do you think I'm hiding things?"

"Yes," Cass yells. "You're hiding pot. Where is it?"

ASPEN

I squeeze Cass close. "I'm gonna miss you so much next year." I talk into his shoulder, which smells really good. I hold his shirt to my face. "You smell like sunshine."

"Saying no to drugs is a joke." Cass stomps his foot. "Now I definitely want to eat an apple. I'm gonna go find one." He walks away, and I go back to my dancing. I close my eyes and sway. Time disappears. Songs melt together. And all I do is swing back and forth and keep my head up. It's like the music and I are one, living in each other.

But when the next song starts, the pain in my head comes back.

"Don't play this song," I mutter as "Touch of Grey" comes through the speakers, but the sudden ringing in my ears covers up my voice. I try to be louder. "Don't play this song."

It comes out like air. No one hears me.

And then I get mad. High people aren't supposed to be mad either. I try to shake the pain away, but it stays, pinching at my brain. Lazily, I bring my hand up to my head and rub my scar.

When I look down at my fingertips, they're covered in blood.

Stumbling to the side, I clutch my chest. Maybe getting high wasn't the best idea. I try to wipe the blood off on my jeans, but it's stuck to me.

Forcing my legs forward, I push through the crowd, searching desperately for anything that will clean me up. I push past a girl, my fingers touching her long brown hair.

It stops me in my tracks, an ice-cold sensation that starts in my toes and creeps all the way up my spine.

194

Katelyn.

All the air that I was feeling is sucked away in one breath, and my chest caves in. My hand reaches out to touch her. She's so real, dressed in her purple and gold soccer uniform. When the room begins to spin and all the colors from the strobe lights blend together to make a rainbow, I think she'll disappear. But she just stands there.

"I'm bleeding," I say to her.

She mouths the word, "Liar."

I choke on it. My body rocks back and forth, not to the beat, but like I'm on a ship and I might get seasick.

"I didn't mean to hit you," I say. "It was an accident." My head hurts, like gears are turning in my brain. I can feel their every movement. I try to knock my head clear on my hand, but the pressure doesn't go away.

Katelyn was so bloody. It dripped down her face and on the pavement. I didn't know a person could bleed that much. And the smell. Metallic.

I taste it in my mouth.

"Are you okay, sweetie?"

"I didn't mean to do it." Panic chokes me.

"Didn't mean to do what?"

I close my eyes, hoping for darkness.

"You're high, sweetie." I look at the person talking to me. I'm holding her long brown hair in my hands, but it's not Katelyn anymore. It's a stranger. "It'll wear off. It'll go away."

I look at my clean palms.

"No it won't. It'll never go away."

ASPEN

I push past the people in the ballroom and burst out of the building, scrambling for air. Reaching into my purse, I pull out my phone and squeeze it in my palm until my nails pinch my skin.

Then I cock my arm back and throw my phone against the building, shattering it to pieces.

I take off down the street. At first a slow jog, and then a dead sprint until I can't hear the noise anymore. All I hear is wind in my ears.

CHAPTER 18

I run until I'm standing in front of a one-story box house. I've never been inside. A blue tarp covers the roof and a red hummingbird feeder hangs from the tree in the front yard.

I knock on the front door.

Less than a minute later, a little girl with short black hair stands in front of me.

"Why are you sweating?" she asks without saying hello.

"I went for a run."

"I recognize you from the homecoming game." She furrows her brow. "You're that girl named after a tree who won with Ben."

"Yes. Are you that girl named after a boy?"

"Yeah," Sam says. "You're weird."

I nod.

"What are you doing here?" she asks.

I look around, rocking back on my heels. "I don't really know."

"Do you want me to get my brother?"

I nod, and then shake my head. "I don't really know that either. Do you ever feel like there are no answers in life?"

"I'm only ten."

I snap my finger and point at her. "You're lucky."

Sam leans on the doorframe, scanning me from head to toe. "I like you better than the other one. She cried too much."

"Katelyn?"

Sam nods and walks away, yelling, "Ben, Cottonwood's at the door for you."

He appears a few seconds later, out of breath. Ben's eyes widen as he sees me, but he doesn't say anything. We just stand there, staring at each other under the porch light.

"I'm high," I finally say.

"And sweaty. Good concert?"

"Why aren't you at the basketball game?"

"Because it's over. Why aren't you at the concert?"

"Because I'm high." I pause for a second. "I can't feel my arms."

"That's probably because it's thirty degrees and you're in a short-sleeved shirt."

"Or because I'm high."

"How'd that happen?"

"A hunter in a ski hat gave me drugs."

"Do you want to come in?" Ben leans on the door.

"I don't know," I say, trying to peek past his tall frame into the dimly lit house. "I'm high."

"Are you high?" He laughs, and his eyes are sparkly in the porch light.

"Has anyone ever told you that you have Snuffleupagus eyelashes?" I squint at him. My eyes are so dry I think my eyelids might stick to the ball.

"The elephant from *Sesame Street*?"

"I think technically he's a wooly mammoth, elephant and dog combined. I could eat a pizza right now."

"Probably hungry from the run."

"Or because I'm high."

"Or that." Ben smiles. "You're watching my eyelashes right now, aren't you."

"Totally." I lean into his face.

"Come on." Ben's arm wraps around my shoulder and he pulls me into the house. I trip over the doorframe.

"What about your dad?" I whisper, paranoid, and stop still. "And Sam saw me."

"He's at work. And Sam's seen worse."

"Is your dad picking up cars that don't work?" Ben nods, and I lean against the door, tired. "We should all just ride bikes. It's better for everyone. Cars are messy."

"But faster than bikes."

"Exactly." I point my finger at Ben. "Why are we in such a hurry?"

He carts me through the living room. A battered recliner sits, directed at the TV. Over the fireplace are pictures: Ben's senior photo, Sam in a baseball uniform, a scruffy dad in coveralls standing beside a car with a proud look on his face. I stop at one and pick it up. It's old and looks fake, like the photo that comes with the frame. A young couple with a small child stand in front of a small stucco house. All three faces are bright with smiles.

"Those are my grandparents and my mom at the first house they bought in the States," Ben says over my shoulder.

"Where are they from?"

"Mexico."

"I've never been to Mexico."

"Me neither." Ben smiles.

"Where do your grandparents live now?"

"They moved to Texas a few years ago."

"I've never been to Texas, either," I say. I set the picture back. "Sam looks like you."

"She's part Snuffleupagus. From our mom's side."

"I like when you talk about her."

"Sam?" Ben asks.

"Your mom." I smile. Or at least I think I smile. I can't really feel my face.

Ben leads me into his room. The smell of folded laundry fills the air, making me want to curl up in his clothes. He sets me down on his bed and wraps a blanket around my shoulders. Then he squats in front of me. I try to concentrate on one spot, but the room is spinning. He steadies my swaying body and pushes my hair out of my face.

"Your room is a mess," I say.

"I wasn't expecting company."

"I like it this way."

"Messy?"

"Exposed." I smile.

Ben cocks his head to the side. "Water."

"A combination of two hydrogen molecules and one oxygen."

"You need some. Wait here."

When Ben leaves the room, I start investigating his mess. He's got an old TV, as old as my car, sitting on a desk. It has bent antennae sticking out of the top and a DVD player attached to it. I sit down in his desk chair and pick up the one DVD sitting next to the TV. *The Wizard of Oz.*

I swivel back and forth in the chair, examining the DVD, and then set it down on the desk. Ben's soccer letter and a picture of the team are tacked to a corkboard hanging on the wall over the desk. I lean forward, finding Ben in the sea of uniforms.

"Please tell me you didn't look in the desk?" he says, as he walks back into the room.

"No." I sit back in the seat. "Is that where you hide your porn collection?"

He pops a pretzel in his mouth. "Maybe."

I take the bag. After a few bites, the pretzels feel like paste in my mouth. Everything is so dry. I chug the entire glass of water.

Pointing at a stack of folded boxers sitting in a laundry basket, I say, "You weren't lying."

Ben laughs and sits down on his bed. I wheel myself over until I'm directly in front of him. If my brain actually felt like it was sitting in my head right now, I probably wouldn't do this stuff, but right now it's on vacation. Or oozing out of my ear. Or left behind me in the Boulder Theater with Katelyn.

ASPEN

"Isn't it weird that we never really see ourselves? We just see reflections," I say.

"It's a good thing I like your face."

"It's kind of depressing, though, that we never really see ourselves," I say.

"Maybe life isn't about seeing ourselves. Maybe it's about letting other people see us."

I smile and blink too slowly. "You sound like Dr. Brenda."

"Who's Dr. Brenda?"

"My shrink. I'm not sure if you know this but I've been through something 'traumatic.'" I exaggerate the word and make quotation marks with my hands.

"Life is traumatic," Ben scoffs.

I lean in closer, so we're almost nose-to-nose. "Tell me something I can't see."

Ben studies me for a second. "Your left eyebrow always pops up when you're about to say something smart."

"I'm not smart."

"That's another thing you can't see. You *are* smart. You just don't try." Ben smiles and moves closer. I can feel his breath on my face. It smells like pretzels. "Now do me."

I pucker my lips and squint my eyes like I'm trying to think of something. But I really don't have to try. "Your eyes change color depending on your shirt."

"What color are they now?"

"Dark blue, almost brown." We've never sat this close before. Or maybe we have; we sit practically arm to arm in physics class, but it doesn't *feel* this close.

202

"Anything else?" Ben asks.

"You're the best person I've ever met."

Ben's gaze moves down to his lap. "Don't say that."

"Okay. Pretend I didn't. I'm stoned."

He gets up and paces the room. "It's just . . . unreasonable standards lead to unreasonable behavior. And I never want to be . . . "

"Unreasonable?" I turn the chair to face him.

Ben stops in front of his desk. "Yeah."

"Are you speaking from experience?"

"Maybe."

"Was Katelyn . . . unreasonable?" I ask.

"Sometimes."

"Sam said she cried a lot."

"When did she say that?"

"Just now."

"Well, Sam should mind her own business." Ben's hand grips the desk hard.

"Do you still miss her?"

Ben hunches over, resting his elbows on his thighs. "It's getting better."

"Are there pictures of her stuffed in your desk drawer? Is that why you don't want me to look in there?"

"I can't seem to get rid of them yet. But I can't look at them either."

"I guess we all try to hide the stuff we don't want to see," I say.

"Yeah." Ben pushes off the desk and comes to squat in front of me. His eyes are stormy now, tense. "Let's talk about something else."

Aspen

As he holds my gaze, so many more questions wrap around my brain. I don't want to talk about something else. I want answers to who Katelyn was. I feel like knowing them might make everything better—or maybe it would get worse, but at least it wouldn't be the same.

Ben puts his hands on my thighs, holding himself steady. The longer he keeps his eyes on me, the more I'm reminded that I know how he feels. I take a deep breath and let my questions go for tonight.

"Why do you have *The Wizard of Oz?*" I say.

"It was my mom's favorite movie."

"Maybe we could watch it?"

"Right now?"

"Well, I'm stoned, so now seems like an appropriate time."

Ben puts the movie in the DVD player. I crawl across his bed and lie down, my head resting on one of his pillows. Ben scoots back and says, "I'm glad you're here." Then he nestles down beside me. His arm touches my arm and his leg touches my leg.

"Sometimes when you look at me I want to kiss your eyelids," I say. "That's what you can't see in your own reflection."

"Sometimes when you look at me I want to throw all the pictures away."

"Don't tell Ninny I got high," I say, gazing up at him with tired eyes.

"Your secret's safe with me." Neither of us moves. For once, we just stay where we are.

When I wake up, Ben's face is inches from mine. Everything is warm. His body curls around mine, holding me, his hands pressed into my back. I run my hand over his cheek and touch his hair.

Tears sting my eyes. I need to get out of here. The room is dark except for the television in the corner. The *Wizard of Oz* home screen sings on repeat.

I peel back from Ben and slide out of the bed, inch by inch. My clothes and shoes are still on. I run my fingers though my hair and pull out a pretzel. Oh, my God, I was high. Like floating in a hot air balloon with the Wizard himself about to soar over the Emerald City high. Ninny would be so proud of me. I vow at this moment never to tell her.

Holding my breath, I tiptoe out of the room. Before I leave, I take one more look at Ben. My clothes are still warm.

In the living room, I stop still when I see a grown man asleep in the beat-up recliner, *Automobile Magazine* spread out across his chest. Ben's dad snorts, rolling over onto his side, and I jump. Shuffling across the floor, I open the front door, praying it won't creak. Ben's dad is a tow truck driver, which I know isn't the same as a *truck* driver, but it's the same genre of jobs. Truck drivers have hooks to replace the hands that they lost in Iraq—they've got bad tempers or prostitute problems. I don't want to encounter that when my head is still kind of cloudy from the hash brownie.

ASPEN

I close the door as quietly as possible. Standing on Ben's front porch, I'm cold. My breath crystallizes as it hits the air; I bend my knees until they crack. There's only one way to get home.

Running down the street, I pass dark house after dark house of people asleep in their beds. I make it back just as the sun is starting to come up. Going in through the kitchen, I chug a glass of water. Sweat rolls down my forehead. It's cold on my already cold skin. I pass Ninny and Toaster, asleep on the couch, spooning. His bare leg is draped over her waist and he's snoring in her ear. Toaster's greasy scalp is nestled into the arm nook of the couch, and I make a mental note to Lysol that spot later.

In the shower, I stand under the water until my body warms to an acceptable level and my fingers turn into little shriveled raisins. My skin is red and raw with overexposure, but I don't care. It feels good to just stand and listen to the sound of water hitting the cracked tile around the bathtub.

When I'm done, I twist my hair into a bun, crawl into my bed and just lie there, eyes open.

At one point, I hover in that state between sleep and wakefulness when you sometimes dream about a ball coming at your face and jump, waking up. Except I don't dream about a ball coming at me. I dream about a car coming at me. Two bright headlights.

I shoot up in bed, my lungs about to burst.

Light pours through my window, haloing Katelyn as she stands at the end of my bed.

"Please, no more blood," I whisper, my voice wobbly. "It's a bit dramatic, don't you think?"

Her face is like stone. She points at me.

I squeeze my eyes closed. "Please go away. Please go away. Please go away."

When I finally make it downstairs for the day, my skin feels tight around my eyes and my stomach is a ball of knots. Ninny lies on the couch, watching TV. She looks me up and down. "How was the concert? You didn't eat any apples, did you?"

And all I can bring myself to say is "I want a bike for Christmas."

"You want a bike for Christmas?"

"Global warming is a real bitch." I say, picking up a banana and then setting it back in the fruit bowl. My stomach is too sour. "It's time I did something proactive about it."

CHAPTER 19

I gnaw on my lip as I sit in Dr. Brenda's office Monday morning. The coffee I chugged down on an empty stomach feels like acid burning its way through my system. And the caffeine isn't even working.

Dr. Brenda sits in front of me, her trusty notepad and pen poised to jot down anything I say. I'm so tired that I have to hold my head up with my palm. And my entire skull hurts. I barely strung together a few hours of sleep last night. I was afraid to close my eyes for too long. But then, I was afraid to keep them open, too.

I rub my temples and wish my headache would go away.

"You're studying physics, right?" Dr. Brenda asks.

"How'd you know?"

"You talked about a test once. How'd that go, by the way?"

"I got a C."

"Average. Not bad. So you know Isaac Newton and his laws of motion?"

"Some would say biblically."

"Pardon?"

"I know him," I say.

Dr. Brenda moves forward in her seat, pulling down on her black pencil skirt. Her hair is darker today. Almost a cherry red, where it used to look more fiery. I like the new color better. It's more natural. "So you know an object in motion stays in motion until it runs into something."

"Newton's first law of motion: An object in motion remains in that state of motion unless an external force is applied to it."

"And you only got a C?"

"Definitions are my specialty." I shrug.

Dr. Brenda brings her hands to prayer position over her chest and says, "I have a theory of motion myself. I'm not sure if Newton would agree, but in my experience it holds true. Would you like to hear it?" I nod lazily and pull my eyes wide so they'll stay open. "When that object in motion runs into another object, all the energy moving forward at the time of impact gets caught."

"Okay."

"You've been in a traumatic car accident, Aspen, and somewhere inside of you is all the energy from that night. We need to figure out how to get it out of you so you can heal."

"I am healed," I say, and yawn.

"Physically, maybe. But there are some scars people can't see." Dr. Brenda puts her notebook down on the table. "I need you to tell me everything that happened that night."

"I told you: I don't remember anything." I look at the clock.

"I think you don't *want* to remember anything."

I sit up straighter. "What?"

"The memory of that night is somewhere inside of you, and it will come out. If you shake a bottle of soda long enough, eventually the top will pop, Aspen."

"Do shrinks take a class in analogies?"

"I can help you get the bubbles down, but we have to start at the beginning."

I look at Dr. Brenda's awful snow globe collection. "Can I leave early?"

I don't wait for an answer. I leave Dr. Brenda's office and vow never to set foot in there again. After all, what kind of person puts a deer head in their office?

Kim hounds me at lunch, waiting by my locker, arms crossed over her chest. The scowl on her face contorts her lips until they're crooked and makes her eyes sharp like razors. She looks like Uma, all scrunched up and evil. This usually happens when she's about to start swearing at me in Korean and flailing her arms.

"No goodbye." Kim starts ticking things off on her hands. "No text. No anything. You just up and leave the concert without telling me?"

"I lost my phone." I kick the ground with my sneaker. "And I had food poisoning."

"Food poisoning?" Her hip pops out.

"I ate a bad brownie."

"Cass said you were high."

"I ate a bad brownie with hash inside."

"Are you crazy?" Kim throws her hands out to the side. Arm flailing has commenced. "What's gotten into you?"

"Nothing." I push past her to my locker.

"No. Something very weird is going on. Drugs? Ninny does drugs. You don't do drugs."

"It was one brownie. And you're the one who said we needed to try new things our senior year."

"It's more than that." Kim leans her hip against Tom's locker. "You're irritable. You don't talk to me about stuff. You're having trouble sleeping." She points to the bags under my eyes.

"Sounds like I'm a teenager."

"Just tell me. I want to help."

I yank open my locker. Resting my forehead against the cool metal door, I close my eyes. "I'm just so tired," I whisper.

"Why aren't you sleeping?" she asks.

"I have bad dreams," I admit.

"About the accident?"

I can't bring myself to look at Kim when I say, "About everything coming to an end."

"What do you mean?"

I exhale the tightness in my lungs. "You and Cass are leaving next year. You'll be making out with some dude who reads poetry to you on a college green. You'll be fancy. You'll start drinking coffee without sugar or cream in it. You'll cut off all your hair. You'll wear jackets that look like sweaters that look like jackets. And I'll be working at Shakedown Street."

Kim rubs my back. "I hate poetry. And drinking black coffee is for communists."

"You *are* Korean."

"That's North Korea, you racist, not South Korea."

"There's a North and a South Korea?" I ask and smile. My shoulders relax. "Maybe playing ExtermiNATION isn't such a good idea," I say.

"I told Cass those video games are a fucking nightmare."

"But the sex is cool."

We laugh. I grab Kim and wrap my arms around her small frame, squeezing my best friend into me as hard as I can. And I don't let go. Kim slumps down into my arms, and we just stand there in the hallway, breathing into each other's ears.

"Was it fun being stoned?" She asks as we walk down the hallway.

"I can honestly say I'll never do it again."

And I'm telling the truth. Finally.

I get to physics early, sitting myself in my seat, my eyes trained on my sketchbook. My foot shakes underneath the desk, and I try to control the bile coming up my throat. I could barely eat at Moe's. I sipped on a soda, thinking it might cure my stomachache, but all it did is remind me of Dr. Brenda's terrible analogy and how much I hope I never see her and her red hair again.

When Ben sits down next to me, he says, "You didn't say goodbye."

"I was afraid of your dad's trucker hook hand."

RebekaH CranE

"He doesn't have a hook hand."

"My bad." I stare down at the sketchbook.

"He has a wooden leg."

"Well, I love a man with a wooden leg. I'll stay next time."

"Next time?"

"I didn't mean that. I hate drugs."

Ben laughs and grabs a notebook out of his bag. "That's a bummer."

"That I hate drugs?"

"That or the other thing."

My heart stammers inside my chest, swelling seven sizes larger. I settle back in my chair, exhaling.

Mr. Salmon slams a book down on his desk. The noise makes me jump, and I knock my sketchpad to the ground.

"Let's see who did their homework this weekend," he says.

I bend down to grab my sketchpad as Mr. Salmon continues.

"Let's say I'm driving in a car and there's a red light ahead. I slam on the brakes, but I'm not wearing a seatbelt."

I sit up. Did Mr. Salmon just say car? A few people glance at me. Or at least I think they glance at me. My stomach gets tight.

When I look to the front of the room, it's like we're alone in the classroom and Mr. Salmon is narrowing his eyes on me. "What causes me to go flying through the windshield?"

My stomach drops to the floor. I can't take my eyes off Mr. Salmon. He's staring at me.

"Aspen," he says my name.

My heartbeat pounds in my head. The longer people stare, the faster it gets. I feel the blood drain from my cheeks.

"Aspen," Mr. Salmon says again.

213

ASPEN

"I need to go to the bathroom." I grab my backpack and rush out the door. As I run down the hallway, past the bathroom, my legs don't feel attached to my body. I'm just glad they don't give out completely.

When I burst out of school into the cold winter day, sun beams into my eyes, making me go blind for a moment. I'm having a heart attack at school. I bend over, heaving. That'll be great for all the rumors.

"You've come . . . to see me . . . die on the front lawn of school . . . haven't you?" I say in between gasps to the girl standing next to me.

Katelyn doesn't move. Her eyes stay locked on the spirit rock. It's painted for the holiday choir concert. I pull on my shirt like maybe it's the thing suffocating me and shake out my numb hands. The stars in my vision start to fade. But Katelyn doesn't.

"At least you left the theatrics at home." I manage to squeak out in one breath. "The concert was a little much, don't you think?"

But Katelyn just ignores me and walks up to the rock. She places her hand on the new paint. I stand back and watch her as my heart rate slows to a normal pace. I feel like all my energy has been drained.

"You're covered up now," I say to Katelyn. But she still doesn't move. She doesn't nod. She doesn't speak. She doesn't even cry.

And then we just stand there as snow starts to fall.

When I walk in the back door, Ninny's sitting on the couch, watching TV. Her shoes have left tracks across the floor to her seat. I leave my shoes by the door and wipe up her mess with a kitchen towel.

"Thank God you're home," she says over her shoulder. "There's a girl upstairs in your room with way too much energy. She needs a Xanax, pronto. Or a joint."

"What?" I drop the towel and go upstairs. In my room, Suzy paces the floor, biting her nails. When she sees me, she flings herself into my arms and holds on tight.

"Don't ever do that to me again," she squeals in my ear.

"Do what?" I choke through her strong embrace.

"Disappear. You never came back to physics." Suzy's voice is tense and shaky, like she might cry.

"I didn't feel good, so I bailed. I'm sorry."

"I texted you like a million times. And you didn't answer. You need to answer."

"I lost my phone at the concert."

Suzy eases back and takes a breath. "Oh." She sits down on the end of my bed. "I didn't know that."

"Are you okay?"

Tears wet Suzy's eyes. Her hands are shaking. I've never seen her like this.

"I can't lose another friend, Aspen. Not on my watch," she says. And then Suzy pulls me into a hug and doesn't let go. I fall into her.

"I'm not going anywhere," I say.

When Suzy finally releases me, she says, "We have something else to discuss."

"What?"

"New Year's Eve. Tom's having a party and you're coming with me."

"I'm not sure that's a good idea."

"I don't care. You're coming." Suzy grabs my hand. Her eyes might be the kindest I've ever seen. I get sad for a moment that I didn't know Suzy before this year.

"Okay," I say. I guess going to another party isn't *such* a bad idea. It's my senior year, after all.

Chapter 20

Ninny gets me a used bike for Christmas. It's an orange banana-seat thing with only one gear and rust around the chain. She even gets me a bike lock, though I'm pretty sure anyone desperate enough to steal this bike can have it. I ride it around the block a few times, just to get the wheels moving before it starts to snow.

Ninny and I stay in our pajamas all day long and watch movies. She spends the majority of the day not high, as a Christmas present to me, which I appreciate. When I've eaten her entire stash of candy and Ninny's leg won't stop tapping on the ground, most likely because she's jonesing for a joint so badly, I retreat up to my room.

"I'm just going to Uncle Salvador's for a while," she calls after me.

"Whatever," I yell back. The door slams so fast, I think Ninny must be sprinting to her van.

I sit at my desk and turn on my computer. Logging onto Facebook, I pull up Katelyn's page. And then I click off of it. And then I click back to it. Then I send a message to Kim. Then I go back to Katelyn's page, then click off of it. Then I check my newsfeed. Then I click back to it. And then I shut my computer down.

I'm a stalker.

Then I roll a charcoal pencil around a sheet of paper until my room gets dark. When a noise in the kitchen catches my attention, I go downstairs, expecting to find Ninny, wandering around with bloodshot eyes. Sure enough, the fridge door is open.

"Munchies?" I say, leaning on the counter.

"Just looking for ice cream." Ben stands up from behind the door. I practically jump out of my socks, totally thrown by his presence.

"What are you doing here?"

"Looking for ice cream," he says again. His words are slurred and his eyes are wobbly. He grabs a container of mint chocolate chip out of the freezer and takes a spoon from the drawer. "Merry Christmas," he says, and gives me a kiss on the cheek. His lips are icicles and his breath is coated in booze. I rub my hand over the spot on my face. "I tried to call you, but you didn't answer, so I thought I'd just come over." Ben stumbles into the living room.

"My phone is broken. Permanently."

"Right." He sits on the couch, bouncing a little bit. "I've been drinking." Ben's droopy eyes travel up my body slowly until they meet mine. "You're wearing reindeer pajamas."

"It's Christmas."

Ben takes a heaping bite of ice cream. "Where's Ninny?"

"At Toaster's."

Some ice cream drips off Ben's spoon onto the floor. "Shit. Sorry." He bends down to wipe it up with his shirt and almost falls over into the coffee table. I grab his waist and hoist him back up onto the couch, giggling at his compromised state.

"Don't worry about it," I say.

Red rims his eyes. He looks like he's been crying. It makes my heart hurt.

"See. That's what I'm talking about," Ben says.

"We were talking about something?"

He grabs my charcoal-covered fingers and holds them in front of his face. "You're messy. You don't try to hide it."

"Thanks. I think."

Ben examines my fingertips, his body wobbling. "I hate Mrs. Ryan."

My posture gets straight when I hear Katelyn's mom's name. "Hate is a strong word."

"Well, I strongly hate her." Ben lets go of my hand and slumps back on the couch in a huff.

"Why do you hate her?"

"Because she's so clean and tidy and . . . clean." Ben's eyes hang at half-mast, and anger fills his voice. "She hates me, too, but she'd never admit it. She'd rather pretend to like me." Ben's head rocks back.

For a moment, I think Ben has passed out. His eyes stay closed, and his breath falls even. I want to grab his shoulders and shake him awake.

And then Ben sits up on the couch, alert again.

"Why did you come over?" he asks.

"Ben, you're at my house, remember."

"I know that." He taps my nose playfully. "Not now. Before."

"Why did *you* come over?" I counter.

"Because I had an important question to ask you."

"What's the question?"

"Why did you come over?" A grin lifts Ben's mouth, but then his face falls. "Oh, shit. I'm spinning."

"Come on." I pull Ben off the couch and drag him upstairs to my room. Setting him on the bed, I prop up his head with pillows. "Put a foot on the ground, it'll help the spins," I say. Ben's leg flops over the side of the mattress. He spreads his arms out to the side.

"Remember when I laid down in the street with you?" He blinks slowly, like it's getting harder for his eyes to stay open.

"I do." I sit down on the end of the bed.

"Will you lie down with me now?"

Ben's hair is extra messy today, almost like he got caught in a windstorm. Or like he drank a bottle of booze and got caught in a windstorm.

He pats the spot next to him on the bed and I can't resist. I crawl up next to him. It's not like we haven't done this before.

He wraps his arms around my waist, pulling me in tighter, like he's trying to make our two bodies one. Or like he's grasping for me, holding onto me in case I disappear. It makes my body heat a hundred degrees warmer. I rest my face against his chest.

"That night was the beginning," he whispers.

"The beginning of what?"

"The beginning of the end." He runs his fingers over my forehead, brushing my curls away. I don't respond, because I don't know what to say. Instead, I pull the blanket over Ben and me, snuggling down under the covers.

For a long while we don't say anything. Then Ben's voice comes through the silence in the room.

"She cried on Christmas every year," he says, breathing into my ear. "And the fucked up part is that I miss it."

"Katelyn?" I ask. Ben nods slowly, his eyes closed. "Why did she cry?"

"She was always looking for a way out. And always sad when she couldn't find it." His head tilts back on the pillow, finding a more comfortable position.

"A way out of what?" I ask.

"Just so you know," Ben pulls me closer. "It would be okay if you kissed my eyelids." And then he falls asleep completely.

"A way out of what?" I repeat to myself. I lie there, listening to his breathing. Squeezing my eyes shut, I press my face into Ben's shirt. The smell of laundry detergent fills my head. And eventually, everything goes black.

~∿∿∿⟊

Ben's leg is hooked over my waist, his arm resting lightly on my shoulder, as I wake up face down on my bed the next morning. I lift my head from the pillow and gaze around the room. Sun pours in my window. The weight of Ben's body holds me down to the point where I can't move.

ASPEN

Stuffing my face in the pillow, I blow out a breath. Then, ever so slowly I attempt to scoot out from underneath him. It doesn't work. Ben's body curls even more, wrapping around me so we're in a spoon position, my back resting against his front. He breathes in my ear, his face nestling into my hair. It's better than any physical contact I've ever had with a boy.

I slide, inch by inch, out of the bed. First my legs, so my feet can touch the ground. Then my torso, peeling away from Ben's. Finally I flop on the floor like a dead fish, then stand up. Ben rolls onto his stomach, overtaking the entire space of the bed and sprawling out like a giant starfish.

I tiptoe through the room and down the hallway to brush my teeth. Running my fingers through my hair, I pull my curls into a messy bun on my head. I'm still dressed in my reindeer pajamas from the night before, so I find a basket of clean clothes in the laundry room and change into grey sweatpants and a tie-dye T-shirt. Then I peek through my door to check on Ben. He's sitting up in bed, rubbing his temples. I grab a glass of water from the kitchen before going back into the bedroom. He looks up from checking his phone, a nervous smile on his face.

"Hi." I hand him the drink.

"Hi." Ben's voice is deep with fatigue. He looks at me with guilty eyes. "I'm sorry I took over your bed." He downs the glass of water.

"That's okay. I did it to you first." When Ben rubs his temples, I ask "Headache?"

"Life-ache. My dad's not so happy about my disappearing act last night." Ben holds up his phone and rolls his eyes. "I better get out of here."

"He might beat you with his wooden leg." I say, and Ben laughs.

"Ouch. Even laughing hurts." He wobbles to his feet and catches himself on the bed.

"Do you remember anything from last night?"

Ben squeezes the bridge of his nose. "I broke in to your house. There was ice cream. And then it all goes kind of black." His face falls. "Did I do something embarrassing?"

"No." I help Ben to his feet, letting go of my questions and the disappointment along with them.

As I'm walking Ben to the front door, Ninny emerges from her bedroom at just the right moment to catch him leaving. She yawns, arching her back in a stretch. "So this is what happens when I go to Salvador's. I'll make sure to leave more often."

"Classy, mom."

"Just keeping it real. It's always good to see you, Benny. You can sleep with Aspen anytime." She winks and disappears into the kitchen.

"Is it wrong to say I love Ninny?" Ben asks. I swat him in the arm. "Ouch. Life-ache, remember."

"Do you want a ride or not?"

"I thought you'd never ask."

At the garage, I wheel out my new orange bike. I hand him Ninny's helmet, which has flowers all over it, and put on my own.

"There's snow on the ground. Why aren't we taking your car?"

Aspen

"You need some fresh air. This'll be better." I climb onto the seat and point to the pegs jutting out from the back wheel. "Hop on, Benny."

Ben hesitates for a second, and then he straps on Ninny's helmet and climbs onto my bike. I giggle as he holds my shoulders to balance himself.

It takes a running start to get up enough momentum for any kind of speed. Banana-seat bikes aren't really built for teenagers. More like five-year-old girls with flower baskets strapped to the front handlebars. But as Ben and I wind through the streets of Boulder, the wind in our ears and the snow sloshing around our ankles, it feels right.

CHAPTER 21

Being back in Suzy's room is weird. Her party wasn't that long ago, yet it feels like forever. I tried to convince Kim and Cass to come with me tonight, but they decided that after the last party, it would be safer to play video games at Cass's house while he babysits his little sister so his parents can go out. I'm sure they'll manage to sneak some liquor from his parents' cabinet. They might even get drunk enough to stop fighting and start taking their clothes off.

Suzy scuttles around in the bathroom behind the closed door and reappears in her tie-dye T-shirt. It's beginning to suit her in a rebellious way. Kind of like our friendship. I know Olivia must hate that Suzy wants to be my friend, but she does it anyway.

"Ta-da!" Suzy spins in a circle. Smiling, I want to jump up and hug her for her loyalty. "What?" she says when she notices my goofy grin.

"The tie-dye looks good on you. It's your color."

"It still smells like the Crystal Dragon, too." Suzy take a sniff of the shirt.

As she finishes up in the bathroom, I poke around her room. A dried red rose with a purple and gold ribbon tied around it sits on top of her dresser. I pick it up. It's the rose from the homecoming crowning celebration. I threw mine in the garbage at Shakedown Street afterward.

Suzy walks out of the bathroom and notices the rose in my hand. "Do you still have yours?"

"No." I spin the stem around in my fingers.

"I actually meant to give it to Katelyn, but I forgot."

"Give it to Katelyn?"

"For her grave." Suzy's voice is soft. Her eyes get sad for a moment.

"Oh." I set the rose down.

She sits on her bed and slips a pair of brown knee high boots over her jeans. "Mrs. Ryan had us all go visit her on Christmas. It was Katelyn's birthday."

"Christmas?" I perk up.

"I know. It's such a shitty time to have a birthday. You don't get nearly the number of presents you would on any other day." Suzy laughs. "Katelyn hated it."

"Was something wrong with Katelyn?" I blurt out.

Suzy gets stiff and scoots back from me on the bed. "Why do you ask?" I ease back, feeling bad that I made my friend so tense.

"It's nothing. I just . . . " I stand and pick up a lipstick from the pile on Suzy's dresser. I can't I think of what to say. Suzy doesn't move.

"I had to wrestle scissors out of her hands once," she says.

"What?" I look at Suzy's reflection in the mirror. Her eyes aren't on me. They're fixed on her knotted, white fingers.

"Katelyn wanted to cut all her hair off. I grabbed the scissors just in time. She only managed to snip a few strands."

"But she had such nice hair."

"She sliced me, she was so mad. I had to get stitches." Suzy spreads her palm out on her lap, turning her hand to face me. She runs her finger over the light scar. "It was an accident. She apologized."

"Suzy . . . " I begin, but she cuts me off when she notices the shocked look on my face.

"Don't tell anyone. Mrs. Ryan would kill me."

I nod slowly, still clutching the lipstick.

"That color would look good on you." Suzy points to it.

"It's not really my style." I set it down.

"I'm wearing a tie-dye. You can wear lipstick."

Suzy paints my lips with rosy pink and tells me when to press together.

"It's totally you." She turns me toward the mirror.

I don't look at my lips. I can only focus on the girl standing behind me.

"You're a really good friend," I say.

Suzy's eyebrows rise. Her chin starts to shake, like she's holding back a waterfall of tears that want to break free. "Thank you."

ASPEN

Tom's house looks totally dead. From the street, it looks like no one's home. No lights are on. We tiptoe up the driveway—and I hear someone whispering our names from the side of the house.

Tom's blond hair shines in the moonlight, a cigarette hanging out of his mouth. He needs stock in hair gel. He motions for us to come around back.

"It's good to see you, locker buddy." He pulls me into a hug, his cigarette smoke going up my nose. "You too, Suz." She curtsies as he offers me his cigarette. "You want a hit?"

"No thanks."

He tosses it on the ground and rubs it out with his shoe. "Let's get you guys a drink."

The inside of Tom's house is a stark contrast to what it looks like from the outside. Music blares; people stand around his kitchen, drinking and talking too loudly. Someone yells Suzy's name the second we're in the door and she gives me a hug before disappearing into another room.

The inside of Tom's fridge is lined with condiments, beer and shots. He hands me a silver beer can.

"Happy New Year, beautiful." Tom pops the top of my beer, and it foams, almost dripping down the side. "Why don't you take off your coat and stay awhile?" He moves to help me out of my jacket.

"That's okay." I step back. "In case of a quick getaway," I add.

Tom taps his temple. "Good thinking."

I glance around the party, as more people walk in the back door.

"You look hot tonight."

228

"Did you just call me hot?" I ask.

"Maybe." Tom puts his arm around me.

I peel it away and say, "I'm gonna go find Suzy."

"Find me at midnight," he hollers after me.

People are scattered everywhere in the house, laughing and talking loudly over the music. I look for Suzy's shirt in the crowd and see she's not the only one wearing tie-dye. There are at least three other people. I shake my head and chug the rest of my beer, setting the empty down on a table. Through the windows, I can see a beat-up old teeter-totter in Tom's backyard. I make a quick exit out the back door.

In the cold, I push the air out of my lungs. I sit down on the teeter-totter and gaze up at the stars. The cold air makes everything seem clearer and brighter. The moon hangs in the sky, half full, lighting the black to grey. Almost like a light shining down on everything. It gives the trees a shadow even in the darkness.

"These things usually work better with two people." Ben sits down on the other end of the teeter-totter, lifting me into the air.

"I was actually saving that for Tom. He just needed to gel his hair first."

Ben laughs and pushes off the ground. I come down, my knees pulling up toward my stomach. We ride back and forth like this for a while, and then he says, "I'm sorry again about Christmas."

"Don't be. Are you going to do it again tonight?"

"I'm off the hard stuff for a while."

"Bummer. How am I supposed to get you in my bed again?"

Ben floats back down to the ground as I rise in the air. He's smiling.

"I like long walks on the beach and a band called Beta Particle, but you've probably never heard of them."

"Never. They must be new."

"It was Katelyn's birthday," he says, practically into his shirt. "Her mom made us go to her grave. I hate cemeteries."

"I think that's a good thing. You're not supposed to *want* to be there."

"Right," Ben says, a smile returning to his face. "Wanna play a game?"

"That's my line." I push myself high into the air as Ben floats down.

"I ask you a question and you answer with the first thing that pops into your head."

"This isn't a game. It's a trick."

"Maybe."

"Bring it on."

"Okay." Ben rubs his hands together. "Favorite season?" he asks.

"Spring."

"Favorite fruit?"

"Raspberries."

"Favorite flower?"

"Daisies."

"Favorite song?"

"Anything by the Dead."

"That's cheating but I'll let it go." Ben grins. "Run, bike or swim?"

"Swim."

"Outside or inside?"

"Outside."

"Warm or cold?"

"Warm."

"Windows or air-conditioning?"

"Windows."

"Best thing you did today?"

"This." I smile and push off the ground.

"The teeter-totter or me?"

"Technically, I didn't *do* you today."

Ben wags his finger. "There's still time. Tom will be disappointed, though."

I laugh as Ben lands on the ground. He stares down at the teeter-totter, his once relaxed face turning perplexed. "Don't leave me hanging here," I say, and tap on the wood.

"I could have answered all of those questions for you."

"I'm that predictable?"

"I know you that well," Ben says. He gets off the teeter-totter, slowly setting me on the ground. He paces back and forth, hands stuffed in his pockets. I wipe my pants as I stand, checking behind me to see if I have any residual dirt on my butt.

A moment later, Ben is standing in front of me, almost nose to nose. Instinct makes me want to take a step back, my stomach flying to my throat, but I manage to stay still.

"I'm not supposed to be happy with you." Ben's eyes are serious. More serious than I've ever seen them. My heart pounds in my ears.

"Why?"

"Because it makes me forget."

"If you ask me, forgetting isn't so bad."

Ben runs his hands through his hair, his brow knitted tight. So tight it might stay that way. He holds my shoulders, like he's worried I might run away. I suck in a breath when he presses his forehead to mine.

"I can't make the past go away," he whispers.

"Even though it's already done."

He pulls back. My forehead goes cold. "But maybe it's not about making it go away. Maybe it's about moving on," he says.

Ben's hands are shaking. He leans in, inches from my face. I can practically feel lips on mine.

"You can't leave me, Aspen," he whispers.

And then Ben's lips really are on mine. They're warm and soft, and for just a moment, I feel as though I've fallen out of my body. That I'm floating somewhere inches above the ground.

"I need you," he says in my ear.

"Like air." I whisper back. Ben nods. And we both breathe.

"Look at what we have here." Olivia's voice is like cold water splitting pavement. Ben and I separate. She stands with Claire, arms crossed over her chests. Olivia clicks her tongue on the roof of her mouth. "The king and the queen."

"*Puta*," Claire spits at me.

I stumble over the words in my head, but I can't get anything out. Everything turns red . . . then blue . . . then red.

A second passes, then two. Tom's back door flies open and a sea of people come streaming out.

"The cops!" Suzy yells as she takes off down the driveway. People scatter in different directions. Olivia and Claire dash into the neighbor's yard. There's yelling and running and beer cans everywhere. It's a quick getaway. But somehow in the chaos, Ben manages to grab my hand.

CHAPTER 22

My house is dark from the outside. Ben and I haven't said anything. I'm not sure I want to.

He stops on my front porch. I can't read the expression on his face.

"What did Claire say in Spanish?" I ask.

Ben shakes his head. "I don't know."

"I thought you said your mom was from Mexico." I nudge him in the shoulder.

"Yeah and she moved here when she was like two. She's more American than Ninny. The jury is still out on where *she* actually came from."

I laugh too loudly and then look around like the cops might be following us.

"That was . . . " Ben trails off, his eyes searching around, looking anywhere but at my face.

"Nice," I say.

He exhales. "It was?"

"You don't think so?" I step back.

"No."

"No, you don't think it was nice?" I take another step.

"No," Ben yells and grabs my arms, yanking me back to him. Before I can take a breath, his lips are on mine. My knees give out a little, but Ben holds me steady. When he pulls back, he says, "That was more than nice."

I smile, my lips warm again.

In my house, we both stand at the end of the bed. It looks different now. Bigger or smaller or sexier. I become acutely aware that there's a box of condoms in my drawer. Neither of us moves.

"Ninny is at Toaster's," I say, flatly.

"Maybe I should go." Ben points to the door.

"Don't." I grab Ben's hand. When I crawl back on the bed, he takes off his shoes. I pull down the sheets. We don't say a word as we nestle down in the bed. I rest my cheek on Ben's chest and listen to his heartbeat.

"I sleep better when you're next to me," I say, and yawn.

"Me, too," Ben says. "Happy New Year, Aspen"

"I hope so," I say.

I don't wake up until there's sunshine spilling through my window. I pick my head up and feel my cheek. The pillow crease has left an impression. My head swims with grogginess. I get lost for a moment, after so many hours of sleep.

ASPEN

When I feel Ben's chest rising and falling under my head, it all comes back to me. The party, the cops, the kiss. The fact that I'm pretty sure Claire called me a not-so-nice name in Spanish. I turn to glance up at Ben, resting my chin on his shoulder.

His lips are parted slightly as he exhales. I reach up and almost touch them. But he looks so peaceful. I can't disturb that.

When he finally does wakes up, I'm sitting at my desk, fully changed out of my clothes from the night before, teeth brushed.

"I want to do something with you," I say before he can even speak.

"Okay." Ben rubs his eyes and stretches his arms over his head in a yawn.

I ride us over to Shakedown Street on my bike. The lights are off inside and a "closed" sign hangs on the door. The shop's shut for New Year's Day. I use my set of keys to unlock the place. Ben grabs my hand as I turn the handle to let us in.

"Are you sure this is okay?"

I grab Ben's hand and yank him into the store. I flip on just a few lights and turn on the radio. Jam band music fills the shop. I bob my head to the beat as I pull food out of the fridge. Ben walks over to my mural and examines it.

"You did this?" He runs his finger over the picture painted on the wall. When I nod, he says, "You're really talented, Aspen."

"You don't have to flatter me. We've already made out." I roll my eyes, but can't stop my cheeks from heating. Ben laughs.

When I'm done cutting and mixing my concoction, I pour us two heaping glasses full of shakes.

"Here." I set one on the counter.

"What is it?"

"I call it the John Lennon."

"Why?"

"Because it's one of a kind."

Ben takes a sip, licking his lips clean. "Oh, my God, that's good. Why isn't it on the menu?"

I smile and take a sip of my own. "Because I don't like sharing. I've never actually made it for anyone but myself before."

"Does this mean I'm special?"

"Maybe."

He sets his glass down and comes to stand in front of me. I search his face for what's different today and stop on his eyes. They seem lighter, like he's carrying less weight. Like the new year really is new.

And then his lips press to mine for the first time today. They're cold and sweet. I taste the flavor of the vanilla shake on his tongue. Ben leans into me further, pressing my back against the counter, pinning me in place. I wouldn't want to move even if I could.

The moment breaks apart when Ben's phone beeps. A text message. My heart jumps into my throat; the sound scares me. I pull back quickly. My hands shake as I grip the counter.

A glass moves from one of the shelves.

Ben sees the surprise on my face. I feel the blood drain from my cheeks clear down to my toes.

"Sorry." He pulls his phone from his pocket.

Katelyn holds the glass high in the air.

"Shit. It's my dad," Ben says.

"Don't do it," I say to Katelyn. I use the counter to brace myself, my knees wavering.

"Don't do what?" Ben stares at the screen, typing.

"Please," I whisper.

Katelyn lets go. I close my eyes, but hear the glass shatter on the ground. Like every sliver and every shard is a crack of thunder in my ears.

I grab my head.

"Aspen, what is it?" Ben cups my cheeks with his hands. "Look at me."

I can't open my eyes. I can't look at all the tiny pieces of glass on the ground, like razor sharp rain.

"I think I'm getting a headache." I step back from Ben and force my eyes open. There's no mess. No Katelyn. "I'll take you home."

"A headache." Ben doesn't sound convinced. "That's it?"

"That's it."

We clean up, returning everything to its proper place so no one will know Ben and I were even here. I turn off the lights and lock up, staring for a moment at the counter where Ben and I just kissed.

I don't go home after I drop him off. I make a quick stop at Walgreens, and then ride across town to the one place I never thought I'd go. Nerves make me peddle faster, but fast and banana-seat bike don't really go together.

I search row after row of cement headstones, looking for Katelyn's name. *Katelyn Grace Ryan*. It takes three hours of searching through the mashed-down grass at the cemetery to find it. When I do, I'm struck still, my breath tight in my throat. A dozen red roses sit wilting on the ground. I shake out my numb hands at my side.

Standing in front of her name, I stare at the numbers. They're so close together. Seventeen years.

"Here." I toss a pack of No. 2 pencils at the stone. "Better late than never." And then I wait. I don't know what I'm waiting for. But I wait. One lone white cloud passes overhead. "I'm pretty sure no one is satisfied with the number on their gravestone." I finally say. "No matter what you have, it never feels long enough."

And as I ride away, I can't help remembering what I said to Ben about cemeteries. How no one wants to be here, yet this is where we end up. No matter how hard we fight against it.

My house is dark when I ride up the driveway on my bike. Parking in the garage, I see that Ninny's van is gone. When I get inside, a note sits on the counter.

Gone to Salvador's. Don't wait up. Happy New Year, baby.

The kitchen is a mess. Ninny's bowl of mushy half-eaten cereal sits on the counter; the coffee pot is still on, filling the house with the smell of burnt coffee. I groan and clean the bowl, slamming it down too hard on the counter. When I dump the sludge of coffee down the sink, I bite the inside of my lip, tears threatening to pour down my face. I'm so tired of cleaning up after Ninny. For once, I'd like her to act like a grown-up and me like a child.

Aspen

I light incense to get rid of the Starbucks smell and microwave leftover spaghetti for dinner. As I sit eating, the only sound in my house is my chewing.

I sat at this same table while Ninny was in Taos, waiting for her to come home. I learned to hate the sound of silence. To hate anticipating a person walking in the back door, only to be horribly disappointed when they don't.

I drop my fork into the container of spaghetti and pinch my ears closed, grinding my teeth together. Nothing moves but the shadows on the wall.

When my heart beats like it might explode, I rinse my dirty dish in the sink, running the water just to hear something else. Then I jumping on my bike and ride over to Ben's. I can't be alone tonight.

His house is lit up. The gentle blue hue of a TV shines out into the street. I creep around until I find Ben's bedroom. I tap on the window. When nothing happens, I knock harder. The thin glass vibrates like it might shatter at any second. A light flicks on in the room.

"Shit." I duck into the bushes. A few seconds later, I hear someone outside walking towards me. I try to be as quiet as possible.

"Aspen?" Ben finds me crouched close to the ground. "What are you doing?"

"Hiding?"

"Why are you hiding?"

"Can I blame your dad's wooden leg?"

"You know he really doesn't have a wooden leg, right?"

I crawl out from the bushes and dust my pants off. "Ninny's at Toaster's again." Ben cocks an eyebrow at me. "And I was thinking maybe I could stay here."

"So you want to sleep with me."

"You make it sound like I want to *study* with you."

"Do you?" Ben gets a shit-eating grin on his face, and I swat him in the arm. "I'll sneak you in the back," he says.

The tension in my shoulders releases as I walk back into Ben's room. I take off my shoes and climb in, hugging one of Ben's pillows to my chest. Ben watches me before getting in behind me and cupping his body around mine. He kisses my ear.

"I can't reach your eyelids, or I'd kiss those." And then he whispers good night.

Before I can say it back, I'm asleep.

I try to run down the street, but everything is moving in slow motion. At least it feels that way. I'm locked in some sort of quicksand that's holding my feet to the ground. But I need to move. It's coming. I can feel it behind me.

I take another step and fall, catching my heavy body. The cement is cold on my hands.

I need to get away from here. Clawing at the ground, I pull myself along the cement. My nails dig in and rip from my fingers.

When my arms collapse under me, someone takes hold of my legs. She's got me; she's dragging me across the road, the weight of her body like a ball and chain meant to drown me in a sea of blood. I kick and punch and scream at the top of my lungs, but her hold is strong. And I know she won't let go. She'll never let go.

I sit up in bed, wheezing, a scream caught in my throat. I choke with every painful breath. My head is covered in sweat.

"What is it?" Ben sits up, brushing my hair out of my face. "Aspen, what's wrong?" His voice is panicked. Even in the darkness, I see fear in his eyes.

Grabbing Ben as hard as I can, I press him to me and squeeze my eyes shut. I grab a fistful of Ben's shirt and knot it in my hand. Tears break from my eyes, but I choke them back.

Ben strokes my hair with one hand as the other presses into my back. I listen to his breath in my ear. Eventually, everything starts to slow down. My muscles let go and I loosen my grip on Ben's shirt. He pulls back to look at me. Ben's eyes still look worried, and I want to make it go away. I want to make it all go away.

I press my lips to Ben's. He kisses me back. I grope at his back and arms, holding him to me. I let my mind go. The world only consists of Ben's lips and Ben's hands.

I grab for the bottom of his shirt.

"Are you sure?" he asks breathlessly.

I nod, kissing him again, and pull his shirt over his head. He does the same to me. I lose track of what time it is, what day it is, if I'm living in the past or present or future. All that exists to me is Ben.

CHAPTER 23

I hesitate outside of Shakedown Street the next morning, looking at myself in the window reflection. Nothing looks different. My hair hangs curly around my shoulders, still a little damp from my shower. My dull brown eyes are still dull. I place my hand on my stomach. It's tight today, trying to hold in the butterflies that have taken up residency there. Did I really *study* with Ben Tyler? My body tells me yes. It aches this morning, like it ached the first time.

I take another breath and walk into Shakedown Street. Warm air from the heating vent over the door blasts my head and I shiver. The place is quiet this morning. Too quiet. The radio isn't even on. I'm switching out my sweatshirt for my green apron when I hear a sniffle come from behind the counter. I look to see what it is and find Ninny curled up on the floor.

"Mom?"

Aspen

"Aspen-tree." She looks up at me with tear-covered cheeks. Her hair is a mess and she looks like she hasn't slept all night.

"What is it?" I move to sit next to her.

"Salvador broke up with me." Her head falls into her hands, her back shaking with sobs.

I stroke her hair and pull a few tangles free. She's wearing an extra dose of pot perfume, which leads me to believe she's been on a smoking binge. I should feel relieved that Uncle Toaster, the snaggletoothed monster, is finally gone, but I don't.

"What happened?" I ask.

"I wanted to make him dinner last night, so I went to the grocery store and bought a frozen lasagna." Ninny wipes tears from her cheeks. "When Salvador saw it, he got pissed. He asked if I got it out of the Dumpster, and I said no. He said that I needed to respect his freegan lifestyle and not bring wasteful, commercialized garbage into his house. I laughed and said *he's* the one who eats freegan *garbage*, not me. That's when he told me to leave." Ninny's shoulders slump and she starts to cry again.

We sit nestled next to each other on the floor at Shakedown Street for a long while as Ninny gets it all out. I hug her, petting her cheek and clearing away fresh tears. She's clearly upset but at least she showed up for work, which is a positive sign.

"I'm sure he's regretting it today," I say.

It takes a few seconds, but eventually Ninny sits up straighter. "He better," she says through clenched teeth. "Who does Salvador think he is?"

"A freegan, I guess."

"Well, he's freegan crazy to let go of this." She wipes her cheeks with her damp sleeve. Slowly, a resolved look grows on her face. Ninny stands up, pulling her V-neck shirt down lower so her cleavage pops out. "You know what I need?"

"I hope whatever you say is legal."

"A distraction. I'm going to Whole Foods later. I need some organic meat."

"Organic meat." I shrug. "That's one way to put it."

"Like Salvador is the only man in Boulder." Ninny looks at herself in a metal cup, like she's giving herself a pep talk.

"That's the spirit, Mom."

Ninny turns to me. "By the way, where were you last night?"

I turn away from Ninny and stuff an empty napkin dispenser with paper napkins. "I spent the night at Cass's since we didn't see each other New Year's Eve."

"I hope Ben's not jealous." Ninny rummages around in her gigantic purse. My stomach flip-flops. She pulls out a tube of red lipstick and applies a generous layer, checking her reflection in the metal blender cup. "I should wear my 'Namaste' shirt tonight."

"What?" I ask.

"To Whole Foods."

"Right. Organic meat."

"Are you okay, baby?" Ninny sets the cup down on the counter.

"Yeah." I try to sound indifferent.

She comes over to me and tucks my hair behind my ears. "So how *was* the party? Did you kiss anyone at midnight?"

"It was fine," I say quickly without making eye contact.

"And . . . " Ninny's eyes get big.

"And what?"

"Did you kiss anyone?"

"No," I say with an annoyed edge, how a teenager is supposed to when her mom asks about kissing boys. It sound disingenuous coming from me. From the quizzical look on Ninny's face, she notices.

"You're sure you're okay?" she asks.

I busy myself by grabbing a rag and a bucket of soapy water to wipe down the tables. "I'm fine."

She grabs my in a hug, squeezing me tightly. "I don't know what I'd do without you, baby." Ninny kisses my forehead.

"Definitely wear your 'Namaste' shirt," I say.

"Works every time." Ninny smiles and blows me a kiss with bright red lips.

"It better work," I mutter to myself. I can't have Ninny checking out of her life again.

To keep my mind busy, I scrub Shakedown Street until it sparkles. I clean behind the refrigerator and the gigantic box freezer, and even scour the bathrooms until they're spotless. My hands are red and my knuckles are cracking, they're so dry.

Ninny goes home early to get ready for her night at Whole Foods, leaving me to close Shakedown Street alone.

"Wish me luck." She crosses her fingers and kisses me on the forehead.

As I'm about to wipe down the tables and clean the glasses for the night, Suzy walks in the front door.

"I've let this go for a day, but I need answers." Suzy purses her lips at me.

"Answers?"

"Did you kiss Ben on New Year's Eve or what?"

I squeeze my eyes shut and nod. Suzy squeals and jumps to hug me. "How do you know?" I ask into her shoulder.

Suzy rolls her eyes. "Olivia and Claire said they saw you."

I sit down in a chair, tired. Suzy pulls up the seat next to me.

"Don't worry about them. They suck. You and Ben deserve this."

"Why do we *deserve* it?"

Suzy sits back in her seat. She exhales a long breath and then says, "Because Katelyn could be a bitch, and she treated Ben like shit. There. I said it."

"I thought you said Katelyn was like 'the best drunk of your life.'"

"Well, sometimes drunks are assholes. And sometimes they're fun."

"Is that why you don't comment on her pictures on Facebook?" I ask.

Suzy looks down at the scar on her hand. "I don't comment because it doesn't matter what I think."

"But she was your best friend."

"Exactly," Suzy says. "And the people on Facebook are her 'friends.' They can have their Katelyn and I can have mine." She stands up, pulling her car key out of her purse. "Can I drive you home?"

The dangly crystal ball keychain catches the light. The flash makes my eyes hurt.

"That's okay." I rub my eyeballs with my palms. "I have to close up."

Aspen

I don't move after Suzy leaves. I just sit still as the Phish Pandora station plays over the speakers, filling the silence.

When I walk out the back door into the cold January darkness, I pull a rag from the back pocket of my jeans and stop still. I forgot to wipe down the tables. I've never forgotten to wipe down the tables.

An empty can rolls down the alley, banging along the cement. My heart jumps into my throat at the sound.

I squeeze the rag in my hand until my knuckles turn white and then toss it into the Dumpster.

CHAPTER 24

It hits me: I had sex with Ben Tyler.

CHAPTER 25

I pick up the house phone and dial Ben's number. I hang up before it starts to ring.

It's dark in the kitchen. It's dark outside.

A stranger's jacket and messenger bag sit on the counter. Two pins are attached: *I like mainstream because hating mainstream would be too mainstream* and *Composting = Compassion*. Ninny's organic meat from Whole Foods.

I dial Ben's number again. I hang up.

It's three in the morning.

I take everything out of the fridge and clean the inside. I put everything back.

I pick up the phone and listen to the dial tone.

But she doesn't go away.

Katelyn just stands in the corner screaming.

CHAPTER 26

"A-hole. Wake up." Kim pokes my side with a plastic fork. I pick my head off the table at Moe's. A napkin sticks to my face and Kim peels it off my cheek.

"Dude, you fell asleep in your food," Cass says.

I yawn and arch back. Every knuckle on my hands is cracked. Dried blood sits in the crevasses. I can smell in my hair the lemon cleaning product I used last night.

"I'm sorry. I'm just really tired."

"Are you pregnant?" He wags his finger at me. "I gave you those condoms for a reason."

I punch him in the arm. He almost falls out of his seat.

"I have an announcement," Kim says.

"Oh, God. You're pregnant, and Jason is the father."

"I'm gonna kick you in the balls. No, ass hat, I'm not pregnant. I got into Stanford early admission," Kim says. "I found out a few weeks ago, but it just didn't seem real until now."

ASPEN

Cass and I sit frozen. Now I want to kick something in the balls. Namely Stanford.

"Well, duh. Of course you got in," I say, sipping my water to cover the frown on my face.

"Don't. Don't fake being happy. I'm not fucking happy. I'm fucking sad. I'm fucking overwhelmed. I'm fucking—"

"You're fucked," Cass says.

Kim plops her head down on the table. "And Uma's over the moon. 'I knew you could do it. I so proud. Both my girls in big American college.'" Kim groans and puts her head in her hands. I rub her back, but really wish I could lay my head down with her and sob.

"You'll be home for Christmas and in the summer," I say. It's hard to push the words out.

"That's not the same and you know it."

I do know it.

The rest of lunch is silent, except for the light ringing of fatigue in my ears. As we walk out of Moe's, Kim pulls me aside. "Are you still not sleeping well?"

I shake my head. The ringing gets louder.

She snaps her fingers, her face bright. The sound is like a needle through my eyeball. "What about seeing a hypnotist?"

"Am I talking to my best friend or Ninny?" I ask as I put on a pair of sunglasses. It's always so damn sunny here.

"I'm serious. Uma saw a hypnotist to quit smoking."

"Uma smoked?"

"Like a fucking pack-a-day when I was little. But then she went to some hypnotist and they, like, I don't know, made

252

her forget that she liked cigarettes or something. She hasn't touched one since. Maybe they can help you sleep."

"I don't think a hypnotist will help." An exorcist, maybe, I think to myself.

"What about Dr. Brenda? You're still seeing her, right?" Kim asks.

"Yeah." I walk faster so she can't see my face. "Good idea. I'll ask her."

Kim grabs my arm to slow me down. "We're still going to be best friends when I'm at Stanford, right?"

My stomach hits the pavement. I adjust my sunglasses and blink away the water collecting in my eyes. "Of course," I whisper.

Kim wraps me in a hug. I press my nose into her hair and smell her coconut shampoo. I might buy a bottle just to have around when she's gone next year. "So, we haven't talked about Tom's party. Did anything happen?" she asks in my ear.

My throat closes. I wrap my fingers tighter around Kim's jacket, and I feel my dry knuckles split open.

"No," I say.

I walk into physics with my sunglasses still on. The pain behind my eyeballs won't go away. Everyone stares at me. For, I'm sure, a list of reasons. I try not to care. I really try. But the heartbeat in my ears tells me I'm doing a bad job of it.

"Are you okay?" Ben asks.

"Kim's going to Stanford."

"That's great."

"And my head hurts."

"That's not great." Ben runs his hand over the top of my head, lightly pulling on one of my curls.

Him touching me is the only good thing that's happened today.

He rubs my shoulders as Mr. Salmon walks around the classroom passing out our new assignment. Joey Roscoe leans back to hand me a stack of papers and says, "Here, Katelyn."

Ben's hands drop from me. I sit up in my seat, the papers cascading to the ground.

"What did you say?" Ben's voice is flat.

"I mean Aspen. *Aspen.*" Joey smiles with exaggeration. The entire class looks at us. Even Mr. Salmon. For a moment, no one moves.

I bend down to grab the dropped papers. A metallic smell hits my nose. Fresh blood seeps out from one of the cracks in my knuckles. I quickly wipe it on my jeans. The smell doesn't go away.

When I stand up, Katelyn sits in one of the empty seats across the room. She quietly screams, like her voice is choked in her throat. I press on my forehead, right on top of my scar.

"*Is there anything you want tell us? Anything we should know?*" Mr. Salmon seems to say. But his lips don't move. And he sounds like Officer Hubert.

Katelyn keeps screaming. The papers rattle in my hand.

"Can I go to the nurse?" I ask Mr. Salmon. "I have a headache."

When he nods, I rush out of class and down the
the bathroom. Locking myself in the stall, I bend over a
for breath. For a second I think I might pass out, right here
the bathroom floor.

I sit on the toilet a moment before my knees give out, and
put my head down. When I finally gather the energy to walk
out of the bathroom, I find Ben pacing back and forth in the
hallway.

"Is everything okay?" He grabs my face between his hands.
"Aspen, you have to tell me if something is wrong." Ben's
voice is panicked. His eyes search my face like he's trying to
memorize me.

"It's just a migraine. They make me nauseated." The words
slide out of my mouth naturally. "I think I'm gonna go home."

"I'm coming with you."

"You don't have to do that," I say too quickly. "I'm fine."

"I've made this mistake before, and I'm not doing it again.
I'm coming."

I pull back from Ben. "What mistake?"

"I've lost two people already, Aspen," he says, moving to
hold me again. "I'm not losing you."

We get two steps into my house and Ben is on me, covering
me with his hands and lips. It makes the pain in my head
disappear. But when we climb back onto my bed and Ben goes
to take my shirt off, I push him back.

"I think Ninny's going to be home any minute," I say, even
though I know she's working until close at Shakedown Street.

Ben kisses me and goes for my shirt again. "Ninny did say
I could sleep with you anytime."

"I can't." I stop his hands.

"Okay." Ben backs up, a look on his face like he did something wrong. "Is this about what happened at school?"

I don't move. I just stare at one of the empty spaces in the Grove.

Ben gets off the bed and paces my room. "People don't know what they're talking about. They only know what they saw in the halls."

"Suzy said that Katelyn treated you badly." I pause. "Actually, like shit is what she said. Katelyn treated you like shit."

Ben stops still. He pulls on the collar of his shirt. "She did sometimes."

"Why did you stay with her?"

"Because sometimes she loved me, too."

The pain in my head comes back. My eyes burn like someone poured acid in my room. But I'm so fixed on the Grove, I can't even blink to clear them.

"But Katelyn and I never had what we have," Ben says.

"What do we have?" I ask.

"Something real." Ben kisses the palm of my hand. The feel makes me snap out of it. Then he moves to my lips. And this time, I don't stop him.

Ninny gets home from work after Ben's already left for the night. She sticks her head in my room and asks if I've had dinner.

"No." I'm sitting on the floor next to my bed. My sketchbook in my lap.

"Do you want anything, baby?"

256

"No. That's okay."

I don't move the rest of the night. When I wake up in the morning on the floor, my sketchbook sits next to me. The word liar is written on the blank page. I don't remember writing it.

CHAPTER 27

Suzy pulls up in her SUV as I'm undoing my bike lock. It's so cold my hands are practically frozen to the metal. She rolls down the window.

"What are you doing?"

I glance up, my hair in my face. "Saving the planet, one bike ride at a time."

"It's freezing. And riding bikes is for losers and seven-year-olds." She gets out of the car. "I'll give you a ride."

"That's okay."

"Stop being silly. We can put your bike in the back of my car." She picks up the lock and makes a wrinkled, gross face. "Do you seriously think someone is going to steal this thing?"

Suzy and I hoist the bike into the back of her car, and I climb in the front seat.

"Thanks," I say.

"What are friends for?" She turns up the heat so it's blasting our faces. It melts my frozen nose. "Where to?"

"Shakedown Street."

We drive toward Pearl Street, both of us quiet. Suzy taps out the beat of the song playing on the radio and bobs her head. Big sunglasses cover her eyes. I watch her.

"Why are you friends with me?" I ask.

"What?"

"You didn't talk to me once last year."

"I didn't know you."

"But what made you want to get to know me?"

Suzy's easy demeanor shifts. She sits up straighter in the seat, eyes glued to the road. "Because I felt bad for you," she says.

I exhale but can't respond. The truth sits on me.

When Suzy stops at a red light, she turns to me and says, "Aspen, what is it? What's going on?"

The air in the car is thick. Too thick. It's getting caught in my throat.

"I just . . . I . . . "

Suzy's eyes are wide. "Do you not want to be friends anymore?" The words sound like they hurt coming out of her mouth. Her bottom lip starts to tremble.

"No." I say. "I just need some fresh air. I'll ride my bike from here." I jump out and grab my bike from the back.

"You'd tell me if something were wrong, right?" Suzy says through the rolled down car window. I nod and ride down the street as fast as I can, never looking back.

By the time I get to Shakedown Street, my entire body aches. I squat and rest my head against my knees, pressing on my forehead.

ASPEN

Mickey walks out of the back room, clipboard in hand, and says, "You look tired. Go home."

I stand up, a little wobbly on my feet. "I'm fine."

He points his pencil at me. "No, you're not. I can tell. Go home."

"Just leave me alone," I bark.

Mickey's face freezes. Even I freeze. I can't believe I just snapped at my boss. The man who's given my mom the only job she's managed to maintain in my entire life.

"I'm sorry," I say.

Mickey walks over and grabs my shoulders. "Go home, Aspen. Get some sleep. You'll feel better tomorrow."

I grit my teeth. *Get some sleep.* But even when I get home, I can't close my eyes. Keeping them open doesn't help the pain either. I down three Advil and wait. They don't help. I chug seven glasses of water. My head still hurts. I open Ninny's pot stash. And then I close it.

When I hear Ninny and a muffled male voice walk into the house giggling, I lock my bedroom door. At least Ninny's laughing. That's a good sign.

I log on to Facebook. Olivia has posted a video of Katelyn. The caption reads, "I found this today and can't stop crying. I miss you, K!" I hold the mouse over the play button, but don't click on it. Over a hundred people have liked the video. And there are thirty-seven comments. I turn off the computer screen.

I walk around my room for an hour. Then I clean my closet so all my clothes are hung up and color coordinated. Then

I rearrange the entire Grove, trying to get rid of the empty spaces. No matter what I do, they're still there.

I finally click on the video. When Katelyn comes on screen, I hold my breath.

"What do you want to do when you're older?" Olivia's voice comes through speaker.

Katelyn shrugs. She's sitting in the middle of the soccer field in her uniform. The sun makes her eyes extra blue.

"Come on, this is for posterity," Olivia presses.

Katelyn runs her hands through her hair. "I don't want to get older," she says.

I choke at the sound of her voice. Seconds pass by as the video plays on. I try to stop it.

"Damn it." I click on the stop button. Katelyn freezes on my screen. I shut the computer down. The screen goes black.

"Aspen, baby, what are you doing?" Ninny walks out of her bedroom in her pajamas. I don't know what time it is. Darkness.

"I'm watching TV," I say.

"Baby." Ninny touches my shoulder. "The TV isn't on."

But there is a voice in the room. And she won't stop talking.

ASPEN

"I want to see a hypnotist," I say to Kim at my locker the next day. My foot taps on the ground. I started drinking coffee at five in the morning when I realized I wouldn't sleep at all.

"Okay." Kim's face gets a surprised look. "What's going on?"

"Will you come with me?" I pull on my hair. My head is numb. "Today. I need to go today."

Kim's face goes from surprised to flabbergasted. "Okay. I'll find someone." She looks up a person on her phone and calls. "She has an appointment this afternoon at four." I nod my head repeatedly. After Kim hangs up, she says, "I'll get Uma's car at lunch and drive you."

"Thanks. I'll meet you here later." I walk out of school. I need some more coffee.

~\/\/\/\/~▶

Sky's hypnotism office is worse than Dr. Brenda's. It's actually a living room with seven cathouses and crystals hanging from the windows, sending glistening prisms all over the furniture. Kim and I sit on an old leather couch as new age yoga music plays over a small stereo tucked in the corner. The room smells like cat food and pot.

"Which one of you is Aspen?" Sky says in that hippie-kind-of voice, slow and slurred. Most likely she just ripped a bong hit. She's wearing a flowing brown dress down to her ankles and about seven silver necklaces that jangle when she moves. I raise my hand.

"I'm just the best friend," Kim offers.

"A best friend is never *just* anything." Sky smiles and pets one of the cats. "So what can I do for you today, Aspen?"

"I'm having trouble sleeping."

Sky nods, looking at my jittery hands. "Let's go back into my office." When Kim gets up to move with us, Sky stops her. "You can wait out here, best friend. Aspen will be fine." Sky winks at Kim, who slumps back on the couch.

"I'll be here when you're done," Kim says.

We enter the back of Sky's house through a set of large wooden doors that slide closed. Sky motions for me to sit in an antique armchair as she pulls up an ottoman covered by a colorful tapestry. I wipe the cat hair off the chair before sitting down.

"So you can't sleep," Sky repeats. She pats my hand in a motherly way. "You know, Aspen, the only way to get out of the forest is to go through it."

"Okay." My voice wobbles.

Sky takes off one of her seven necklaces. "Lean back, love. Get comfortable." I wiggle down in the seat and rest my head back. "Now, I want you to focus on this necklace. Clear your head of everything and just look at my pretty necklace."

A silver ball hangs from the end. Almost like a sleigh bell. I stare hard at the rounded edges. I focus on the way it moves in Sky's hand, back and forth.

"I'm going to start counting," she says, "Ten, nine, eight . . . "

But I block Sky out. All my attention is on that ball. How it hangs in the air, moving through invisible energy.

Aspen

"Mickey, I'm out of here," I say, placing my dirty rag in the laundry bin. The tables in Shakedown Street gleam. "Don't forget the lights," I say.

Mickey pops out to the front of the shop. "I don't need to be reminded how to close my own damn store." I cock my head at him. "Get out of here. Enjoy your youth while you have it."

I walk into the back alley, where my car is parked, and check my phone: one text message on the screen. It's from Kim.

R u coming over?

I don't respond. I need a moment. Just one moment to myself. The warm summer air blows lightly as I roll down the windows of my Rabbit. When I pull away from Shakedown Street, Mickey walks out.

"The lights," I yell out the window. He scowls and stomps back into the shop.

I head west up my favorite road—it winds out of Boulder and into the mountains towards the small town of Nederland. Within a few miles, traffic and congestion disappear. All that I can hear is wind howling down the canyon. I rest my head back against the seat and turn up the Grateful Dead song playing on the stereo.

As I get higher up the mountain and my phone rings. Another text message. I grab the phone and glance down at the screen. It's from Kim again.

Where the fuck r u?

I laugh. God, she loves the word "fuck." But then my laugh fades. Soon, I won't be able to hear her swear like a sailor. I won't have my best friend in the same town as me. Kim and Cass will be off at college in less than a year.

I turn the car and make my way back down the mountain, anxious. We're seniors. Seniors. It's our final year together. I press down on the gas and grab my phone to text her back.

The road is darker now. Twilight is hanging over the mountains. I lift my foot from the gas pedal and let my Rabbit coast. I know this part of the drive, how the road will curve to the left next to a large aspen grove that sits just down the embankment. I'm almost back to town. Looking down at my phone as my car winds around the curve, I text Kim.

It only takes a moment for my body to sense the mistake I've made. Like the zing of static before someone gets shocked. But once it happens, it's too late.

I look up at the road as two headlights blind me, blurring my vision. There isn't time to swerve. There's barely time to slam on the brakes, but I do it instinctively.

Blackness comes first. For a moment, I wonder if it really happened. Like waking up from a realistic dream, and you're not sure what to believe anymore. But the light comes eventually, making everything illuminated and so real. I'm begging for this to be a dream.

I open the door and crawl out of the car. My leg hurts, a burning sensation down to my bone—or what's left of my bone. I wipe my forehead with my arm. Red stains my skin, and a metallic smell fills my nose. The hood of my car is still hot to the touch. It burns my fingers.

And then I see her, brown hair splayed out on the pavement, her face down toward the ground. And blood. There's blood everywhere.

ASPEN

I throw up. It isn't the right thing to do and I know it, but the shake Mickey let me make for dinner just comes spewing out of me. It hurts my chest.

I crawl through the mess of glass around me. It looks like rain on the pavement. My leg hurts, but her leg looks even worse. It's bent out to the side in a backwards L. I try to remember what Mrs. Andrews said in health about moving someone who might have a spinal injury, but my mind is blank.

"Oh, my God," I whisper, rolling her over. Her hair falls back from her face as I cup her cheeks in my palms. Like my car, she's still hot.

Blue eyes look up at me. I know this girl. Everyone knows this girl. She blinks.

"Aspen?" Katelyn Ryan says. "I'm so sorry."

That's when I start screaming.

CHAPTER 28

I come to in Sky's office. She's frozen in front of me. My head hurts; it's like my scar has reopened and is bleeding all over again.

"Aspen, I think—" Sky starts to say, but I don't let her finish. My entire body shakes. It rattles me down to my bones. I can't stand being in my own skin. I need to take it off of me.

I run out of Sky's office in a panic. Kim sees the look on my face and goes white.

"She was alive," I whisper.

"What?"

"Katelyn was alive," I say louder.

The weight of what I've said hits Kim and she grabs me. "What do you need?"

"I need you to take me to Ben's."

Kim begs to come inside with me, but I refuse. I watch her drive down the street and disappear around the corner. Then I bang on Ben's front door like a madwoman. I'll bang until my fists bleed if he doesn't answer.

When Ben answers, he looks surprised.

"What's going on?" Ben looks around like someone's chasing me. "Aspen, what is it?"

"She spoke to me," I blurt out.

"What?"

"Katelyn," I say.

Ben grabs my hand and pulls me through his house into his room. Everything blurs around me. He sets me down on his bed. But I feel like I'm floating.

"What did she say?" Ben's voice shakes.

My mouth is dry. "She said she was sorry." The words come out as light as air.

Ben stumbles back from me and almost falls over. He catches himself on the desk and starts to pace the room. "It's impossible," I say.

"What?" Ben bites his nails. I've never seen him do that before.

And then it's like I'm out of my body. Seeing things I've never seen before.

"I was texting. The accident was my fault," I say.

Ben hands fall to his sides and he comes to sit in front of me. He wipes tears from my cheeks with the fingers he was just biting. I didn't know I was crying.

"No, Aspen. The accident wasn't your fault."

"Yes, it was. I was texting." I say it again and finally feel the tears in my eyes.

"No," Ben grabs my face and holds his eyes to mine. "Katelyn killed herself."

CHAPTER 29

The world stops spinning. The air holds no breeze, no oxygen, no energy. I stand up out of Ben's grasp. Blood drains from my face, all the way down to my toes.

"No," I whisper.

"Aspen." Ben moves towards me, but I step to the side.

"That isn't true."

"I'm so sorry." He goes to grab my arm, but I yank it away.

"No. It was my fault."

"It couldn't have been," he says.

"How do you know?"

"Katelyn wasn't wearing a seatbelt, Aspen."

"So what? People make mistakes all the time."

Ben looks at his hands. "She told me what she was going to do."

"What?" I yell the word.

"Please, Aspen, let me explain." Ben reaches for me again, but I dodge his move. "Katelyn was depressed. She needed help. It got so bad that Suzy and I confronted her parents."

My head splits open in pain. Black spots speckle my vision.

"Katelyn came over the night of the accident totally crazed. She found out that I gave her mom an ultimatum: Either she get Katelyn help or I would. Katelyn was beyond pissed. She was manic. She scared the shit out of Sam, throwing things and screaming about how Suzy and I betrayed her. I swear, I meant to help. But Katelyn was convinced I was out to ruin her. She said that she'd rather kill herself than be sent away to some psych ward. You should have seen the look on Sam's face. I've never seen her so scared. I didn't know what to do."

"What did you do?"

Ben's head falls to his chest. "I kicked her out."

"You kicked Katelyn out."

He grabs my hand. "If I thought she'd really go through with it, I never would have let her go, I swear. I thought she was just being dramatic. But when Suzy showed me the text message she got right before the accident, I knew I'd made a huge mistake. The biggest mistake of my life."

"Suzy got a text from Katelyn that night," I say, barely feeling the words on my lips. Ben nods slowly. "What did the text say?"

"Please don't make me repeat it."

"What did the text say?" My voice gets louder.

Ben's eyes focus on his lap. His voice shakes as he says, "I'm going to hit the next thing I see. I hope you're happy." He grasps at me, pulling me toward him like I'm his breath and he can't bear to let go. "I'll never forgive myself for kicking her out. Please, you have to believe me." He kisses my face and my neck and my hands. But I'm numb. Completely numb.

ASPEN

"I was the next thing she saw," I whisper. My knees give out. Ben catches me before I hit the ground. He sets me down on the bed.

"I'm sorry. I'm sorry." Ben says it over and over.

"Don't say those words."

And then it starts to burn. A fire rages up my limbs and into my chest and all the way to the top of my head, where the blood poured down my cheeks and mixed with hers and I thought it was all my fault. I hear the skid of the tires, the crushing sound of metal. And the screams. Like the howling wind that grows until it's the piercing shriek of life obliterated. I pinch my eyes closed. Ben grabs my hand.

"Please. Talk to me," he pleads. "I'm sorry."

"Don't say those words."

When I open my eyes, she's there. In Ben's room. And for the first time, I see Katelyn for who she was. All the blank spaces filled.

"Go away," I say to her.

But she just stands in the corner of Ben's room, screaming.

"I'm not leaving you," Ben says frantically.

"I hate you!" I yell at Katelyn. "I hate you!" I run out of his room. Ben tries to stop me, but I wiggle out of his arms. I take off down the street. My leg hurts like it's broken again. I feel the impact of the steering wheel crushing my chest and my head. I stumble and almost fall into the road. A car horn sounds.

And the blood. On my hands. On my clothes. It's on my clothes.

I burst in the front door of my house covered in blood. I trip up the stairs to my room.

I have Katelyn's blood on me. I need to get it off.

She stands in front of me, her voice so loud in my ears, I can't hear anything else.

"I'm sorry I didn't give you a damn pencil!" I scream.

Angry, I go to my desk and grab my sketchpad. The noise won't stop. And I need it to stop. Like I need air.

I stare Katelyn in the face. I look into her blue eyes and see her on the ground that night. My hand moves on the paper. I feel her hair in my hands. And the crunch of glass on my knees as I knelt beside her. My arm is tired, but my hand doesn't stop moving on the paper. I feel the gurney they strapped me to and how fast the ambulance drove back to town. I feel Kim's hands in my hair, rinsing the blood away.

My hand moves.

I feel everything.

And realize Katelyn now feels nothing.

The pencil drops to the ground. I breathe. But Katelyn doesn't. My eyes stare into hers.

And at the same time, we both say, "I'm sorry."

CHAPTER 30

"Aspen, baby?" Ninny's voice comes through my ears. "Oh my God, what's going on?"

I'm lying on the floor of my room. My charcoal pencil is in my hand. Ninny pulls it out of my grip. She wipes my wet cheeks.

"Why were you late?" I whisper, barely seeing her through my tears. "I needed you. You promised you'd never do that to me again. After Taos, you promised." My voice sounds faint, like something hushed off in the distance. Ninny scoops me up, rocking me back and forth like a baby, petting my hair over and over.

"I'm so sorry, baby. I'm so sorry." Ninny whispers the words in my ear. It's those words again. But they don't hurt anymore. She picks me off the ground and lays me down in bed. "I'm right here, baby," Ninny says, grabbing my hand. "I'm not going anywhere."

Ninny covers me with layers of blankets. She lies down next to me, running her fingers through my hair, and then Ninny starts to sing in my ear. "You are my sunshine, my only sunshine. You make me happy, when skies are grey. You'll never know, dear, how much I love you. Please don't take my sunshine away."

My toes warm first, followed by my legs. Before I fall asleep, I look at the Grove. A new sketch hangs on my wall. I don't remember hanging it up. A beautiful girl with long brown hair and eyes that sparkle.

And at that moment, the screaming stops.

Everything hurts, inside and out. I lie on my bed, staring at the ceiling, my mind quiet for the first time in months. Ninny knocks twice on the door and then walks in.

"Do you want some pizza?" she asks in a whisper. She's carrying a Domino's box like a delivery person.

"No, thanks." I sit up, and Ninny places the box on the end of my bed.

Her face is tight, her eyes pulling downward like last night aged her ten years. She looks down at her hands. "You know why I was so sad after I got back from Taos?"

"Because Uncle Steve left you."

Ninny shakes her head, her eyes never leaving her hands. "I couldn't believe I did to you what my parents did to me. I left you. I was ashamed, Aspen-tree. And when I got the call about the accident . . . " Ninny trails off, a tear rolling down her cheek. "Every parent knows they aren't supposed to outlive their babies. And I came so close that night."

"But I needed you. I still need you."

"I felt so guilty." Her face collapses into her hands.

"Guilty?"

"I was so mad that you almost died." Ninny looks up at me. "Because I needed *you*. I bought you that car to begin with. I should've made you get something safer, something with air bags. But I was trying to do what my parents didn't. To give you freedom."

"I don't want freedom. I just want a mom," I say.

Ninny grabs my cheeks and focuses her eyes on me. "I don't deserve you. I'm gonna change, baby. I am." Ninny brushes a few curls from my face. "I'm so sorry."

Her hair hangs long down her back. There are random braids throughout. I touch a hole in the neckline of her shirt. And I realize for the first time how much strength it must have taken for Ninny to raise me by herself. How she accepted her past mistakes and moved forward. She might be the strongest person I know, with or without the punctuality.

Ninny wraps one of my curls around her finger and opens the pizza box. "I got your favorite. Olives and extra cheese. Sure you aren't hungry?"

We sit back on my bed and eat, the pizza box between us. Ninny picks the cheese from her pizza and sets it aside. "Ben was here earlier," she says, staring down at her pizza-turned-breadstick.

I sit up straighter. "What did he want?"

"To see you. He looked bad, Aspen. And it would take quite a beating to make that boy look bad."

The pizza turns sour in my mouth. I set my piece aside.

"It's just so complicated."

Ninny holds up her hands in surrender. "I'm not going to tell you your business. You're old enough to make your own choices when it comes to boys. But can I give you one piece of advice?" When I nod, Ninny scoots next to me on the bed, resting her head on my shoulder, and continues, "Life is complicated, baby. But that's what makes it worth it. You asked me once what love is, and I said I didn't know. But that wasn't true. It's hard to believe in something you can't see, Aspen. I've never been good at it. But I know the wind blows, even if I can't see it. Sometimes what we feel can't be defined, because it would take every word, every sound, every emotion ever created to do it. That's what I think love is. And some people don't think teenagers are capable of understanding that kind of thing, but I'm here to tell you, that's total bullshit. They're the most capable. And I should know. I fell in love at sixteen."

"With who?"

"You, baby."

Ninny wraps her arms around me and I curl into her, letting her familiar smell envelop me. "How's it going with your distraction from Whole Foods?"

"I'm done with distractions for a while. I've got a more important person to focus on right now."

I nuzzle into Ninny more, pressing my face into her shirt, her patchouli oil filling my nose. "Mom?"

"Yes."

ASPEN

"Could you maybe take the van in for a detail? It's about time we got rid of the ice cream stain."

"Whatever you want, baby."

"Thanks."

"No, Aspen, thank you," she whispers in my ear.

Ninny calls me out of school the next day, claiming I'm sick, which isn't that big of a stretch. I did end up lying on my bedroom floor after drawing a dead girl. She should probably have me locked up in the loony bin.

I'm watching *The Price is Right* and eating candy from Ninny's secret stash when there's a knock at the door. I groan and ignore it. A few seconds later, the back door flies open, thudding against the wall. It scares the shit out of me, and I jump on the couch. Kim and Cass walk into the house, arms crossed over their chests.

"Skipping school without us? What the fuck?" Kim says.

"I'm sick." I cough once.

Cass comes over to me and places his hand on my forehead. "You don't feel like you have a fever. I think you'd better get naked so I can make sure."

"You're sick." I swat his hand away.

"No, you're sick. I'm a guy." Cass smiles at me.

"Shouldn't you be in school?" I ask.

"It's Senior Skip Day." Kim sits down on the couch next to me.

"It is?"

"Well, technically, no." Cass says, sitting on my other side. "But we're pretending."

"Is this like my un-birthday celebration?"

"Skipping on actual Senior Skip Day is for fucking amateurs. Why would you skip a day of school when the entire grade is gone? No teacher is going to teach a class to one person. It's the best day to be *in* school."

"So you skipped today for me?" Kim nods, resting her head on my shoulder. "Kim Jong Uma's gonna kill you."

"She can't kill me. I'm going to fucking Stanford. She'd never jeopardize that."

"I love Senior Skip Day," I say as all three of us sit together in the quiet of my house, watching *The Price is Right*. When the show ends, I turn off the TV. "I have an idea."

I run up to my room and grab my iPod. Back in the living room, I hook it into the stereo and sit back down with my friends. When "Strawberry Fields Forever" by the Beatles comes through the speakers, Kim and Cass smile.

"I buried Paul," Cass imitates.

Halfway through the song, Kim says, "I think I've decided what name I want to use at Stanford next year, and it's fucking perfect."

"Let me guess . . . Candy. No, wait, wait. Destiny," Cass says.

Kim swats him in the arm. "I've decided I like the name Kim. Kim Choi is going to Stanford."

"Finally," Cass says.

We sit together, listening to music for hours, until the sun has moved toward the mountains and it's almost dusk. Kim braids my hair. Cass eats Cheetos until his fingers are orange.

ASPEN

We don't talk about what happened. But they don't look at me with puppy dog eyes, either, wondering if I might break apart again. It's as if my best friends know what I need right now is not to talk about the past, about what happened a few days ago or a few months ago, but to be reminded of the present.

When they leave, I stop Cass and say, "Do you think you could help me put together an art portfolio?"

"Why?"

"I think I might apply to college." I shrug my shoulders. "I hear video game designers have better 401Ks than employees at Shakedown Street."

Cass smiles, a wide grin. "Sure."

At that moment, my fear of losing Kim and Cass lessens. No matter where we go, even if we're dead and buried and all that's left is our breath floating over the mountains, we'll still be friends.

Ninny comes home from her shift at Shakedown Street with a bag of groceries and a determined look on her face. She's making dinner, she proclaims. She even cleans up the kitchen without me.

"It's a start," she says, wiping down the counter.

I smile. "I hear that's the only place to begin."

Later that night, I stand in front of the Grove looking at Katelyn, my dictionary out on my desk. I see Suzy pop up in the doorframe. The makeup she's usually wearing is wiped clean, and I can tell she's been crying.

"Can I come in?" she asks in a shaky voice.

Suzy doesn't wait for a response; she comes rushing into my room and hugs me.

"I'm so sorry, Aspen. I should have told you," she whispers. "Katelyn told me she wanted to kill herself, and I didn't believe her. It was just once. And then I got the text message that night. When Ben told me everything that happened, I knew it was my fault. If I'd just done something more . . . "

I hug Suzy tighter, knowing the pain Suzy's held onto for months. And the guilt. I know what that feels like.

"It wasn't your fault," I say, pulling back from her. Then, for the first time, I utter the truth. "And it wasn't my fault or Ben's fault. It was Katelyn's."

The words echo around inside of me. For a while, Suzy and I sit in silence, letting the moment sink in.

"Do you think it will ever go away?" Suzy asks, resting her head on my shoulder.

I take a second and answer truthfully. "No. I don't think it will. We'll have to live with it. But that's the point. We *live* with it."

After Suzy leaves, I grab the sketch of Katelyn from my wall. I open my dictionary and flip to a word. I've been waiting for this moment all year.

The end: the final point, finish.

I write the definition on the back of my sketch and hang Katelyn back in the Grove, so she can be a part of all the pieces that make up my life. Then I stand back and admire my work. Even the blank spaces. All the choices I have left to make. My future of unexpected and unintentional moments.

I don't think the Grove will ever be complete. That's the funny thing about endings. They're usually the start of something new.

Chapter 31

Ben is standing by the bike racks when I pull up to school in my Rabbit. His shoulders are hunched, and dark circles rim his eyes. When he sees my car, he stands up straighter.

"You drove," he says, walking up to me.

"Riding bikes is for losers and seven-year-olds." I repeat Suzy's words.

"I like your bike."

"That's because you get to ride on my pegs."

"I like riding your pegs." Ben smiles. "I mean, I like riding *on* your pegs."

I laugh and kick the ground with my shoe.

Ben steps closer to me and grabs my hand. I don't pull away. His palm is warm, like every other part of him. "Aspen, I'm so sorry. I never should have—"

But I cut him off.

"I think I'm in love with you." My heart pounds. In a good way. A bursting way.

I take a tube of Chapstick from my pocket and apply a layer to my lips. Holding it out to Ben, I ask, "Do you want to share my Chapstick?"

He takes it from me and puts some on his own lips, a smile spreading on his face. "Well, now that we've officially shared Chapstick, I guess I should tell you that I love you, too," Ben says, taking his finger and wiping my bottom lip.

"Does this mean you're my boyfriend?"

"I prefer lab partner. It's more intimate. There's *studying* involved, after all." I elbow Ben in the side as we walk into school, hand in hand.

"Well, lab partner, will you do something with me after school?"

Ben stops, taking my face between his warm hands. "Anything," he says.

When he leans in to kiss me, I don't hesitate. I kiss him back. I know people will stare at us, but I don't care. They've been staring all year.

Ninny and Ben sit in my car. They both promise they'll be here when I get out.

"I'm not going anywhere," Ninny says.

"Me neither," Ben says.

I shake out my hands at my sides. I'm nervous to be back here. Walking in the office building front doors, the familiar smell of hand sanitizer hits my nose. It tickles like I might sneeze.

Aspen

Dr. Brenda's office doesn't look different, except for the addition of a few new snow globes. I pick one up and spin it around in my hand.

"It's good to see you, Aspen."

"It's good to see you, too." And it is. I like Dr. Brenda, even if her analogies are terrible and her hoarding problem seems to be getting worse. I guess we all have our things.

She points to the couch, the spot where I've sat a handful of times before. But it's never been like this. I sit down slowly, clasping my hands in my lap.

"Where should we start?" I ask.

"The beginning is usually the best place." Dr. Brenda takes out her notebook and sets it on her lap.

I settle back in my seat, finding a comfortable position, knowing this might take awhile. But I'm ready. Finally.

"Katelyn Ryan sat in front of me in chemistry. I'd stare at the back of her head and wonder what it would be like to have straight brown hair instead of the curly, dirty blonde mess that protrudes from my head, like a perm on a troll doll."

Dr. Brenda laughs and makes a note. "What else?"

"She asked to borrow a pencil once."

"Did you give it to her?"

"No," I say. "I'm not very good at sharing."

THE END

Acknowledgments

First and always, I want to thank my husband, Kyle, for his never-ending love and support. Even when I don't think I have it in me, he does. This book would not be without him.

To Claire Heffron, the strongest person I know, who read this story from the beginning, who knew Aspen like she was her best friend, who reviewed draft after draft and held my hand and always answered my phone calls—you are a gift to me.

Thank you to my wonderful, amazing, determined interns Riki and Tawney. You joined this ride without knowing where it would go and never lost faith. You dedicated your time, your mind, your love to this book and for that I am eternally grateful.

Carey Albertine, you are a goddess. You saw the writer I wanted to be even when I couldn't see it. Thank you isn't enough, but it's a good place to start.

Genevieve Gagne-Hawes, your enthusiasm for this story kept me afloat at times. We *will* meet for drinks some day when we are both in New York City and I'm buying.

Thank you to Saira Rao for being the energizer bunny of publishing. I don't know a person more determined than you. And I'm proud to be part of your genius.

Thank you to my writing therapist, Cara Vescio, who kept my head on straight. You are the Joey to my Chandler.

To every blogger, every fan, every person who helped spread the word about this book. You make the difference— and I couldn't be more thankful.

And to Caroline—who stayed.

About Rebekah Crane

Rebekah Crane fell in love with Young Adult literature while studying Secondary English Education at Ohio University. After having two kids, living in six different cities, and finally settling down in the foothills of her beloved Rocky Mountains, her first novel, *Playing Nice*, was published. She now spends her day carpooling kids or tucked behind a laptop at 7,500 ft high in the Rockies, where the altitude only enhances the experience. *Aspen* is her second novel.

Join the Bek Effect:
http://www.rebekahcrane.com/media.html

#BEKHEADS

OTHER BOOKS BY
IN THIS TOGETHER MEDIA

Middle-Grade (8–13 yrs.):

The Soccer Sisters Series by Andrea Montalbano
  Lily Out of Bounds
  Vee Caught Offside
  Tabitha One on One

Kat McGee Adventures
  Kat McGee and The School of Christmas Spirit by Rebecca Munsterer
  Kat McGee and The Halloween Costume Caper by Kristin Riddick
  Kat McGee Saves America by Kristin Riddick

Carly Keene Literary Detective Adventures
  Carly Keene Literary Detective: Braving the Brontës by Katherine Rue

Young Adult (14+):

Playing Nice by Rebekah Crane
Personal Statement by Jason Odell Williams

www.inthistogethermedia.com
@intogethermedia

Made in the USA
Charleston, SC
09 August 2014